Praise for *COLD SLICE*

"One cool dude of a novel. . . . A fine piece of work.
—Joe R. Lansdale, author of *A Fine Dark Line*

"Anyone who doubts that men can bond with one another and be there in good times and bad must read *Cold Slice*, an upbeat mystery that proves males have emotions and are not afraid to show them to those they trust. Terry and his friends are all blue-collar workers and their lack of pretentiousness will be enjoyed by a whole different segment of mystery readers. L.T. Fawkes has written a very exciting mystery starring a protagonist who will appeal to men and women." —*Midwest Book Review*

"Full of enjoyable characters. From Terry, who is trying to walk the straight and narrow, but knows he still has issues, to Bump, who can get you whatever you need (even an attoney) wholesale, to Gruf, the night manager who feels a responsibility to watch out for his entire crew, but is able to weed out the slackers that make his life not as easy as he'd like it . . . Astute sleuthing . . . A great introduction to a bunch of fun guys." —*The Mystery Reader*

Other Working Man's Mysteries

Lights Out
Cold Slice

EARLY EIGHT

A WORKING MAN'S MYSTERY

L. T. Fawkes

A SIGNET BOOK

SIGNET
Published by New American Library, a division of
Penguin Group (USA) Inc., 375 Hudson Street,
New York, New York 10014, U.S.A.
Penguin Books Ltd, 80 Strand,
London WC2R 0RL, England
Penguin Books Australia Ltd, 250 Camberwell Road,
Camberwell, Victoria 3124, Australia
Penguin Books Canada Ltd, 10 Alcorn Avenue,
Toronto, Ontario, Canada M4V 3B2
Penguin Books (NZ), cnr Airborne and Rosedale Roads,
Albany, Auckland 1310, New Zealand

Penguin Books Ltd, Registered Offices:
80 Strand, London WC2R 0RL, England

Published by Signet, an imprint of New American Library,
a division of Penguin Group (USA) Inc.

First Printing, September 2004
10 9 8 7 6 5 4 3 2 1

To Bob, Bryan, Marc and Susan,
and Aaron and Angela.
Thanks, too, to that guy in Newbury.
You know who you are.
Many, many thanks to my editor, Claire Zion.
And thanks to my agent, Carol Mann.

Chapter 1

Procol Harum's "Salty Dog" was playing on the juke-box. I could barely hear it over the commotion in the busy kitchen at Smitty's Bar and Eats, but that didn't stop me from singing along while I watched the seconds tick down on the bread timer. My name's Terry Saltz. I'm a carpenter. I also moonlight a few nights a week at Smitty's. Technically, when I'm at Smitty's I'm a bouncer, but at Smitty's you pitch in where you're needed. That's why I was baking bread.

Suddenly Danny Gillespie was beside me, elbowing me in the ribs. "Boss. Seven-thirty. Time for pool league. Let's go." His freckled face was all serious. That was an unusual condition for him. He was chewing the inside of his cheek and the chewing action was making his strawberry blond mustache bounce.

Me and Danny have been best friends since we were little kids. When we were fifteen, my brother P.J. got us jobs as gofers for Red Perkins Construction and we learned carpentry together. Danny eventually got fed up with Red, went to work for Miller Roofing, and we lost touch for a while. But when I went to jail, there was Danny on his white horse. He visited me in jail and mostly kept a straight face as he listened to my sad stories.

I guess I'll have to go ahead and explain how I ended up in jail. Get that right out of the way. One night I did a bunch of shots along with some controlled substances in a bar, and then I trashed the place and hit some people. I don't remember anything after the first few shots, but when I came to, I was in a cell. My skinned knuckles and assorted lumps and bruises were solid evidence I'd had a pretty interesting night.

Because of my one-man rampage, I'd lost my job, my wife, and my trailer. There was gonna be no place for me to go when I got out, and nothing for me to do when I got there. Danny was living in the crappy little attic of an old house just down the hill from the town square in Spencer, Ohio, which is in the northern part of Grand County. As my release date approached, he saved my ass by offering to let me crash at his place till I got back on my feet. Moving in with Danny kept me off the streets.

Moving in with Danny had an added benefit. If I'd gone back to my old stomping grounds in the southern end of the county, odds were I'd have slid right back into my old bad habits, and I didn't want that. I didn't want to end up back in jail.

I swore off the booze and drugs and moved in with Danny in Spencer. He even carried me awhile till I found a job as a pizza driver. Now, a busy year and a half later, I still hadn't touched anything stronger than coffee and Marlboros, we had us a bunch of new friends, and we were sharing an awesome double-wide with a rookie cop out in Chandler's Trailer Park. We were carpentering together again, and moonlighting together as bouncers at Smitty's, and our brand-new pool team was about to kick off its winter session.

I told Danny, "Hang on. I gotta get these loaves out of the oven when the timer goes off. And don't call me Boss."

Danny snickered. Then Hammer spoke up. Which I didn't even think he was paying any attention. He'd been standing there with his hands tucked under his armpits like he was in a hypnotic trance or something, watching the hot new waitress as she tried to reach the take-home cartons that were stacked on a high shelf.

Hammer said, "Go on, Boss. I'll take care of the bread."

I glared at him. Skinny, goofy, redheaded kid. He was grinning at me. Because he'd called me Boss.

I said, "Now he's got you doing it, too? It's not funny, Hammer. Do not call me Boss."

I stepped over to lift down the boxes the new girl was never gonna reach without a stepladder. Then Danny dragged me out of the kitchen. I glanced at his profile and saw he was still smirking about Hammer calling me Boss. I got my arm free and followed him across the busy dining room. Sexy-ass dining room with thick burgundy carpeting, dark green wainscoted walls, sparkling brass chandeliers dimmed down to half light, and oak captain's chairs with sexy green leather seats at sexy oak tables. Most of the tables were surrounded by happy, chewing customers.

I was about to tell Danny he seriously had to stop calling me Boss, and stop instigating everybody else to do it, too, when we came to the doorway from the dining room to the pool hall and I saw the crowd. I stopped and stared. "Holy shit. Where'd all these *people* come from?"

Both of Smitty's teams were shooting at home that first night of pool league. You figure, four pool teams with six to eight players each, okay, that's a lot of people. But that didn't account for the crowd all along the front of the bar. Besides a lot of unfamiliar faces, I saw that Smitty had come out from behind the bar to watch, and I noticed that some of the regulars, who we call the Members, had even come around from their reserved seating area on the back side of the bar. Mule, wearing his usual stained Carhartt overalls, leaned against the pinball machine, his longneck in his hand. Big ol' Tiny was right beside him. Tiny's huge Carhartts were plenty stained, too. Tiny runs a septic service. Mule works for him.

Danny threaded his way between the pool tables to where our team, looking tough and menacing in their black Smitty's T-shirts and black jeans, was huddled by our scorer's table. I followed him, looking around with my mouth open.

The Elliot twins, Luther and Reginald, were our co-captains. They were sitting at our scorer's table, study-ing the score sheet. The rest of our team was hovering over them. A fat guy I didn't know was also hovering there. He was talking to the twins. As I walked up, he said, ". . . to shove it, ya know? I mean, I need a job, but I don't need *that* job."

One of the Elliot twins said, "No kidding. You can make *that* hourly working at Burger King these days. That one up in Fairfield has a sign out in front."

The fat guy said, "No shit? Huh." He looked at his watch. "Well, I guess we oughtta get started. Who're you putting up first?"

Luther Elliot said, "Saltz. New player. Unranked."

The fat guy bustled back to his team's end of the table.

Bump Bellini was standing behind the twins, screw-ing a stick together. Some of his long blond hair had gotten loose from his ponytail. He blew it away from his nose. I looked closer at the stick. It was mine. The new one I'd bought two weeks earlier. He saw me and walked over, holding my stick out.

I couldn't stop staring at the crowd. It was a total clusterfuck, all around the pool tables and in front of the bar. People were glancing my way, rubbing their chins, putting their heads together and talking quietly, like they were discussing something important. I didn't like the look of things at all.

I pushed past Bump so I could talk to the twins. We had six players on our team, and only five sets are played in a match, so I was thinking I could sit out that first week. You know? Get a feel from the sidelines for what these matches were like.

I said to Reginald Elliot, "Dude. Play somebody else first. And where the *fuck* did all these people come from?"

Reginald grinned up at me. "Believe me, precious. It's better to go first when you're new. If you wait, your jitters will only get worse."

Don't get the wrong idea about that "precious" thing. The twins are like that. They call everybody precious.

"But Danny, Bump, and Gruf are all new, too. Seriously. I'm not ready."

The twins were shaking their blond heads. Reginald said, "Danny, Bump, and Gruf have all played in leagues before. You're the inexperienced one, so you're up. You've got a five-minute practice session as soon as your opponent finishes. Then it's a race to three. That means, whoever wins three games first—"

"I *know* what it means."

I stole a glance across the pool table toward the other team's end. I remembered we were playing the team from Four Corners Tavern in Woodcrest. The team that called themselves the Terminators.

I said, "Who's my opponent?"

"They're discussing it now. Ah, here comes their captain."

The fat guy was waddling toward us. He said, "We're playing Tiffany," and jerked his thumb to indicate a fat, messy girl who had stepped up to the table and was beginning to rack the balls.

Tiffany was wearing a school bus–yellow T-shirt that said I'M WITH STUPID and had a big red pointing arrow. I watched the arrow, but no matter which way she turned, I didn't see Stupid anywhere. I wondered if maybe Stupid had gotten a load of her T-shirt and decided she wasn't with him after all.

A voice beside me said, "Wouldja?"

It was Danny. I saw he was watching Tiffany, too. I said, "Not even with *your* dick." Then I turned back to tell Reginald that I wasn't shooting first, but he wasn't there anymore. He was over at the bar getting his gin and tonic refreshed.

Gruf Ridolfi straightened up from the score book. He ran his fingers through his long black DA, grinned at me, and gave me the thumbs-up.

I said, "No. Dude. Somebody else has to go first. I—"

"New guy always goes first," he said firmly. "It's easier on the nerves that way."

"*Whose* nerves?"

Tiffany's five minute practice session seemed like it was over before it started. Then it was my turn to practice. There was no one left to turn to. No mercy available anywhere, except that Reginald came back to the scorer's table carrying an iced tea for me along with his gin and tonic. Iced tea for me because, like I said before, I don't do alcohol anymore.

There was nothing I could do but suck it up. I racked the balls, positioned the cue ball, lined up to break, and totally biffed. My stick glanced over the top of the cue ball and the cue ball rolled sideways about two inches. I'd forgotten to chalk the tip of my stick.

Tiffany snickered. Behind me, people groaned. Somebody said, "Noonan." It sounded like Gruf. I turned around. Gruf was scratching his head and looking up at the ceiling. Mule was frowning at me. Fuckin' Mule. Frowning at *me*. I turned back to the table and found the chalk. Somehow I got through my practice session, even though my bridge hand seemed to have developed a slight tremor.

Then it was time to shoot for the break. At least I knew how to do that. We'd gone over it at our team practices. What you do is, the two players stand side by side at the head of the table and both shoot at the same time. The idea is to hit the end rail, and the one whose ball stops closest to the end rail after touching it, wins the right to break. Tiffany's ball bounced off the end rail and stopped in about the middle of the table. So did mine, only mine stopped there after it came all the way back to the head rail and bounced back to the middle. Her break.

I racked the balls and stepped back out of the way. Reginald came to stand beside me. He reached over and brushed bread flour off the front of my black Smitty's T-shirt. Tiffany broke and the thirteen ball dropped into the corner pocket. She walked around the table, decided to try a rail shot on the eleven, and missed. I started for the table.

Danny said, "Boss. Don't forget to chalk up."

Which was irritating, because I would've forgotten.

I decided to go for the four in the side, but just as I was lining up on it, Reginald stopped me. "Time out."

I stood up and turned around. *"What."*

Reginald stepped close beside me, cocked his hip, frowned, cupped his chin, and stared at the table. "Let's talk about your strategy."

I said, "My strategy is: Sink all the solids and then drop the eight." Like, What the fuck?

He allowed a tight smile. "Well, yes. In a perfect world."

Across the way, Tiffany said loudly, "Tick tock, there, Shitty's. In this lifetime, huh?"

The Terminators all snickered.

Reginald ignored her and gave me my first four shots, telling me what English to use and where to leave the cue ball. I paid attention. The Elliot twins are far and away the two best shots in the entire bar league.

I lined up on the one ball to the corner like he'd said. The one dropped, but I shot a little too hard and ended up with the cue ball behind two stripes and no good shots on a solid. I'd only managed to get one lousy ball down and I was already screwed. I stood up from the table, baffled.

Reginald said, "Time out."

Tiffany yelled, "*Foul.* He already had a time-out."

Reginald looked over with his mouth open, but her fat captain was already telling her that I was a new, unranked player and was entitled to unlimited time-outs in my first two matches.

The captain was fat and Tiffany was fat. Matter of fact, just about everybody standing and sitting around the opposing scorer's table was fat.

I said to Reginald, "Those guys must have a lot of team dinners, huh?"

But he was studying the table and seemed not to hear me. He said, "We'll call a safety. Remember, to make it a legal shot, you have to hit one of your own balls first. Then something has to hit a rail." He showed me what to do by sketching lines in the air above the green felt surface with his finger.

I nodded and lined up for the shot. Reginald said, "Call the safety, precious."

Tiffany said, "Yeah. Call the safety, precious."

I straightened. "Safety." I stood there breathing for a few seconds. *Jeez.* Up until the last ten minutes or so, I'd been pretty good at pool. Now, I felt like I'd never played the game in my life.

I chalked my stick and managed to do what he'd told me. My team and most of the people standing in front of the bar nodded and clapped. The safety worked like it was supposed to and Tiffany scratched. I sank a couple of balls and then blew an easy shot. Then she blew an easy shot, and then I managed to run out the table. One–zip.

Tiffany racked the balls, swearing to herself. I chalked my stick. I broke and the four ball dropped. I lined up on the three ball to the corner pocket. Tiffany suddenly appeared in my line of vision, twirling her stick. Distracted, I glanced at her, and in that glance I caught sight of a face in the crowd just over her shoulder. I went back to lining up my shot before I realized whose face it was. I stood up and looked again, but he had disappeared.

I took a few steps toward the bar, craning my neck, trying to find him. I took a few more steps so that I could see down the back hall, but there was no sign of him. Danny, looking puzzled, had stepped up beside me. I said, "I thought I saw my brother. Berk. Did you see him?"

He shook his head. "What would Berk be doing here? Are you sure it was him?"

I wasn't. It'd been years since I'd seen Berk, and it'd been only a split-second glance. I shrugged it off and went back to the table, but I couldn't get my head clear. My shot went wide, and my cue ball didn't end up where I meant for it to, either. It was lined up to give Tiffany a bunny shot, eleven to the side. She made her shot, and three more, before she blew a bank shot and scratched.

I shook out the cobwebs and settled myself down. Then I ran the table. Two–zip. The fans went wild. Gruf and Bump stood on either side of me, pounding me on the back.

Bump said, "One more game, dude."

Gruf said, "Bring it on home now."

I laughed at them. I broke, sinking the two ball, and missed a rail shot to the corner. Tiffany sank two but missed a bank shot into the side pocket. As I stepped up to the table, I noticed for the first time that the eight ball was sitting on the side rail, dangerously close to the near corner pocket. I dropped four balls, but then I hesitated. I looked back to the scorer's table to see if Reginald was going to come out to talk to me. He nodded at me to go ahead and see what I could do.

I thought I could maybe clip the six ball into the side pocket, but then the cue ball would be heading up toward that eight ball. You never want to risk an Early Eight. Early Eight is instant death. Sink that badass black eight ball before it's time and it's insta-matic Game Over. I looked for a safety, found one, and made it. My team applauded.

Tiffany stepped up, called the nine in the side, and made a tough bank shot. But the cue ball kept going. It banked around to make a perfect rail shot on the eight. The eight dropped into the corner pocket with a thud. Early Eight. My team and most of the bar erupted into cheers. I'd won my first-ever bar-league set, three–zip. I was suddenly swallowed up by laughing, back-slapping teammates.

Then the other end of the room erupted in cheers. A bunch of people from Lo-Lites Bar in Ladonia were cheering for the tall, slender blonde who had just won her set. She strutted back to her table laughing, pumping the air with her hands in that "raise the roof" gesture. I heard her say, "That's me. Red Hot. Just like my license plate says."

None of us knew it on that frigid January night, of course, but Red Hot didn't have much longer to *be* red hot. In just a few hours, she was going to be as cold as ice. The long, tall blonde from Lo-Lites in Ladonia was about to experience the ultimate Early Eight.

Chapter 2

Luther was up next. While he and his opponent took their practice sessions, I walked through the bar looking for my brother Berk, or a guy who looked like him. I kept on looking for him even after I knew he wasn't there.

Berk is eight years older than me. I thought about that as I searched the bar, and realized that made him thirty-four. As a kid, I worshiped Berk like a god. Everything he did seemed golden. Sometimes he'd let me ride shotgun and we'd cruise around southern Grand County. Go get a Coke or something. I'd ride as tall as I could and keep my eyes peeled, hoping to see kids I knew. When I did, I'd make Berk honk his horn so they'd look around and see me riding with my brother. Then I'd hoist the high hard one at them.

Even after I was sure Berk wasn't in the bar, I kept my eyes moving around. Now that my set was over, I was back in bouncer mode. But "bouncer" doesn't really cover it. Odd-job boys, that's what we are. Whatever needs to get done, we do it. Danny and Bump are bouncers at Smitty's, too. Gruf is Smitty's son, so he helps manage and does a little bit of everything else, including bounce.

The co-captains of our pool team, the Elliot twins, are servers at Smitty's. They're ranked as sevens in the pool league. That's the highest ranking there is, and those two are amazing to watch. Luther Elliot's opponent that night was ranked a four. Under the handicapping system the league used, that meant Luther had to win seven games before his opponent won four. Everybody settled down for a long one.

There was quite a crowd gathered around to watch Luther shoot—including, I noticed, the tall blonde from Lo-Lites. She was very slender and had that kind of long, straight, glossy blond hair that looks so perfect it seems like it must be fake.

Since I'm six-five or so, I stayed toward the back so some of the short people could see better. Danny, Gruf, and Bump are all right around the same height as me. We can see from the back of a crowd.

Luther and his opponent shot for the break. Luther left his ball leaning against the end rail. You can't do any better than that. His opponent was a little ruddy-faced guy who'd lost about half of his brown hair and who was nearly as wide as he was tall. I noticed that the first thing he did was look around for a bridge. I imagined, as short and wide as he was, he was probably pretty good with the bridge by now.

Somewhere behind me, I heard a guy clear his throat in a nervous way and say, "I was watching your set. You really spanked that guy."

I looked for the speaker and found a pale little pocket protector–looking dude standing behind me and a little to my left. He was staring up through his cloudy glasses at the blonde from Lo-Lites. His eyes were wide with awe and wonder.

Without looking at him, she said, "That's me. Red Hot. Just like my license plate says."

The first time I'd heard her say that, it sounded kind of cool. Hearing her say it a second time, I realized it was her rap, and now it sounded kind of corny. Kind of annoying in a vague sort of way, like, Oh, license plate? *Golly.*

The nerd cleared his throat again. "Boy. You sure are a tall drink of water."

She ignored him for a few seconds, then she looked down her nose at him and said, "Long." Her attitude was nasty.

The guy said, "Huh?"

The girl said, "It's not tall. It's long. Long drink of water."

She looked back toward our team's table, where Luther was lining up for his break. I watched her, thinking her bitchy attitude with her shy admirer was out of line. I mean, the guy was harmless. Why'd she have to go ahead and bust his balls like that?

An older guy in a chocolate brown suit with a lighter brown tie stood beside her. He had a soft, tired look about him. His cheeks drooped like some of the air had leaked out. Even his thin brown hair looked tired. He had the posture of a guy who has to stand up all day on his job—toed out, with his knees bent a little, like he had a slightly lower center of gravity than most people.

A spot opened up in front of the pinball machine so I moved over there and leaned against it. I was curious about the guy in the brown suit because that suit and tie made him look so out of place. Like he belonged over in the dining room, chewing on a twenty-six-dollar steak, instead of out here in the pool hall. I noticed that every time a girl walked by, his eyes followed her. Each time, it looked to me like his eyes were firmly focused on ass.

It didn't occur to me then that they were together, the old guy and the tall blonde. I watched him when he headed over to the bar. After a few minutes of watching Luther's set, I glanced over and saw that the guy was on his way back and he was carrying two drinks. He handed one to the blonde and I thought, Huh. They still didn't speak to each other.

Ten or fifteen minutes went by. I glanced at the couple a few times, but mainly I watched Luther shoot. The couple was standing so that the blonde had about a quarter profile to me and Brown Suit faced me head-on. They never seemed to actually look at each other. They were too busy watching the people who passed back and forth between the bar and the pool tables.

The blonde finished her drink. She rattled her ice at Brown Suit and he headed toward the bar for another refill. As he walked away, she slowly did a three-sixty. Her eyes paused briefly on me as she scanned toward the bar. Then the scanning stopped and she smiled. She raised her hand and wiggled her fingers at somebody. By the obvious change in her breathing and the way she began to squirm just a little bit, I could tell she was happy to see him, whoever he was.

I turned to look. The somebody had his chin on his fist, his head tipped sideways, and was staring at her. He flicked his tongue at her like a snake. He was dark and dangerous-looking, with long, black, curling hair which he wore loose, a menacing black mustache, and a black turtleneck full of muscle.

Over the turtleneck, he wore his colors. By colors, I mean his leather jacket. One glance at that weathered, studded leather jacket told me that he was a club biker. I couldn't see his back, so I didn't know which club until much later.

I got curious what would happen, since the blond chick was already with somebody. Brown Suit returned with her drink refill and she shifted so that she was facing the bar where Snake Man was. I had a chance to really look at her now. She had a long narrow nose, big green eyes that were slightly too close together, high cheekbones that gave her a hungry look, and an indentation in the middle of her chin. She wore a black stretch-lace T-shirt and you could see the shadow of the black bra underneath it. Tight black straight-leg jeans disappeared into tall black leather boots with some serious spike heels.

She'd stopped smiling. She was restless and fidgety, like she had an interesting itch.

Over at the pool table, a loud *Wo* went up. Luther had just won his set, and he'd apparently done it decisively, since the eight ball and all the solids were gone but all the stripes were still there, spread across the table. Bump was pounding Luther on the back. I caught Luther's eye and gave him the thumbs-up.

As the noise died down, I heard the blonde finish her sentence: ". . . filthy pig."

I looked over. So did several other people who were standing near enough to hear her. She was glaring at Brown Suit and breathing hard. I couldn't hear what he said. Then she said, "You're a fucking pig, Ray. Get me another drink."

He shrugged, took her glass, and headed for the bar. She looked over at Snake Man, smiled, pursed her lips, and kissed the air at him. I didn't look at him right then. I didn't need to see any more of his flicking tongue. Brown Suit came back from the bar and stopped beside the blonde, so now they were both more or less facing me.

She took her glass from him and knocked some back.

He said, "Now. Have you calmed down?"

She said, "You disgust me. I can't even stand to look at you." Then she noticed me staring at her. "What're *you* looking at?"

I frowned. "Nothing special."

She said, "Well, then, mind your own fucking business."

I said, "I am." Which, *she* was my business at that particular moment, since I was the nearest bouncer. When she finally succeeded in provoking Brown Suit into swinging on her or something, it was probably gonna be up to me to pull him off. So I went right on watching them.

She turned back to Brown Suit and snarled, "You fat fuck."

He'd had enough. He said, "Get your coat. I'm taking you home."

"I drove my*self* here, remember?"

"You're drunk. I'll drive you home."

She laughed. "I'd rather walk home to Ladonia in a fucking blizzard than ride with you. But why don't you go? That's a good idea." She tossed her glossy blond hair and looked toward the pool tables.

He said, "Don't tempt me. But you're drunk. If I left, how would you— Oh, I get it. Who is it this time?" He began to look around. I glanced over at Snake Man. He was hunched over his beer mug, studying his knuckles.

Brown Suit sucked in one cheek and stared at her, nodding. "One of these times, Gwen . . ."

She looked back at him, sneering. "Are you still here?"

He said, "One of these times, you're gonna go too far." He raised one eyebrow at her.

She twinkled her fingers at him. "Drive carefully."

He turned around, carried his glass over to the bar, walked down the back hall, and disappeared out the door. Before the door had even swung closed behind him, the girl was heading for Snake Man. He stood up. She walked right into his open arms and they kissed.

I thought, Wow. She's some piece of work. Then I caught a patch of brown in my peripheral. I looked. Brown Suit had returned and was standing at the far end of the bar watching them kiss. He stood there blank-faced for a full five seconds. Then he turned and walked back outside.

The thought went through my mind, He's going out to his car for a gun. I moved to a position beside the cigarette machine and leaned my elbow on top of it. I figured that way, when he returned, which I was

sure he would, I could step up behind him and grab
his arm.

I waited and watched the back door. Five minutes
went by. At the bar, the blonde and Snake Man were
sitting side by side now. She had her arm up around
his shoulders and they had their heads together. He
was whispering something in her ear.

Another five minutes went by. Danny finished his
practice session and his set got under way. A few people came in the back door, but none of them was a
pissed-off old guy in a brown suit with a big ol' gun.
After five or ten more minutes, I went outside into
the icy January night and walked up and down the
rows of cars in the shadowy parking lot, looking to
see if he was sitting in a car out there anywhere, but
he wasn't. The only people I saw were Gruf and Tiny,
who were standing about halfway up the narrow alley,
sharing a doobie. I said, Cool, and headed back inside
to catch the end of Danny's set.

I stopped beside Bump. "There's a tall blonde on
the Ladonia team. Gwen something. She's sitting over
there—"

He interrupted. "Yeah. What about her?"

"What's her last name?"

"Dillon. Gwen Dillon."

Danny won his game and his set in his next turn. I
was listening to his triumphant play-by-play when I
felt a light nudge in the ribs. I turned around to see
Mule standing there. His cloudy burn-out eyes blinked
shyly up at me. "Tiny wants to buy you and Danny a
beer." He jerked his thumb over his shoulder. I
looked to the back of the bar and saw Tiny hunched
there, watching us. His nose and cheeks were still pink
from being out in the alley with Gruf.

Danny said, "Cool." We followed Mule around to
the Members Only seating area on the back side of
the bar, which Gruf had created so the regular barflies

wouldn't be bothered, and vice versa, by the well-dressed yuppies and grays who were flocking in droves to our fancy new dining room.

Princess was working the back side of the bar. Tiny gestured along the line of Danny, Mule, and me, and told her, "Beers."

But Princess knows I don't drink, so she looked at me and said, "Iced tea, Terry?"

I nodded.

Mule gave me a funny look. "Are you an alcoholic, Terry?"

I nodded. I don't know what the technical definition of alcoholism is. My definition is, if screwing up your whole life seems like a good idea to you when you're drunk, you're an alcoholic. By my definition, I'm the fuckin' poster boy.

Where was I? Oh, yeah. I sat on the back side of the bar with Tiny, Danny, and Mule for a while, enjoying my iced tea and watching the action. I noticed that the Red Hot blonde left Snake Man sometime along in there and wandered back over to the table where her team was shooting. Off and on I noticed her circulating around the bar, chatting up one guy after another.

Then I got interested in Bump's set and before long Danny and I thanked Tiny for the drinks and walked back over to the table to watch Bump's tiebreaker game, which he won. After Bump's set, Gruf took a girl from the Terminators to school. His win gave our team a clean sweep.

I got caught up in the celebration and forgot all about the blonde and Snake Man. Sometime later, when I glanced around the bar looking for them, it seemed like they were both gone.

Chapter 3

After breakfast at Brewster's Thursday morning, Danny leaned so far back on his chair I thought he was gonna go over on his head. Then he stretched back even more and lit a smoke. Our usual breakfast group was in the process of breaking up. John Garvey had already left. Nelma Wolfert, who started out as my parole officer and ended up as my friend, and Alan Bushnell, a sergeant on the Spencer PD, were up at the cash register chatting with Ilene as she totaled their bills. That left me, Danny, Bump, and Gruf sitting at the table, sipping coffee and smoking.

Me and my friends eat breakfast at Brewster's every weekday morning. We push three tables together so there's room for everybody. Brewster's is a big ol' hometown place where you can smoke and joke and hit on the waitresses and nobody cares. The food's good and the atmosphere's friendly.

A sweet-natured waitress named Mary takes our table every morning. She's got me so spoiled I don't think I could face the world if I didn't start my day seeing her pleasant smile.

I mentioned John Garvey. John's a rookie cop, stands about five-eleven or so, and wears his brown hair buzz-cut. He left his home in Indiana to enter Ohio Highway Patrol School and came straight onto the Spencer force from there. Staying in Danny's and my spare bedroom in our super-fine double-wide three bedroom trailer out in Chandler's Trailer Park was supposed to be a temporary thing until he could find a place of his own. But John's a friendly, square, likeable guy who can cook like a sonofabitch, so it wasn't long before Danny and me invited him to make the thing permanent.

I already told you about Danny. He's tall like me and he's got long, golden red hair which he usually wears pulled back into a ponytail. When he doesn't have his hair tied back with the customary leather shoelace, and there's a little wind, and the light's right, he looks sort of like a freckled, goofy Jesus.

I tie my black hair in a ponytail, too. I got it all cut off a year or so ago, but that was a bad mistake. I knew it almost right away. So I grew it back. Grew back my mustache, too. The mustache grew back faster.

Anyway. Danny stretched back in his chair and lit a smoke. I glanced at the clock. It was a few minutes past eight. The weather forecasters had said we were gonna get hit by a blizzard, but they predicted it wasn't gonna arrive until late afternoon. They were wrong. The front edge of the blizzard had blown into northeastern Ohio overnight and by breakfast time the storm had been hammering us for several hours.

Mary came around with the coffeepot and we all nodded yes to one last cup. As she poured mine, she glanced toward Brewster's wide front windows and sighed. "Look at that snow."

Gruf nodded. "How much of that shit are we supposed to get today, anyway?"

Danny said, "All."

Gruf said, *"All?"*

"All."

Gruf grinnned. "That could be quite a bit of snow. You think we can make it out to Ladonia in this stuff?"

We'd just started a job out in Ladonia. A friend of ours, Bud Hanratty, hooked us up with it. Three of his lawyer friends bought a big old two-story farm-house and wanted to convert it to offices for their law firm. They wanted it remodeled, from the attic (climate-controlled for files and storage space) to the basement (kitchen, lunchroom, bathrooms, and con-ference room). It was an awesome job. It would take several months, and Bud had told us to charge them top dollar. We said, That'll work.

Danny bounced his eyebrows. "We'll make it out there, but will we be able to make it back in?"

Bump laughed and slapped a tip onto the table. "I'll give you guys two days, and if I haven't heard from you by then, I'll send out the weiner dogs."

The rest of us stared at him. Gruf said, "You mean the St. Bernards."

Bump had stood and was looking around for Mary. He spotted her back by the waitress station and blew her a kiss. Then he turned back to Gruf. "No, I mean weiners. You do the math." We watched him saunter out the front door.

Danny said, "Oh. I get it. He's saying we're a bunch of weinies. What a funny guy."

I said, "We'll cram into my truck. My truck can go through anything." My black Toyota Tacoma has the four-wheel drive. The odomoter had just rolled past a hundred twenty-five thousand and the thing still ran tight as a drum. I love my truck.

We drove east on Third Avenue out of town, then cut over toward Ladonia on Route 89. It was slow going. Heavy snow and strong wind all the way. I barely made it out of second gear.

Danny was folded into the backseat. He leaned for-ward between the headrests and propped his elbows on the corners of the seat backs. When he belched, you could smell the bacon. "I bet the power goes off.

All that heavy snow on the lines. I bet the Highway Patrol closes the roads. Aw, look at this guy."

A county plow roared toward us. He was going so fast his blade was throwing the snow a good twenty feet in the air. He flew past us and my windshield got pelted with the salt that was being whipped out from the back of his truck. We all turned to watch him go by. Just after he passed us, his blade caught a mailbox and sent it flying with a loud *thwack.*

Danny yelled, "*Hooo.* No mail for you."

Ladonia, Ohio, is about ten miles northeast of Spencer. It pretty much consists of the Ladonia Volunteer Fire Department, the house we were working on, and Ladonia Hills Apartments. Oh, yeah—there's the Lo-Lites Bar, too, but it's on down the highway another half mile.

I turned into the driveway and pulled all the way back to the garage. We each grabbed a snow shovel from my truck bed, spaced out along the driveway, and started throwing snow. The wind howled in our ears as we worked.

Danny had the middle section. After a few minutes, he walked over to the Dumpsters we'd rented, shoveled snow off the lid of one, and looked inside. He yelled, "Sonofabitch. They *did* come and empty these things last night."

I could barely hear him over the wind. I shouted, "They did? That's great." I wanted to yell that I took back everything I'd said and I guessed he did know how to sweet-talk refuse hauler dispatchers, but it was too hard to yell into that wind. I decided to save it for later. I worked my way out to the edge of the highway, threw my last shovelful, and bent over to stretch my back. I saw that Gruf had already worked his way to the part Danny had cleared, and Danny had another shovel or two before he reached my part.

Gruf was carrying his shovel toward my truck and

I saw that he was going to drop it in the bed. I had my mouth open to yell that they were extra shovels, and we'd leave them in the garage for the duration, when the air was suddenly filled with a bloodcurdling scream. I jerked straight.

Danny yelled, "What the fuck was that?"

It sounded again, high and shrill in the thin, cold air. I turned and began to run up the driveway. Danny was just ahead of me. Gruf was turning his head this way and that, trying to hear where the noise was coming from. That second scream seemed to last forever. You could hear the terror in it.

As I got closer to the house, I realized the screams were carrying from the apartment complex next door. I yelled, "The apartments. Come on."

Danny said, "I'll call 911." He'd yanked off his gloves and was already fumbling his cell phone from his inside pocket.

I began to run toward the sound. Gruf pounded along right behind me. We crossed the wide strip of side yard and ran between two of the apartment buildings, following the screaming sound. Two long rows of three-story redbrick buildings faced each other across the long, wide parking lot. Now we could see the screamer toward the far end. She stood on the far side of a parked, snow-covered car, screaming, staring at something inside. We raced down the length of the parking lot toward her. The plow hadn't been through yet. We followed the tire tracks of some earlier vehicle.

The girl saw us coming and began to point into the snow-covered car. She was hopping up and down now and still screaming. She was trying to make words but the screaming was getting in her way.

We ran around the back of the car, stopped, and stared. Danny came pounding up behind us. The driver's side door was open and there was a blonde sitting behind the wheel, not moving. The girl continued to scream.

Gruf took her by the arm and pulled her away past the back of the car, out into the driveway, telling her, "You gotta stop screaming now."

Danny and I stepped up to the open door and leaned in, being careful not to touch anything. A section of the gray dashboard casing stuck up out of plumb from where the blonde had evidently kicked it as she struggled. A length of yellow rope was looped over her shoulders, and you could see frozen blood stuck on it up near her neck. Her face was so distorted it was unrecognizable. Her eyes bulged and her jaw seemed to be dislocated.

Danny and I drew back like a single organism. Danny said, "God." The other girl had stopped screaming. Gruf was talking to her, trying to get her to stay quiet.

There were two little purses sitting on the front passenger seat, one black, one brown. I looked past the tangled blond hair of the dead girl and saw a black leather cue stick case sitting on the backseat.

I got a sick feeling in the pit of my stomach. I said, "Oh, *shit*."

Danny said, "What?"

I moved to the back of the car and brushed snow away from the license plate. It said REDHOTZ.

Gruf said, "What?"

I said, "It's Gwen Dillon."

The girl began to scream again. Gruf told her, "You're really gonna hafta stop that."

I looked over at them. The girl was a little brunette. Now I recognized her as another member of the Lo-Lites pool team. All she was wearing was a fuzzy little white sweater, jeans, and high-tops. She stood there hugging herself, shivering. Her teeth were chattering and there was a voice sound, too, like a low-grade scream, or a hum. Like there was an engine running inside her or something.

I said, "Come on. Let's wait for the cops inside."

Trying to stay on the tracks we'd already made in the snow, Danny and I high-stepped away from the car and then all four of us made for the nearest building entrance. Once we were inside, I peeled off my Carhartt and wrapped it around the girl. Gruf opened his own Carhartt and hugged her against him inside it. She was still humming.

I said, "You were at Smitty's last night. You're on the Lo-Lites team."

She nodded.

I said, "What's your name?"

Her words, when they came, gushed out like a dam had broken. Rushing, tumbling words and rattling teeth.

"Allison. Allison Burgess. My boyfriend dropped me off at Smitty's last night because my car's at the BP getting a new battery? So then I didn't have anyplace to put my purse. So then Gwen says, Well put it out in *my* car. So then I did and I locked her car because she never locks it herself. So then after my set was over my boyfriend was there to give me a ride home. So then Gwen's car was locked and I couldn't find her to give me her keys. So then he's all, I gotta get up and go to work in the morning let's *go*. So then I go, Well if you're in such a fucking hurry let's just go and I'll get my purse tomorrow and you'll hafta give me a pack of *your* cigarettes. I'm dumping him. I swear to God."

Danny said, "You and Gwen share an apartment here?"

She shook her head. "She's on 2C and I'm on 3B."

I said, "In the same building?"

She nodded. "See the three doors? A, B, and C." She pointed a shaking finger at the building across from the doorway where we huddled.

She said, "Gwen's got a fucking two bedroom with a balcony and everything. I just have a one bedroom.

I can't afford the two bedroom. I don't have help like some people I could name. I just have my jerk boyfriend. Soon to be ex."

I said, "Your boyfriend brought you home without your purse last night and you figured you'd get it back from Gwen this morning?"

She nodded. "So then this morning the BP called that my car was ready and my boyfriend goes, I don't know what time I'll be over, but I'm not waiting around. You better be ready. I gotta dump him he's such a jerk. So then I had to get my purse back from Gwen's car so I could pay for *my* car. So then I thought, Well maybe I won't hafta wake her up because she doesn't like that when you wake her up. So then I thought, Well maybe she didn't lock her car. Because she usually doesn't, like she thinks nobody would *dare* rob her. So then her car was all covered up with snow and all the windows were all covered with snow and I couldn't see in and then when I tried the back door to get my purse and it wasn't locked but she was sitting there in the front seat. I go, Gwen? Gwen?"

The hum started again and began to pick up some volume. Gruf said, "Don't start screaming again, okay? Please."

She nodded and the volume of the hum dropped.

I said, "Last night. You couldn't find Gwen?"

She nodded. "Somebody got a cigarette?"

Danny was first with his pack out.

Gruf said, "Are you allowed to smoke here in the hall?"

She said, "I'd like to see somebody try and tell me not to," and gave us all a hot glare. Danny thumbed his lighter and she sucked flame.

I said, "So, Allison. Last night."

"Yeah."

"The bar was closing and you couldn't find Gwen?"

Allison said, "Somebody better call the cops."

Danny said, "Already did."

It occurred to me that Ladonia was too small to have a police department. I wondered if the highway patrol would handle this. I said, "Which cops are coming, anyway?"

Danny grinned at me. "Spencer PD."

I said, "Shit."

Gruf grinned, too. Because we were all thinking the same thing. If Spencer PD were the responders, that meant it was gonna be Alan Bushnell's case, and he was not gonna fucking *believe* we were right in the middle of it.

Gruf said, "Well, at least Alan won't be out here this morning. At least it's not on his shift. . . ."

Alan pretty much works third shift. Works third shift, and then stops at Brewster's and eats breakfast with us before he goes home. He's got the seniority to work any shift he wants, but he says first and second shifts are too boring.

I said, "We oughtta call Bump."

Bump doesn't carpenter with us. He's got his own business on the side to tend to during the day. He buys stuff and sells stuff. He's got a garage full of stuff. But even though he doesn't carpenter with us, he's still an important part of our crew. Any time anything's going on, Bump's included.

Danny pulled out his cell phone and dialed Bump's home number. He got the answering machine. He left a quick message and was just finishing up when he saw something outside. He slapped his phone closed and shouldered the door open.

"Folks. *Hey.* Stay back. That's a crime scene." He looked back at us. "I'm going out. They're gonna be all over that car in a minute."

I watched from the doorway. Three guys in ski jackets and jeans were shuffling uncertainly on the sidewalk across the way. They really wanted to go have a look for themselves. Danny walked toward them, gesturing, explaining. There was a sound on the wind. I couldn't tell if it was the wind howling or if it was a siren. I stepped back in and pulled the door closed.

I said, "Allison. I got a couple quick questions for you before the cops get here."

She peeked up at me from behind Gruf's sheltering arm and her own shaggy brown bangs.

"You said after you played last night, you couldn't find Gwen?"

"It wasn't the first time she went off with somebody without telling anyone." She smirked. "It was just the first time *last* night."

"But her car was still there in Smitty's parking lot?"

She nodded.

"Do you know where she went, or who she was with?"

"I've got a pretty good idea, but I'm not saying."

Gruf said, "You're gonna hafta tell the cops, anyway."

Her jaw stuck out. "Says who? I'll just say, Gee, I don't have any idea where she went, Officer."

Gruf said, "I hear the siren."

I said, "Allison. Do you know who killed her?"

Her eyes skittered toward the door. Her voice went soft. "She turned twenty-nine last September. She was a Virgo."

I nodded. Virgo. Got it. Whatever that means.

She said, "I remember the night of her birthday. We were all in Lo-Lites. We all work there. Guys were buying her drinks all night and she got *lit*. She was upset that she was twenty-nine already. After we closed, it was just a few of us girls. She told us, 'I'm making a solemn vow. I'm gonna get a rich husband before my thirtieth birthday.'" Allison drew a ragged breath. "Now she's not gonna get the husband *or* the birthday."

I said, "Allison. Do you know who did this?"

Gruf said, "There's the cop car. Let's go out. Hey, is that John?"

I said, "Hang on." I didn't want to let her get away from us until she told us what she knew. But Gruf, distracted by the arrival of the cops, was already half-way out the door, taking Allison with him.

Chapter 4

The wind was so cold it sucked your words away when you tried to talk. I glanced up and down the parking lot at the solid row of snow-covered parked cars. "How come Spencer PD responds to an emergency call in Ladonia?"

Our trailer mate, John Garvey, was one of the responding officers. The other one was Brian Bell. John said, "Ladonia only has a part-time constable. He only does traffic offenses. Everything else gets routed over to us."

Danny said, "There sure are a lot of cars in the lot here. Don't any of these people work? Or did they close everything down because of the weather?"

John nodded. "About an hour ago the Highway Patrol ordered everybody off the road but emergency vehicles."

John had wrapped Allison in a heavy blanket he pulled from the trunk of his cruiser and I had skinnied back into my warm Carhartt. While John and Brian were helping Allison into the backseat, her boyfriend arrived in his big, growling Ford pickup truck. John assured him the cops would get Allison where she needed to go after she'd been questioned, and Allison assured him that it wasn't any of his concern anymore, anyway, and also he should go fuck himself.

The boyfriend drove away with a glazed look in his eyes, John and Brian draped the area around Gwen's car with their yellow crime scene tape, and now we were all standing around beside their purring Crown Vic.

John blinked away a snowflake and two more landed on his cheek. "Oh, man? Alan's gonna go ballistic when he finds out you guys are all over this."

Gruf chuckled. I stepped sideways so I could turn my face a little out of the cold, stinging wind. The wind was a bitch that day. Keeping your back to it was *key*.

Brian Bell said, "I'll call it in, huh? It isn't gonna get any better if we wait."

John nodded. Brian slid onto the driver's seat and reached for the radio. Allison, tucked away in the backseat and wrapped in her blanket, was whimpering.

John said, "You guys didn't touch anything, did you?"

I said, "I brushed off the license plate. I had gloves on."

"And you're sure the victim's name is Gwen Dillon?"

I nodded. "John, I think Allison might know who did it."

John said, "Did she tell you that?"

I shook my head. "You guys pulled in. We got interrupted."

John leaned a little to peek at Allison. She'd pulled the blanket up over her head.

Danny said, "What do you do now? Wait for reinforcements?"

John said, "Protect the integrity of the crime scene." Like he was quoting the textbook, which he probably was.

I was freezing my ass off and the clock was ticking. I said, "Can we get back to work? We're working in the house right next door."

John looked where I pointed and thought it over. "Okay, go on. Long as I know where to find you."

Me, Gruf, and Danny tromped back between the

buildings, across the lot, and into the house through the back door. We quickly stomped the snow off our boots and shed our gloves and Carhartts. I said, "I'll make some coffee. We might as well take a few minutes to have a smoke and warm up before we get started."

We'd decided we'd leave the old kitchen alone until we had the new one built in the basement. Gruf had brought over a microwave and Danny and I had brought our old coffeemaker. We'd stocked the ancient refrigerator so we could make lunch there instead of wasting a lot of drive time going back into Spencer every day.

While I got the coffee going, Danny tried to reach Bump at home again, and then on his cell phone, but there was no answer. Then he called the bar, where Smitty and his day cook, Bennie, were already doing food prep for lunch, because we thought maybe Bump was there, but they hadn't seen any sign of him.

After a cup of coffee and a smoke, we clomped down into the old, dark, dirty basement. Danny and Gruf walked around switching on the trouble lights we'd hung from the old joists. I walked back to the area where the big conference room was gonna be and turned on the radio.

The plumbing in the old house was in pretty good shape. It'd all been replaced sometime in the midseventies. But the wiring was a nightmare. At some point, the farmer or one of his relatives had done some DIY work and nothing was like it was supposed to be. I jobbed out the bulk of the rewiring to an electrician I knew from when I worked for Red Perkins. He spent a hectic two days in the basement bringing all the main lines and circuits up to code. Once that was done we could take over. We could wire in the lights and install the outlets and switches and shit ourselves.

We'd already run the new plumbing lines over for

the new kitchen and bathrooms in the basement, and up to the second floor, where each of the three lawyers wanted his own bathroom. I guess lawyers don't like to share porcelain. The existing lines to the first floor were more than adequate for the office staff's bathroom. Back in the basement, we positioned Adjust-A-Posts to hold the load and then we tore out the old jerry-rigged walls which had partitioned off a pantry and a couple of storage areas.

We cleaned, leveled, and resurfaced the crumbly old basement floor and spread several coats of sealer. The top layers would be insulation, carpet padding, and indoor-outdoor carpet, but I didn't want that down before we'd done most of the other work. Now we were working on the new walls for the conference room.

We already had them framed out, the outer wall insulated, and three of the walls covered with the paneling the lawyers had chosen. Now we were working on the front wall. Gruf hung paneling while Danny and I framed up the section where the double doors would hang. By the time Danny started to complain his stomach was growling, the doorframes were finished. We carried the heavy doors down from where they'd been stashed in the front room before we broke for lunch.

I looked out the kitchen window. The snow was still falling heavily. Our tracks from earlier had disappeared completely, and the driveway had two or three new inches. Danny and I made hard salami sandwiches while Gruf popped a Tupperware container into the microwave. Gruf opened the refrigerator and pulled out one of his High Lifes and a Bud for Danny. I mixed up some instant iced tea.

We had brought over one of the old bar tables from Smitty's and three of the old chairs. They weren't much to look at, but they served their purpose, which was someplace to sit and eat lunch. Danny maued a few bites of his first sandwich before he pulled out his cell phone.

Gruf said, "Trying Bump again?"

"You must be a mind reader." He poked in the number, listened for a few seconds, then slapped his cell phone shut. "Still no answer."

I said, "Huh. I don't remember him mentioning any special plans."

Gruf shrugged. "He can't have gone far in this weather."

After lunch Gruf and Danny passed Gruf's bowl back and forth a time or two while I enjoyed another Marlboro Light. Then we clomped back down to the basement, hung the conference room doors, and moved on to the new kitchen.

The first order of business was getting the outer wall framed and insulated. We did that, working around the various pipes and wiring. Then we framed out the rest of the perimeter. Danny began to drag a sheet of drywall off the stack, but I glanced at the red numbers on the face of our radio and stopped him.

"Hang on, Danny. It's ten of five already. We're outa here."

We turned everything off, washed up, climbed back into our snow gear, and went out to the truck. By that time it was pitch-dark outside. I fumbled my key into the ignition.

On the way back into town, Danny tried Bump again. This time he got an answer on the first ring. Danny was trying to get his gloves on, so he handed the cell phone over the seat to me.

I said, "Hey. Heard about Gwen Dillon yet?"

Bump sounded a little breathless. "I'm at the bar. Bud's here, too. Johnny and Brian Bell just walked in and told us. You guys found her, huh?"

Bud meant Bud Hanratty. Bud's the lawyer who'd

gotten us our current job. He's also like a second father to Bump. He took custody of Bump and his younger brother and sister when Bump was fourteen. I wondered what Bud was doing at Smitty's at that time of day.

I said, "A chick named Allison Burgess found her. We heard her screaming and ran over."

"Even so. Alan Bushnell's gonna go apeshit."

I chuckled. "Alan musta led a very dull life until us guys got hooked up together."

Bump said, "Where are you guys now? What time are you gonna be over here?"

"We're on our way. Don't let John leave."

At Smitty's, I parked in the back lot and we stomped into the back hall, through the bar, across the pool hall, and into the dining room. The staff was rattling and banging in the kitchen, getting ready for the dinner rush. There were guys in suits sitting up front in booth eight next to the bay window, and there was a group of silver-haired ladies in booth five, but that was pretty much it.

Bump, Bud Hanratty, John, and Brian Bell were drinking coffee in the back corner booth. Bud looked awful. His eyes were all swollen and red, like he had a bad cold or something. Danny, Gruf, and I got coffee from the waitress station. John and Brian had draped their heavy leather cop coats over the backs of two of the chairs at the nearest table. I shrugged out of my Carhartt and laid it and their leathers over the next table down the line.

Bump saw me staring at Bud. He said, "One of his clients died last night."

Gruf said, "Jeez. There was a lot of that going around last night, wasn't there?"

I gave Bud a sympathetic pat on the arm before I settled down at the table and began to stir sugar and cream into my coffee. Then I sucked needfully. Ah.

That was better. Bud didn't look up from his coffee cup, so I figured he didn't want to talk about his client's accident. I turned to John. "So, John. Did you get any interesting information out of Allison?"

He shook his head.

I said, "Dammit. If we just woulda had another minute or two with her."

John ran his fingertips around the collar of his cop shirt, pulling it out away from his neck.

Reginald Elliot came by with a coffeepot. He peeked into Bud's cup. "More coffee, Bud?"

"No, thanks. I gotta run in a minute."

Reginald ran his eye around the rest of our beverage situation and topped off my coffee.

I said, "What did she tell you?"

John frowned. "Allison? She said she left her purse in Gwen Dillon's car, she needed it this morning, she found the body. That's about it. Why? What'd she tell you?"

I said, "Well, let's see. That girl can really talk once she gets started."

Gruf and Danny nodded.

I said, "She told us something about that Gwen had a two bedroom with a balcony when Allison could barely afford a one bedroom. That somebody was probably helping Gwen with the rent."

Danny said, "And that Gwen wanted to marry a rich guy before her next birthday."

Bump frowned and glanced at Bud. Bud was uncharacteristically quiet. He was staring at his hands, which were curled around his coffee cup.

John nodded. "Oh, that. Yeah. She told us that."

I said, "Gwen was on the Lo-Lites pool team. And she worked at the Lo-Lites, right?"

John said, "I think so. I don't know that for sure. I wasn't around when they questioned her back at the station. I had to go back out on traffic duty."

Danny grinned at him. "Sucks to be you."

John shrugged. "One of these days they'll hire a new rookie and *he'll* get all the bad stuff."

Gruf said, "I'm pretty sure Allison said Gwen worked at Lo-Lites."

Bud's black funk seemed impenetrable. Gruf nudged him with an elbow. Bud didn't respond. Gruf said, "And meanwhile, this other thing happens. What was your client's name, Bud?"

Bud roused himself and ran his fingers through his thinning brown hair. "Ernie. Ernie Burdett. He wasn't just my client. He was one of my best friends, too. Now I—jeez. Now I'm the executor of his estate." He broke off and had a little struggle with his lower lip.

Bump said, "Probably right around the time Gwen Dillon was getting strangled, Ernie was killed in a car wreck downtown."

Bud said, "The cops say he lost control and hit a bridge support on Dead Man's Curve in Cleveland. Then a semi got him from behind."

Danny said, "Bummer."

Bud sighed heavily. "I can't come to terms with it. I can't understand how it could've happened. Ernie was such a careful driver."

Bump said, "That's a bad spot down there."

Bud shook his head. "Even so. I can't imagine Ernie ever losing control of a car like that. I don't understand it. The only witness is the semi driver. Either he's lying . . ."

Bump told us, "Bud wants a look at Ernie's car. I spent all damn day driving a borrowed tow truck around Cleveland looking for it."

Danny said, "Oh, so that's where you were."

"Yeah. They told Bud it was parked in a gas station on Superior, so I go there and they tell me no, it's at a gas station over in Ohio City. On and on like that. Finally a guy says it's in the Central Impound Lot. I go there and they don't know what I'm talking about."

Bud said, "I can't come to terms with this thing

until I see his car. Get it clear in my mind, exactly what happened. And why. *Dammit.*"

Bump reached out and gave Bud's neck and shoulder a squeeze. "We'll find it. The Cleveland cops are looking for it." He turned to me. "Ernie Burdett was a good guy. And his wife, Chrissy, is a friend of mine from way back. Come to think of it, I oughtta go over there. Pay my condolences to Chrissy. Anyone wanna come with?"

We all looked at each other. Danny grimaced, frowned, shook his head.

Gruf shrugged. "I gotta cover the bar tonight."

I didn't have to be anywhere. I said, "I'll go." Then I looked at Bud. Which I totally expected him to come, too, if he was such good friends with Ernie Burdett.

Bump thought so, too. He said, "Bud? You coming?"

But Bud shook his head. "I can't go over there yet. I'm too torn up to face Ernie's widow now. Anyway, what would I say to her? I can't come to terms with this thing myself until I understand how it happened."

He didn't tell us to bring along a message, or anything. When we walked out, he was still sitting there like a statue, staring into his coffee cup.

Chapter 5

We climbed into my Tacoma and Bump directed me north on Third Avenue, out past Pete's convenience store, out past where the streetlights end, out past Carlson's Mill Road where Bump's house is, out past where Third Avenue turns into Route 114. The snow was still coming down big-time and the roads were horrible.

After another mile or so on, he told me to turn into a newish development of tri-levels and colonials called Mallard Pond Estates. Halfway down Drake Lane he pointed to a big colonial on the high ground on the left. There was an old silver Blazer with about a foot of snow stacked on its roof parked at the top of the driveway in front of the garage doors, and the house was all lit up.

The plows hadn't visited Mallard Pond yet. Hell, they hadn't even visited 114 yet. But my four-wheel-drive'll go through about anything, as long as it doesn't bottom out. I cranked the wheel and gunned it up into the driveway beside the Blazer. The Blazer had been there for a while. There was a smooth, track-free sweep of snow between it and the street.

I glanced through the high windows of the two-car garage as we walked toward the porch. There were two shiny new-looking cars parked in there—a Maroon Bronco and a metallic blue PT Cruiser.

We stomped our boots on the front porch even

though it was pointless, since the porch hadn't been shoveled. Bump pushed on the doorbell with his thumb.

He rang twice more before someone answered the door. A woman with a cell phone pressed to her ear pulled the door open and motioned impatiently at us. "Come. Come come come. You're letting all the warm air out."

I had a quick impression of false eyelashes, lots of jangly jewelry, and a platinum mullet. She turned and hurried away down a hall toward the back of the house. She was holding a cigarette in the hand raised over her shoulder, twinkling her two free fingers, and repeating, "Come come come."

I glanced at Bump. "Who's this?"

He shrugged. "Don't know her."

We stepped into a marble-floored foyer about eighty feet high. I caught a glimpse of a large living room with furniture that looked like it was all bought in the same place at the same time. Like the people who lived here had said, "We'll take that whole group, if you throw in the lamps and that statue thingy."

I'd have looked longer, but I really wanted the woman to stop saying, "Come come come," like we were a litter of puppies or something. Bump was already halfway down the hall. The woman was saying "Sit sit sit. I have Coke, Sprite, coffee, hot tea . . ."

Without shedding his pea jacket, Bump pulled out a stool at the breakfast bar. I took the one beside him. The woman was in the kitchen, bending into the refrigerator, her plump ass waving in the air at us. Now she had the phone caught between her ear and her shoulder. She turned to look at us impatiently and gestured with her cigarette hand for us to hurry up and tell her what we wanted to drink.

She was maybe midfifties, wearing a gray sweater

and matching slacks. Dangling earrings. Lotsa rings.
Charm bracelet. Around her waist, over the sweater,
she wore a shiny black belt for some reason.

Bump said, "Cokes'll be good."

I said quietly, "That's not Chrissy, right?"

He shook his head.

She pulled out a two-liter of Coke, lost her grip
because she was trying to hold on to it with the pads
of her fingers to protect her long nails, and dropped
it on the floor. Then she picked it up, slammed it onto
the counter beside the refrigerator, and stubbed out
the cigarette in a little glass ashtray.

I said, "That two-liter's gonna erupt like fuckin'
Mount St. Helens when she opens it."

I could talk like that, because she was involved in
her phone conversation. She said into the phone,
"You're kidding, right?"

She pulled open the freezer and yanked out an ice
cube tray. "What's a little snow? *I* got here, didn't I?"

She opened a cabinet next to the sink and pulled
out two large turquoise plastic tumblers. Her voice
turned a little more strident. "I swear to *God,* Janice.
I've always been there for *you.*"

Bump said, "That's gotta be Chrissy's mom. Drama
queen. Now I know where Chrissy gets it."

There was a loud thump overhead and Bump and
I both looked up at the ceiling. Someone was moving
around up there. Opening and closing drawers, moving stuff around. I became aware of the nearer sound
of machinery running and looked around for the
source. Off the far side of the kitchen there was another doorway and I could see the fronts of a washer
and dryer. The sound I heard was those two machines running.

The woman stood at the counter with her back to
us, one red-nailed hand on her hip, staring at the
glasses, ice cube tray, and two-liter bottle. "The roads

are *fine*. The *plumbers* got here, didn't they?" She glanced back at us. Bump raised his eyebrows.

"*Janice.* Who took you to the Air Show last summer?"

I said, "Does she think we're the plumbers?"

"I *know* I got the tickets for free. What difference does that make? I could have invited anyone, but I invited *you.*"

A wall speaker on the other side of the breakfast bar buzzed and a female voice called, "Ma?"

The woman turned and frowned at it. "Janice. Everything's *crazy* around here." She walked to the speaker and jabbed her pointer finger at random buttons, going, "What? *What?*"

Bump leaned across the breakfast counter. "You gotta press TALK."

She pressed TALK. *"What?"* But then she kept her finger on the TALK button, so that whoever was calling her couldn't be heard until a few seconds later, when she gave up, took her finger off the button, and walked back over to stare at the Coke, ice cube trays, and glasses.

The speaker yelled, "Ma? *Ma?*" Then we heard a loud thud overhead, like a foot stomped in anger, and the speaker yelled, "Oh, just *forget* it."

The woman said into the phone, "I'm sure I don't know how I'm supposed to throw a big funeral *and* get packed for the Bahamas *and* run this house for Chrissy and Sean—the *Bahamas,* Janice. Hot little islands? Margaritas and guys with tiny little butts? We're *all* going. As soon as this *funeral* business is over. Wait a minute."

I glanced at Bump. He was watching the woman with a deepening frown.

She tucked the phone between ear and shoulder, picked up the glasses and ice cube tray with one hand and the two-liter with the other, and transferred them over to us at the breakfast bar.

She told us, "Here. Pour your own. I just, I can't *manage* right now." She turned to glare at the wall speaker.

Bump leaned back and folded his arms. No way he was gonna open that two-liter and have it splooge all over the breakfast bar. I crossed my arms, too. It'd be much more fun to watch her do it.

She stood in the middle of the kitchen with her back to us. "The *Bahamas,* Janice. We're *all* going. All *seven* of us. I gotta buy two new swimsuits. I don't know where you can even *buy* a swimsuit this time of year. Well, of *course* two. We'll practically *live* in our swimsuits. Two weeks, but I'll tell you what. I might just stay there. Find myself a naughty ol' beach bum. How Cheryl Workman got her groove back. You know?"

So that was her name, whoever she was. Cheryl Workman. She said, "No, *seven*. Me and the girls. Chrissy, Holly, Pam, Bridgette, and Barbie. How many is that? Oh, and Sean. *Sean*. Ernie's son. Of *course* he's going. That makes seven, right? Well, *Chrissy's* paying for it, of course. You don't think *I* have that kind of— Oh yes she *does*. She does *now*."

Someone thumped down the stairs and we looked toward the front hall. A guy who looked to be maybe twenty, maybe a little younger, came around the corner and headed toward us, squinting. He wore a wrinkled white T-shirt that look like he'd slept in it, and cutoffs. He was average height, slender, with medium-length brown hair. His hair was all over the place. Some of it stuck up on top, like from the effects of static electricity. His face was a little too pretty for a guy. High cheekbones, big eyes. It made him look a little femmie.

Cheryl Workman said, "Sean. Hold on, Janice. Come here, honey." She held her free arm wide and he stepped into her one-armed hug. His face was turned toward us. He didn't look like he was getting much comfort out of the ordeal. While she was still hugging, Cheryl said loudly, "I said, Hold on, Janice, dammit."

Sean winced from her voice, backed out of her reach, and stood motionless in the middle of the kitchen like he wasn't fully awake yet.

Cheryl said, "How are you feeling, baby?" Into the phone, she said, "He's been sick. Poor baby loses his daddy and he's sick on top of it. What can I get you, honey? Janice, I don't know why you can't drive three lousy *miles* to come and help. *Ten* miles? Well, I think you're exaggerating. As per usual."

Meanwhile, Sean pushed past her and pulled open the refrigerator door. He rummaged around inside, then stood up. "Where's my Dr Pepper?"

Cheryl Workman said, "No, we change planes in Miami. I'm thinking of us staying there a day or two. You know, check out the scene in South Beach. Woo woo."

Sean had turned to look at her. Even from his profile, you could see he was glaring at her. He said, "Where is it? Did someone take it?"

She still paid no attention to him. He spun around and glared at us, but the glare faded when he saw the two-liter of Coke sitting there, and the glasses holding nothing but ice.

He turned back to Cheryl Workman. "Did somebody take it? That Dr Pepper is *mine*. Nobody's allowed to *touch* it." His voice was whiny and angry. Any minute I expected him to start jumping up and down like a little kid. But I thought, Well, when you lose your father suddenly like that, I guess you would have a tendency to fly apart over little things.

Someone thundered down the stairs. Bump and I turned to watch the doorway to the front hall. A bouncy blonde with the face of an angel and the body of not an angel, if you see what I'm saying, hurried into view.

Bump said into my ear, "*That's* Chrissy."

Chrissy Burdett was a stone fox. Bump climbed off his stool and stood with his arms wide. She walked into them.

She kissed him on the mouth like he was her lover. He held her and petted her back, saying into her hair, "Chrissy. I'm so sorry."

I glanced at the kid. He was glaring at them.

After a while she stepped back. She didn't look like a grieving widow to me, the way she was smiling.

She glanced my way and Bump said, "Chrissy, this is Terry Saltz. Friend of mine."

She stepped up against me and gave me a hearty kiss on the mouth. Yikes.

She said, "Thanks for coming, Terry. Did Bump say your last name is Saltz?"

I nodded.

She said, "Do you know Berk Saltz?"

I thought, First I think I see Berk at Smitty's and now Chrissy Burdett asks if I know him. He must've moved up here somewhere nearby. I said, "He's my brother. You know Berk?"

Cheryl Workman interrupted by saying loudly into the phone, "Look, Janice, come or don't come. I can't *deal* with this."

I noticed Sean was staring at me with his mouth open. Chrissy said, "Bump, have you met my mom, Cheryl Workman? And this is my stepson, Sean. Ernie's son from a previous marraige."

Cheryl's voice turned icy. "Do what you want, Janice. But if you don't come help me right now, you can consider our friendship *history*." She thumbed the disconnect button and gently placed the phone on the counter.

She glanced our way. "Chrissy. Pour the Coke for the plumbers." Then she picked up the phone and dialed a new number.

Chrissy had walked over to the coffeemaker on the

counter. She said, "They're not the plumbers, Ma. They're friends of mine. Bump and Terry." She tapped the side of the coffeepot, then pressed her fingers against it. Frowning, she bent to look at the on-off switch on the side of the unit. "Ma. Did you turn this off?"

Sean whined, "Chrissy. Where's my Dr Pepper?"

Cheryl Workman said, "I was gonna make new. Sean, honey, take the plumbers upstairs and show them where that faucet's dripping." Into the phone she said, "Liz? This is Cheryl. I suppose you've already heard about our *tragedy*."

Chrissy said, "Ma. Stop being senile and pay attention. They're not the plumbers. Did the washer shut off yet?"

Cheryl said into the phone, "Ernie's dead. *Ernie.* For God's *sakes,* Liz. *Chrissy's* husband. That's *right.* Killed in a car accident last night."

Sean took a stagger-step to the counter across from us, sagged over it, and propped his head on his hands. His eyes were squeezed tightly closed. Meanwhile, Chrissy quickly filled the coffeemaker and turned it on. Then she peered into the refrigerator, pulled out a two-liter of Dr Pepper, and gently set it on the counter next to Sean. When he opened his eyes, he wasn't looking at his Dr Pepper. He was staring straight at me.

Chrissy hurried into the laundry room, pulled a load of fluffy towels from the drier, replaced them with wet clothes from the washer, pulled a new load of dirty clothes from a basket sitting on top of the drier, dropped them into the washer, dumped in a cup of detergent, and turned both machines on.

During that time, Sean managed to rouse himself enough to get a glass from a nearby cabinet and drop ice cubes into it.

Cheryl was saying into the phone, "I'm over here

now. I need *help,* Liz. I need you to run over here—
Chrissy's house. Where do you *think*? You remember,
you were over here to swim last summer. I need you
to run over here and— The roads are *fine.*"

Chrissy took the bottle of Dr Pepper away from
Sean and poured some into his glass. She said softly,
"You feeling any better, Sean?"

Cheryl was fully engaged on the phone with Liz
now, arguing whether the roads were bad or not.

Sean said, "Maybe a little." He sipped delicately at
his Dr Pepper. Then he turned toward us, glaring
again. He said, "Who are those guys? If they aren't
the plumbers?"

Chrissy said, "That's Bump Bellini and Terry Saltz.
I used to work with Bump out at the Midway."

Sean nodded. Some of the heat went out of his
glare.

Chrissy came toward us, stopped on the far side of
the breakfast bar, and picked up the two-liter of Coke.
"Ma? You just throw the stuff on the counter and you
don't even *pour*?"

Bump said, "Uh, Chrissy, that two-liter—"

Sean said, "I'm hungry. What's for supper?"

Cheryl said, "*Supper*? You *hear* that, Liz? Now I'm
supposed to worry about supper. We've had a *tragedy*
here. People are supposed to be bringing us *casseroles*."

The doorbell rang. Chrissy said, "Oh. That's gonna
be Barbie and Bridgette." She set the two-liter back
down and hurried toward the front hall, calling back
over her shoulder, "Ma. Can't you pour the boys
their Cokes?"

Chrissy's mom said, "What am I, the *maid*?" She
grimaced at us. Into the phone she said, "I swear to
God, Liz. I have to do *everything* around here." She
started toward us.

I elbowed Bump and said quietly, "Let's get the
fuck out of here."

He nodded. We slid off our stools and followed Chrissy out to the front hall, where the door was open and two girls were banging into view. They were both blondes, both foxes, just like Chrissy. Obviously Chrissy's sisters. The three girls filled up the hallway with a lot of hugging and name-screaming.

They were squealing, interrupting each other.

"The Bahamas!"

"I don't know *any*thing about . . ."

"I gotta get a new swimsuit."

". . . on the beach all day . . ."

"Will there be one of those swim-up bars?"

Bump and I stood there, temporarily trapped, watching and listening. I was stunned. I'd been in houses a few times where the people had just suffered a death in the family, but I'd never seen anything like this.

There was a long narrow table against the stair wall. I glanced at it and saw it held a collection of framed photographs. One large one was of a couple. I picked it up. They were turned a little toward each other, smiling. The girl was Chrissy. The guy looked like a car salesman, all slicked back and suited up. His hand rested on Chrissy's shoulder. He wore a pinkie ring with a lot of sparkly stones that looked like diamonds, and there was a diamond stud in his ear.

Bump glanced over. I pointed at the guy's face. "Is that Ernie Burdett?"

He nodded.

The guy in the photo had a full head of brown hair and his face was long and lean. He looked like a sixty-year-old guy, but it was a well-preserved sixty.

The girls finished their hugging and turned toward us. Chrissy said, "Oh, Bump. Are you leaving?"

"Yeah. You'll call me if you need anything, huh?"

She stepped into his arms. "Thanks so much for coming over, Bump."

The other two girls slipped past us. Bump and Chrissy separated and we started for the door. As we pulled it open and stepped out onto the porch, I looked back toward the kitchen in time to see Cheryl Workman pick up the two-liter of Coke and twist the cap. As I pulled the front door closed, Coke exploded all over the breakfast bar.

There was a yellow one of those new VW Beetles parked behind the old silver Blazer now. Bump and I climbed into my truck. I was so disturbed by so many of the things I'd seen and heard in that house that I didn't know where to start. I glanced at Bump. He had a dark scowl on his face.

I said, "That was ugly."

He didn't answer, or even look over. I reminded myself that Chrissy Burdett was a friend of his and kept my mouth shut.

Chapter 6

We left Chrissy Burdett's house just before six. The snow was so heavy and the wind was so bad while we crept back toward town that it was like driving in potato soup. All my headlights showed was a wall of white. At times we couldn't see the hood of the truck.

We wondered if anybody would even still be at Smitty's. Like, maybe they would've all decided to go home. Because for sure there wouldn't be much business in weather like this. Bump suggested we forget Smitty's and go to his house because it was closer. But we were hungry and he said all he had in his kitchen was maybe some Campbell's soup. Which I didn't think that was gonna do it for me.

I said, "Let's go on to Smitty's and see what's what. Maybe some of them are still there."

Bump put his window down and watched the edge of the road to make sure I didn't veer off into the ditch. We didn't see a single car the whole way back to Smitty's.

I could see better once we got closer to town and I had the help of the streetlights. At least the snow wasn't so much in my face. I turned into the driveway for Smitty's and we were surprised to see that there were quite a few cars and trucks in the back lot. They were all buried in snow, of course, so we couldn't identify any of them.

We stomped into the back hall and walked toward

the bar. Jimi Hendrix's Woodstock version of "The Star-Spangled Banner" was blaring from the jukebox. Bump's blond mustache and eyebrows were caked with ice from hanging his head out the window to help keep me on the road.

Smitty and Princess were behind the bar, leaning on it and talking to Tiny and Mule and a few of the other regulars. We waved and walked on through to the dining room. There were only a few booths and tables of customers. A couple of family groups and a few tables of business types. One of the families lived just up the hill. They were Thursday night regulars. Judging by the big, padded, colorful snow boots they all wore, I guessed they'd probably walked down.

The gang was mostly there, sprawling around the back booth and the nearby tables. Bud was gone, but Gruf, Danny, and the Elliot twins were there. John was even there, still in his uniform.

I looked back toward the kitchen and saw that Hammer and his kitchen goofs were back there working. Working? I glanced in that direction in time to see Hammer moonwalk past the doorway with something that looked a lot like a bra wrapped around his head. So maybe working isn't exactly the right word. They were present.

Bump and I burst out laughing that the place was still open and they were all still there. As we shed our coats and draped them over chairs, Bump explained. "We thought you guys would've all gone home. We shoulda known better."

We'd taken to calling Hammer's kitchen crew the Smurfs. I jerked my thumb toward the kitchen. "Are the Smurfs still cooking? Can we get some supper?"

Gruf scooted his chair over to make more room. "They're just about to start closing, but they'll probably whip you something up if you talk nice to them."

Luther was already on his feet, pulling out his order

pad and grinning. "You sit, Reginald. I'm all over this. What'll it be, precious? A nice thick slice of prime rib?"

Bump got the prime rib. I got a pork chop. Nobody cooks pork chops like Hammer. Reginald insisted on getting Bump's Coke and my iced tea. I lit a smoke. When the Elliot twins are on the job, you're not gonna lift a finger waiting on yourself if they can help it.

Naturally everybody'd been talking about Gwen Dillon's murder.

Luther said, "We know a lot of people who knew her from Lo-Lites. She was generally considered to be a nasty bitch. There are a lot of people who really didn't like her."

Gruf said, "Why?"

"There was only one person who mattered to Gwen. That was Gwen. She was selfish, and had a massive ego, and she'd step on anybody to get what she wanted."

I had my mouth open to tell about the shit I'd watched her dish out to that old guy, Brown Suit, the previous night, when I happened to glance toward the bar. A familiar figure stood there with his back to me, leaning on the bar, waiting while Princess set a coffee cup in front of him.

A familiar hulking figure, wearing a snow-covered, heavy, black leather jacket over a black uniform. With a holster and handcuffs and a nightstick hanging off his belt. Alan Bushnell.

I looked over at my buds to give a heads-up, but they were all watching him get his coffee, too. The room had gone silent.

Alan said something and then Princess said something to make him laugh. He turned away from the bar smiling. Then he saw us and got serious. He came toward us gnawing his upper lip. As he got closer, I noticed his upper lip was pretty chapped. He must've been doing a lot of gnawing lately.

He set his coffee cup on the table across from Danny, removed his big black snow-covered cop hat, set it on a nearby table, squeezed out of his heavy black jacket, and draped it over the back of a chair. Then he ran his fingers through his longer-than-regulation-length steel gray hair and looked around at us.

He said, "Isn't this *nice*? All of us here together in this awful storm? And the plows aren't even running right now. They'll be idled for at least the next hour, until this blizzard lets up some. So we can all relax and enjoy a nice, cozy chat."

I glanced around. Everybody else looked about as thrilled as I was that Alan had joined us. I flicked my cigarette above an ashtray. When I looked up at Alan, I was sorry I'd done it. He was staring right at me.

Alan said, "Yeah. I was looking around town for something to do, and I thought, Lemme just take a little cruise through Smitty's parking lot. See if they've closed up and gone home like the Highway Patrol has ordered everybody to do. And there were all you guys' vehicles. And I said to myself, Well now, I wonder why all those guys are hanging around like this. I wonder, could they be having a little meeting about something? Maybe some local event that's happened? I said, Lemme just stop in and see."

Gruf said, "Okay, Alan. You're sore we beat you to another murder scene. We didn't plan it, you know. It's just something that happened."

Alan said, "It's something that's happened for the third fucking time . . ."

I said, "We heard that girl screaming so we came running. What were we supposed to do? Ignore her? It sounded like somebody was murdering *her*."

Alan shrugged me off. "Whatever. Then I start looking into the dead girl's recent history, and come to find out she was right here at Smitty's with you guys all last night. So even if you hadn't been there this morning, I'da still had you guys up my ass again."

Bump said, "Oh, wah wah. So what? It's not like we do this shit on purpose."

Actually, it *was* like we did that shit on purpose. There'd been two previous murders in or around Spencer since I'd moved to town, and both times we'd deliberately stuck our noses into the investigations behind Alan's back. And both times he'd been plenty steamed about it, even though our interference had gotten results.

Hammer, still wearing the bra, came out carrying Bump's prime rib and my pork chop. I noticed we'd both gotten a generous serving of Potatoes Hammer, which is a truly amazing recipe Hammer made up for glorified mashed potatoes with a bunch of garlic and herbs and cheeses. Yum.

Hammer set the plates in front of us and glanced at the faces sitting around the booth and table. Then he sniffed the air and beat it back into the kitchen, where people were laughing and clowning and not talking about things like murder.

Gruf said quietly, "Are we gonna sit around taking shots at each other, or are we gonna get busy and figure out who killed Gwen Dillon?"

I thought Alan would go off on us right then and there. Because the way Gruf said it, it was like, Let's all assume that us guys're gonna be investigating right alongside you, Alan. Which, okay, maybe we were, but the way we'd operated in the past, we did our sniffing around in a sneaky and surreptitious kind of way. Because Alan is not a team player. Okay, he's probably a team player, but he plays on his own team and he hadn't really given any indication he liked the idea of having *us* on it. Crimewise. See?

So I thought Alan would go off. But he controlled himself. He sipped his coffee in a thoughtful and considering kind of way. Then he pulled a notebook and a pen from his shirt pocket. He clicked the pen. It was loud. Everybody sat there waiting for him to say something.

Alan stared at me. I got interested in a callus on my thumb. He blew air out through his lips and even though I was at the next table from him, I thought I could feel his exhaled air move across my face. He leaned an elbow on the table.

Then he said, "What the fuck. All right. Let's hear about the pool match last night."

Bump said, "Hang on a minute. Before we get into all that, did Bud call you about getting Ernie Burdett's car?"

"Bud Hanratty? John gave me a message to call him . . ."

John nodded.

Alan said, "It's about Ernie Burdett's car? What about it?"

Bump said, "I drove a borrowed tow truck all over Cleveland today looking for it. They told Bud it was in a gas station on Superior, so I go there and they tell me it's in the Central Impound Lot. I go there and they don't know what I'm talking about. So then—"

Alan said, "Why does Bud want the car?"

Bump gave him a look. "Come on. You knew Ernie almost as well as Bud did. Ernie Burdett was the carefullest driver that ever lived. The cops told Bud Ernie went into Dead Man's Curve too fast. Went head-on into a pillar."

Alan said, "Then a semi hit him from behind. Crushed him right into the bridge support. Yeah. That's what I heard."

Bump was shaking his head. "Bud doesn't believe it could've happened that way. If the trucker's lying, and the truck hit him first, maybe."

Danny said, "Ernie could've had a stroke or something."

I nodded. "Good point. Or a heart attack or something."

Bump said, "Bud says they'll automatically do an autopsy. If something like that caused the accident, the autopsy will prove it. But Bud doesn't believe it could've been a result of carelessness on Ernie's part. Not a chance."

Alan nodded. "Yeah. I wondered about that myself."

"Bud wants to inspect the car. See if there was some mechanical failure or something. Can you get the Cleveland cops to find it? Get it out here?"

Alan frowned. "The car has to stay in police custody. But yeah, I'll get the CPD to let us tow it out here to the maintenance garage. And I suppose Bud can be present when we inspect it."

Bump said tightly, "He wants me there, too. I know more about cars than he does."

Alan looked doubtful. "I'll talk to Bud about it."

Alan wanted to get back to Gwen Dillon's murder. He wanted to hear about the pool match. What, if anything, had we noticed. So I told about Gwen and the old guy, Brown Suit, and how she'd driven him out so she could be with Snake Man, the dangerous-looking guy at the bar. I described the old guy and the guy at the bar. Nobody had any idea who the old guy could've been. But they all knew who Snake Man was.

Gruf said, "That was Mick Wallace."

I said, "He was wearing colors. What club is he in?"

Bump said, "Blue River Boys."

I said, "No kidding? I've heard of them."

Alan said, "That's an old club. Been around for ages."

Gruf said, "Mick owns the Lo-Lites."

Reginald nodded. "Luther and I know some of the girls who dance out there. At Lo-Lites."

Danny said, "Dance?"

Luther said, "They have topless dancers out there Thursday, Friday, and Saturday nights."

Danny said, "They do?"

Reginald said, "You didn't know that? I thought every guy in the county had been out there at least once. Anyway, we know most of those Lo-Lites people, and they *really* didn't like Gwen. Matter of fact, Allison Burgess was talking about Gwen just last night. She was furious Gwen was over at the bar all cozy with Mick, because she said she knows for a fact that Gwen's been stealing from the Lo-Lites registers."

I said, "Allison? That's the girl who found the body this morning."

Danny said, "They have topless dancers out there? Our pool match next week is out there, isn't it?"

Luther said, "Pool's on Wednesday. They only dance Thursday, Friday, and Saturday."

Danny looked crushed.

Alan had been listening quietly. A few times he wrote a word or two in his notebook. Now he leaned back in his chair and stretched his arms over his head. He came forward and leaned over the table, doodling on his notebook. He drew an arrow. "None of you are to go sniffing around Mick Wallace. And this isn't like the other times, when you sit there and nod and then go right ahead anyway. Stay away from Mick Wallace. Got that? Got that, Terry?"

I shrugged and nodded.

Alan said, "Okay. What else ya got?"

We looked at each other. Danny said that Gwen Dillon had gotten into a nasty little fight with one of her teammates. Right in the middle of her set.

That was a surprise to me. I was shooting on the next table and I never heard any of it. I turned to him. "She did?"

Danny and Bump both nodded. Bump said, "I heard it, too. She started bitching him out for using the bread slicer at Lo-Lites to slice tomatoes before they left to come to Smitty's. Then not cleaning it. She'd found tomato seeds all glued to the blade. He told her he didn't do it, but that she should go fuck herself."

Danny said, "Then she said she was gonna tell Mick and Mick was probably gonna fire his ass. Then he said if she did that it'd be the last thing she ever did."

Alan said, "When did this happen?"

Danny and Bump looked at each other. Bump said, "When was it? You shot first, Terry. So, sometime after seven-thirty?"

Danny nodded.

Alan said, "Okay, so he threatened her. What then?"

Bump said, "Nothing. She laughed at him."

Danny nodded. "That was it. She laughed, and then it was her shot. I don't remember seeing the guy after that."

Bump said. "Me, either."

Alan said, "Do you know the guy's name?"

Danny said, "No, but I saw his face. I'd recognize him."

Bump nodded. "He works out at the Lo-Lites. I think his name is Wes Fletcher, but I'm not positive."

Reginald Elliot spoke up. "Does he have a hideous scar down the right side of his face?"

Bump said, "I don't know if I'd call it hideous, but yeah. You know him?"

Reginald nodded. "That's Wes Fletcher, all right."

Alan said, "Okay. What else?"

Gruf brought up about Allison telling us how Gwen had vowed to marry a rich guy before she was thirty. Alan said Allison had repeated the story to him.

Princess walked over from the bar carrying a coffee

cup, quietly pulled out a chair from the next table, and sat down. She looked tired. I smiled at her.

Alan asked me again about the old guy Gwen had been with when she decided she'd rather be with Mick Wallace. "Did you at least hear her call him by name?"

I nodded. "I did, but I can't think of it right now. Maybe it'll come back to me."

He wanted to say something nasty, you could tell, but he didn't.

Reginald said, "Boy. You just never know, do you? In the space of a few short hours, Gwen Dillon and Ernie Burdett are both gone. What a terrible coincidence, huh?"

Alan was scribbling in his notebook. He muttered, "No such thing as coincidence." He put a period to whatever he'd written and looked up around the table. "Anybody got anything else?"

We looked at each other and shook our heads.

I said, "Allison couldn't find Gwen last night. When she wanted to get her purse out of Gwen's car, it was locked and Gwen wasn't around."

Danny said, "She coulda just been in the can or something."

Alan said, "Yeah. Well, if Gwen left Smitty's, then she came back at some point. She picked up her car and drove back to her apartment parking lot. Somebody was waiting for her there."

I said, "Is that how it was? Somebody was waiting there and strangled her right where we found her?"

"That's what the ME says. She died right there in her car." Alan drained the last of his coffee. "I need to find out who Brown Suit was."

I said, "Ask Mick Wallace. He sat right there and watched Gwen Dillon drive him away."

"Good idea." Alan made a note in his notebook. He pushed away from the table and stood up. "You guys get this place closed and go home." He began to pull on his heavy jacket. "And don't talk to anyone about anything that has to do with Gwen Dillon's murder." He began to walk toward the front door. Then he turned back. "And stay the fuck out of my case."

Chapter 7

I was driving my truck along the beach at Headlands State Park. Lake Erie was violent with wind and waves. The surf crashed, slashed, thrashed against the shore and the wind flung water, spitting and hissing, against my truck, hard enough to rock it.

A horn honked. Then I realized it wasn't so much a horn honking as a phone ringing. It rang again, and I realized I wasn't so much driving my truck along the beach up at Headlands as lying in my bed. By the third ring my groping hand found the phone on my nightstand.

"Yeah."

"You up yet?"

My brain farted, belched, and groggily began to search the index for a name and a face that matched the voice. Ah. Gruf.

I said, "Hey."

He said, "Hey yourself. Getcher lazy ass up outa bed and look out your window."

I turned over, got onto my knees, leaned against my oak headboard, and spread the white miniblinds that cover the windows above my bed. All I saw was a wall of white.

I said, "Holy whiteness."

Gruf said, "Is your power off?"

I glanced at my clock radio. The time showed in red digits. Five fifty-five a.m. "It's on."

"You're lucky. It's off at my house. The whole north side of Spencer is dark. Everything's out from the square all the way out past Pete's."

"Brewster's, too?"

"Brewster's, too."

"No Number Four this morning for a big boy?"

He laughed. "No number anything. And Alan stopped over here at the house a little while ago. Only emergency vehicles are allowed out on the roads. Somebody from the department's gonna call John and tell him to stay home but to be on standby. If they need him, they'll come get him in one of the SUVs."

"Fuck. I could drive him up to town, or just give him my truck keys."

"Don't be so sure. They pulled the plows off the streets again at about three a.m. and they're still off. Alan said the road crews are sitting around in the maintenance garage, drinking coffee and smoking. He said there's drifts across all the roads, particularly the north-south roads, as high as five, six feet deep, and it's useless to plow because the wind just drives the snow back where it was."

"Well, shit."

He said, "Yup. Okay, I just wanted to make sure John got the word. He wouldn't get a foot up your street in that little Geo of his."

"Yeah. Thanks."

"Okay. I've got a lot of loafing to do today, so I need to get started."

I walked out to the kitchen and got the coffee going. The trailer felt like a walk-in cooler. I figured it was that relentless wind. Off and on during the night I'd felt the trailer rocking under the force of the stronger gusts. As the coffee started to drip I walked back to my bedroom to pull on socks, jeans, and a flannel shirt.

By the time I got back out to the kitchen, Danny

was standing at the sink, watching the coffeepot fill up and scratching his ass. He looked over at me. "It's fuckin' freezin' in here."

I said, "I know. This fuckin' wind."

But as I said it, I glanced at the window by the kitchen table and saw a problem. "Well, this accounts for some of it. The storm window's wide open."

It was my fault, too. I'd sat at the table before bedtime, smoking and going over the work ahead of us in the lawyers' offices. I'd opened the window every time the room got too smoky. Apparently I'd forgotten to close the storm window before I went to bed. I quickly corrected the problem and slammed the inner window closed.

Just in that short time, a little pile of snow collected on the kitchen table. I scraped it together, packed it, and tossed it at the back of Danny's neck, scoring a direct hit. He squealed like a girl and brushed it off into the sink, laughing. He said, "Just remember, my friend. Paybacks are hell."

I decided to go out and shovel our little bit of driveway while I waited for the coffee. I gave Danny Gruf's message for John, threw on my snow gear, and headed outside into the predawn darkness.

The key to being out in that storm was to face out of the wind. You turned toward the wind and right away you had a problem because your face froze up and also you couldn't breathe. Facing out of the wind went much better. I got the shovel from the little shed at the back of the carport and quickly began throwing snow. Gruf had been right. Even in our little driveway there was a drift five feet deep, and I'd shoveled it clear last thing before bed.

I was just about finished, and thinking about a steaming cup of coffee, when I heard a scraping noise from across the dark street. I stopped and looked, but I had to look for a while before there was enough of a lull in the screaming, driving snow so I could see that far. There was a small, stooped shadow over there struggling in the dark with a snow shovel. Little old person of indeterminate sex.

Even through the driving snow, even though it was still dark out, I could tell it was someone who was too old to be outside dealing with that shit. As I watched I saw the wind get hold of the shovel blade and wave it around in the air while the gray held on for dear life. After another few seconds, there was a momentary break in the white wall and I clearly saw the yellow scarf tied babushka-style under the red ear-flapped hunter's hat, and the section of red, skinny, bare leg sticking out from under the flimsy housedress and the shapeless black overcoat. It was a woman. Little old lady.

I looked for a way around the deep drift that stretched between her driveway and mine. In order to get across, I had to arc up the street almost half a lot and come back down.

She was facing away from me, and I didn't want to startle her and give her a heart attack, so as I approached, I tried to yell, "Hey. Need some help there?" But the wind caught my words and pushed them right back down my throat. She didn't hear me until I was almost behind her. I yelled, "Ma'am? Hey. I'll do that for you."

She whirled around with her shovel up like a weapon and yelled, *"Get back."*

Now I could dimly see her wrinkled, warty-nosed, runny-eyed, angry face. And she was angry.

I stepped off laughing. *"Wo.* I'm your neighbor. I'm Terry. I live right over there." I pointed across the street.

She yelled, "Then get *back* over there, you little sonofabitch." She feinted at me with the shovel.

Which first of all, I'm six-five and she couldn't have stood an inch over four-eight, all crippled and bent over and humpbacked like she was, so I didn't know who she thought she was calling little. And second, I don't know what she thought she could do with that fuckin' shovel, which by the way was all dented and bent up like somebody had run over it with a car three or four times.

I laughed, but I was getting offended. "Ma'am. I just wanna help you. Why don't you go inside and get warm and let me shovel your driveway?"

She glared at me and gummed her lower lip. I say gummed rather than chewed because I caught a brief glimpse of blue gum and there wasn't a tooth to be seen anywhere in the vicinity.

She said nastily, "I was born at night, but I wasn't born *last* night."

"Beg pardon?"

She was nodding, looking me up and down. "I let you shovel, thinking you're doing me a favor outa the goodness of your heart, and the next thing I know, you're at my door demanding a fiver. Little hippy bastard."

A *fiver*? If I was gonna charge her, I'd charge a hell of a lot more than five bucks. I was starting to think I was gonna hafta kill this old lady dead in order to have the pleasure of shoveling her fucking driveway.

"It's *free*. No *charge*. Get in your *house* and *let me shovel*." I was yelling at her by that time, and it wasn't just to be heard over the wind.

She gave me another long glare, like she was actually debating whether to do me the great honor of letting me shovel her driveway for free or not. Then she began to slowly shuffle through the deep snow toward her trailer. But she stopped several times to look back at me and share a few more thoughts. Such as, "I'm not paying you one red *cent*, young man." And, "Make sure you shovel by the driver's-side door of my car."

Jeez. She crabwalked up the driveway to her porch,

painfully climbed the stairs, and disappeared inside the crummy little trailer. I went to work. I was cold all over by that time, especially my toes and my legs because my jeans were wet up past my knees. I shoveled up to her car, which was parked even with her porch, and I shoveled a wide swath all the way around it. Then I went to work on her little steps and porch. Every time I glanced toward her trailer I saw her glaring out her window at me.

I was just finishing the back edge of the porch, freezing my ass off by that time, trying to concentrate on the comfort I'd soon be getting from a dry pair of socks and that hot cup of coffee, when she startled me by yelling, *"Hey!"*

Her voice was so sharp and so loud I think both my frozen feet left the ground. I looked around at her. Her gnarly old head was sticking half out the window.

"There's rock salt in the garbage can under the porch. Spread it nice and thin, all the way over to the driver's side. And don't try stealing any. I know *exactly* how much is in there." As she slammed the window, I swear I heard her mutter, "Little sonofabitch."

Well, fuck. Running away with all her rock salt was gonna be the crowning achievement of my entire criminal career. But I trudged around to the garbage can, lifted off the lid, and looked inside. She barely had any in there. I had to upend the battered old aluminum garbage can and bang on the sides of it to accomplish a thin layer of rock salt on her porch and steps and over to the driver's-side car door.

When I was finished, I fitted the lid back on and pushed the empty can back under her porch. I looked up at her window, intending to give her a look, like, Now aren't you ashamed of yourself? But of course there was no sign of her. As I walked away I muttered, "You're welcome."

Danny laughed at me when I stomped into our

trailer. By that time there was a layer of ice attached to my eyebrows and mustache. He said, "You were out long enough. What'd you do, shovel the whole fuckin' trailer park?"

I sat at the kitchen table and pried off my frozen work boots. "Just the sweet little old lady's driveway across the street."

"I know. I looked out when you first went over. From what I could see, it looked like she was yelling at you."

I tugged off the first soggy sock. My feet were bright red. My toes were white. "I don't wanna say she was a witch, but if she ever offers you candy to stick your head in her oven, don't do it."

Around noon Bump called. "You guys got power?"

I said, "Yeah. You?"

"Fuck no. But Ray's over and we've got the fireplace cranked. It's almost *too* hot in here. We're roasting hot dogs."

Ray is Bump's younger brother. He looks just like Bump, only smaller and paler. Like he's a diluted version, or something. I said, "Ray. That was the name Gwen Dillon called Brown Suit. I remember because at the time I thought, Hey, same name as Bump's brother."

Bump said, "Huh. I just talked to Gruf. Smitty's can't open tonight even if they do get the power back on and the plows back out on the streets, because none of the jobbers'll come out to Spencer today."

"This morning would've been the beer deliveries. Miller *and* Bud."

"Yeah. Smitty was on the phone with them, and with Sisco. None of them are running trucks out to Grand County today."

"Well, shit. Hate to miss a Friday night."

"Yeah. Busiest night of the week. At least Smitty

and Gruf are making so much money off the new restaurant that missing a Friday night won't hurt 'em too bad. Heard from Mike lately?''

Mike is Bump's sister. A knife twisted in my heart. "Just that letter last week I told you about. You?"

"Naw. I told you about my last one. Fuck. Me and Ray are missing her today."

We hung up. It dawned on me that the whole rest of a day was stretched out ahead of me and I had absolutely nothing to do. I had a sensation like when you fall backwards. I groped for a chair at the kitchen table, sank onto it, and sighed unhappily. After a while I wandered into the living room, flopped onto the sofa, switched on the TV, and surfed channels. I couldn't find anything I wanted to watch, so I turned it off after a few minutes and walked back to my bedroom. I closed my door and stretched out on top of my bedspread.

Mike Bellini is Bump and Ray's sister. I guess I knew the first time I ever saw her that I wanted to spend the rest of my life with her. She's tall for a girl, five-ten plus in her bare feet, and she's got gleaming black hair that she wears curled toward her chin, or sometimes she'll pin it up, only little curls get loose here and there and fall across the pale perfect skin of her forehead and temples. She's got these little rose-bud lips and big dark eyes, and she's funny. Her laugh would melt granite. When we met she was working as a third shift ER nurse at the Cleveland Clinic. Her brother Ray worked there, too, only he worked day shift.

I wanted her right from the beginning. But she was so beautiful I knew she had to be surrounded by guys who were tripping over their dicks because they were so snowed over her. You know? So I stayed cool, even when she started to send signals she was interested in me.

Then one night my patience paid off. She called and said we should go to a movie together. We had a great time and I said to myself that I love it when a plan comes together. My plan was, I wanted to marry her and build us a house on a little land with some water and woods, and she and I would fill it up with kids, and we'd have a bunch of postcard Thanksgivings and Martha Stewart Christmases as we grew old together there.

Things were moving right along. We went to the movies. We went out to eat. Then one night she mentioned a female doctor from Denmark who was at the Clinic developing new kinds of light-weight, adaptable medical equipment for an outfit called Doctors Without Borders. She was going to spend three months at the Clinic, getting her equipment invented, and then she was going to Africa to distribute it and teach the medical people who were already there how to use it.

The doctor made a big impression on Mike. It got so every time I saw Mike she wanted to tell me more about Dr. Mikkelsen. Dr. Bodil Mikkelsen. Mike and Dr. Mikkelsen got in the habit of going to the cafeteria together whenever things got quiet in the middle of third shift. The two of them sat there in the middle of the night in the dark cafeteria drinking coffee, Mike listening, wide-eyed and breathless, while Dr. Mikkelsen talked about her project.

I felt like an asshole when I realized I was beginning to get jealous. Here's this brilliant, fearless doctor who's paid her own way to come to the States to improve emergency medical care in the Third World, and here's ol' Terry Saltz the carpenter getting pissed because his girlfriend talks about her too much.

Then Dr. Mikkelsen asked the Clinic to give her Mike's services for the duration of her stay in Cleveland. She needed an assistant and Mike had a lot of emergency and trauma experience. Mike started call-

ing the doctor Bobo. Then Mike wanted Bobo and
me to meet each other. I spent enough money on a
suit that I coulda bought a pretty decent used car and
we took Bobo out to dinner.

I don't know what I expected, but Bobo turned out
to be a tiny, hyperactive blonde with birdlike manner-
isms and a smile that lit the room. I watched the little
lemon Danish as she perched on the edge of her chair,
her back ramrod straight, and pecked at her food. Her
voice was high and musical and she gestured with her
hands in rapid little twitches and pokes.

As she spoke about the African countries she would
soon be touring, she got so excited she seemed to
shoot off sparks. I felt like I was in the presence of a
living saint or something.

Our plates were being cleared away. Mike com-
mented on the sacrifices Bobo had made to do what
she was doing. Bobo said all she was sacrificing was a
little bit of her time. She'd been very fortunate in her
life. Inherited family money and a successful medical
practice in Denmark had more than set her up to live
well for the rest of her life.

She told us she'd always planned that, at some
point, she'd find a way to give something back to the
world. One day she had stepped back and made an
assessment. Her husband was nearing retirement and
their son was in college. If she was ever going to act,
it had to be now. She could easily afford to volunteer
a year or two of her time.

I looked at Mike. Mike, Bump, and Ray had each
inherited a tidy sum when their father died. She and
I were on the edge of starting our life together. I
watched her play with her coffee cup and I could read
her mind like a book. She was thinking that if she was
ever gonna do something like the doctor was doing,
now was the time for her, too.

A week later she sat across from me in the back

booth at Smitty's and said it out loud. She was thinking about going to Africa with Bobo for a year. She
wanted to know what I thought of the idea.

I kept my face blank, but inside, I was like, Africa?
I can't claim to be up on my current world events, but
my semi-informed idea of Africa was that it's a conti-
nent full of violence, disease, famine, and drought.
War broke out in my brain. Bad Terry said, No. Don't
go. It's too dangerous, and I want you here. Good
Terry said, But if she goes, she'll save lives. Bad Terry
said, Fuck that. I want her here in *my* life. Good Terry
said, You selfish sonofabitch.

Good Terry won. I swallowed back what I really
felt and told her it was a decision she had to make
for herself. If she wanted to do it, I'd support her
however she needed me to, and I'd be here waiting
when she came back.

I really didn't think she'd do it. I thought she'd play
with the idea in her mind, try it out and talk about it
some, but then in the end she'd decide not to go. I
was wrong. She signed on for a year, there was a brief
month of breakneck preparations, and then she was
gone. Her and Bobo.

That had been three months ago. For three months
I'd been trying my best to keep busy and keep the
faith and be satisfied with the occasional breathless
letter and sometimes a couple of blurry photos tucked
into the envelope. I was trying my hardest to be positive, but I was worried sick about her. Every time I
thought about her, which was about every other minute, it was like a knife was twisting in my chest.

As time went by, my thoughts had been trying to
turn bitter. I'd catch myself thinking that if Mike had
loved me enough, she wouldn't have wanted to go. I'd
catch myself feeling envious of how even stupid people seem to stumble into happiness almost by accident.
I wondered how it was that they could go through life

taking their good luck for granted, while, no matter how hard I worked at it, I always seemed to fall short. I wondered if, in setting my sights on Mike, maybe I'd reached a little too high. I fought it, but sometimes I'd catch myself thinking that Mike was never going to come back to me.

But most of the time when these dark thoughts tried to crowd in on me, I smothered them. The thing to do was to work as hard and as much as I could, save every dime I could, and proceed on blind faith. Some way or other, everything would turn out fine if I just kept moving forward. I tried to keep so busy that I'd forget about that knife. Sometimes it even worked for a while.

In the middle of the afternoon I heard an engine idling in front of the trailer. An SUV had come by to pick up John. He was needed at the station. After he left, Danny and I got busy cleaning the place and doing laundry, shit like that. Late in the afternoon the phone rang again. I answered.

The voice said, "Hi, Terry. How are you?"

I recognized the voice. It was my ex-wife, Marylou, formerly known as the Bitch. My stomach clenched. Then I remembered that this was the New and Improved Marylou. The one who was thoughtful and unselfish. The one who had come under the influence of Mike Bellini. The one who was going out with Bud Hanratty. My stomach unclenched.

I said, "Good. And yourself?"

"I'm good. Listen, I have a job for you guys."

I was puzzled. She had a townhouse in Green Acres, which was a very new development out Third Avenue, just past Pete's convenience store. I couldn't imagine what kind of job she might have for us there. Especially on her salary as a bank teller. I didn't even understand how she could afford to live in Green Acres on her salary.

I said, "A job?"

"Yup. It's at Bud's. We want to do some fixing up."

God knows Bud's house needed some fixing up. Except for the beautiful deck me and Gruf had built on the back, his place was a big yellow sprawling slum. But the timing of this surprised me. The last time I'd seen Bud, he was struggling to come to terms with the death of his good friend Ernie Burdett. It was odd that he would pause in the middle of his grief and suddenly decide to remodel his house.

I said, "Sure. We'd be happy to work for Bud again. Tell him to call me."

"Um. Well, *I'm* calling you. I'd like you to come out and meet me there one day next week. I'll show you what I—we—want done, and I've got some magazine pictures."

I thought, Do I just have a suspicious mind, or does this sound a lot like the old Marylou? The one I used to call the Bitch.

I said carefully, "Sure. Just have Bud call and let me know what day he'll be available."

"Well, actually, Bud's awfully busy during the day. And plus this Ernie thing. I thought you and I could just meet out at his house, and I could show you what—"

I said, "Marylou. Does Bud want this work done, or is this all your idea?"

"Well, of course he wants it done."

"Then have him call me and we'll set up a time."

"But Terry, I—"

"I gotta run now, Marylou. Nice talkin' to ya." I hung up the phone and sat there pushing my cigarette around in the ashtray. I was thinking, She's ba-ack. Poor Bud.

Just after dark, the wind died down and Danny and I went outside to shovel. While Danny shoveled our driveway, I did the nasty old gray's across the street. I didn't see any sign of her, although there were lights on inside her trailer.

We turned in right after Letterman was over. There still hadn't been a single plow through the trailer park by the time we went to bed. The snow was so deep that they were gonna need front end loaders and dump trucks to clear the streets. Those rolled in and went to work just about the time I drifted off to sleep. All night long, it seemed like every time I drifted off to sleep another plow or dump truck screamed past my window.

Chapter 8

I got up early Saturday morning because there were a few things I wanted to do before a certain wicked witch of the trailer park was up across the street. I drove into town with my fingers crossed, hoping Pete's twenty-four-hour convenience store was open. It was, and I bought two bags of rock salt there. I parked out on the street, and then I grabbed the rock salt and my snow shovel and crept through the darkness over to her trailer.

I dumped the rock salt into her garbage can, thinking, Let her try to figure this one out. Then I quick shoveled her driveway off, salted it, and hurried back to my own damn side of the street. I never saw her cranky old face pop up in her side window, so I think I got in and out clean.

Then I shoveled our driveway. All that shoveling went much easier than the day before because there wasn't any wind and we'd only gotten another few inches overnight. As I was throwing the next to last shovelful, a big black Lexus purred to a stop at the end of the driveway. The heavily tinted window on the driver-side door lowered smoothly and I found myself looking at Jimmy Chandler, owner of Chandler's Trailer Park. He smiled in the green glow of his dashboard lights.

I leaned on my shovel and said, "Hey, Jimmy. How the fuck are ya?"

Jimmy's kind of a greasy old fish. When you talk to him you have a tendency to want to feel for your wallet in your jeans pocket and keep your hand on it. But he's always been friendly enough to me.

He said, "You're up and at it bright and early."

I nodded.

He said, "Just wanted to drive through the park. Make sure the plow guys gave me my money's worth last night."

"They were roaring around all night long."

He grinned.

I said, "Hey, Jimmy . . ." I stepped a little closer to the Lexus so I could lower my voice. "The old lady who lives across the way there . . ." I pointed to the crappy little trailer across the street. "What's her name?"

Jimmy said, "You mean Mrs. Carmody?" I was like, If I knew she was Mrs. Carmody, would I be asking her name? But the guy was my landlord, so I just pointed to the trailer again. He said, "Yeah. Maude Carmody. Why? She giving you trouble?"

"No. Not at all. I just wondered about her. Living alone over there. She is alone, right?"

He hooted. "Who'd live with that crusty old bitch? Yeah, she's alone."

I nodded.

He said, "What about her?"

I shrugged. "Nothing. Just wanted to know her name, that's all."

Smitty's was slammed Saturday night, even though the temperature dropped into the low teens. It seemed like everybody was making up for time lost due to the blizzard. There was a line waiting for tables in the dining room until past ten, and the bar was rocking. It was a good thing our vendors had resupplied us Saturday morning. It seemed like every time I checked the beer coolers under the bar, they needed restocking. I couldn't tell you how many times I had to go back to the beer cooler, load cases of beer onto that old dolly, and wheel it out to the bar.

Just after ten, I straightened from loading bottles of Miller Lite into their under-bar cooler and stood there looking at the ceiling, acting like I didn't know I was in Princess's way. She realized what I was doing, laughed, said, "Terry, you idiot," and elbowed me in the ribs. As I turned away I saw Gruf on the front side of the bar giving me the signal.

He was moving toward a couple of guys over by the jukebox. Bump was closing in on them from the back pool table. Money was about to change hands between the two guys. Bump lifted one of them by the collar and the back of his pants and started down the back hall with him.

Gruf told me over his shoulder, "Get the buyer, too." He moved to follow Bump down the hall.

I grabbed the second guy the same way I'd seen Bump grab the first and followed Bump and Gruf out the back door, only my guy was kicking me in the shins and knees the whole way. Danny was right behind me.

Bump had his guy out in the parking lot, laid over the trunk of the nearest car. I took my guy to the other side of the car, but as I tried to lay him out, he tried to twist out of my grasp and come around on me. Before I knew what was happening, my guy was flat on his face and Bump had a knee in his back and a handful of his hair and was pushing his face into the snow. When he stopped struggling, Bump lifted his head and asked did he want any more of that. The guy spit snow and gravel and said he didn't. Bump lifted him up and laid him over the car so he and his buddy were facing each other.

The buddy was saying, "What the fuck? We weren't doing anything."

Gruf bent over him. "You were dealing drugs in our bar. *Nobody* deals drugs in our bar."

They started to deny it, but Bump was already pulling stuff from the second guy's pockets. I moved around and started doing the same to the first guy. When Bump had his guy fully unloaded, he stood him up straight. Danny and I did the same with our guy and we stood him up beside his buddy. The contents of their pockets lay in a single pile on the trunk of the car.

I'd never seen either one of them before. It didn't seem like Bump or Gruf knew them, either. The one Bump had carried out was skinny and had stringy brown hair. My guy was shorter and stockier and dark. He was wearing engineer boots. No wonder I felt it when he kicked me all the way out to the parking lot.

Gruf said, "*Dammit.* What do we do now?"

Bump was looking at the pile of stuff. He picked out several small packets of waxed paper and held them up. "What is this?"

The little stocky guy said, "It ain't nothing." There was all snow and gravel stuck to his face.

I never saw Bump move. There was a soft thud and a rush of air, and Stocky suddenly grabbed his gut and doubled over, moaning. Bump straightened him up and said, "One more chance. What's in the packets?"

The skinny guy said, "Don't hit him again. It's horse."

Gruf was way pissed. "You're dealing *horse* in our bar? Holy fuckin' shit."

Bump said, "Danny. Go call the cops. Let 'em bust their asses."

Both guys started to plead. Bump turned toward them and the little dark one broke off in midwhine. The skinny one said, "No. *Please.* I got a wife and a kid."

Bump snorted. "Wow. Little Junior must be proud of his daddy."

Skinny's head jerked back like he'd been slapped. Bump nudged Gruf. "Dude. Call the cops."

Gruf was wrestling with his decision. He glanced at Danny. I knew what he was thinking. On the one hand, these guys'd been dealing horse in the bar. We couldn't have that. On the other hand, Gruf was accustomed to enjoying a pull on his bowl now and then during the day. Danny was, too. Calling the cops on these guys seemed a little hypocritical, even if the substance in question was horse, and not merely good ol' pot.

Gruf said, "I don't know you guys. Where are you from?"

The skinny guy said, "Euclid." Euclid is a suburb of Cleveland.

The stocky guy said, "Mespo." Mespo was short for Mesopotamia, which is a small town east and south of Spencer.

Gruf said, "Why'd you pick Smitty's to do your deal?"

The skinny guy said, "It was just a place in the middle."

The stocky guy from Mespo said, "My cousin'd been telling me about this place. He said you have good steaks and it's a cool bar."

Gruf said, *"Fuck."*

Bump said, "Well, if you aren't gonna call the cops, at least let's give 'em something to remember us by." He turned toward the two guys and stretched his arms out wide, pulling the sleeves of his T-shirt up so he'd have free movement to swing.

Gruf said, "Hold on, Bump. You. Euclid."

The skinny guy, the dealer, looked at him. Gruf said, "I never forget a face. Don't you ever set foot in this bar, or even this parking lot, again, or I'll let my friend here pound on you until his arms get tired. You understand me?"

The skinny guy nodded so hard I thought his head

might fall off. "I won't. I swear. I'll never come anywhere near Spencer again."

"Grab your stuff and get the fuck out of here. And
don't spin your tires on the way out."

Skinny moved cautiously at first, like he was afraid
Bump might overrule Gruf's decision and grab him.
When he was out of reach, he turned and ran for his
car, but he remembered not to throw gravel. He drove
out of the parking lot like somebody's great-grandma.

Stocky watched him go. Then he turned hopefully
to Gruf. "Can I go, too?"

Gruf said, "We're gonna remember you. Any time
you ever come here again, you're gonna be searched.
If we ever find *any*thing on you again, even if it's just
pot, I'll turn you over to this guy here"—he jerked
his thumb at Bump—"and I won't give a shit *what* he
does to you. Clear?"

Stocky nodded, shooting fearful looks at Bump.

Gruf said, "And you tell your cousin, and everybody else you know out there in Mespo, If you're
coming to Smitty's, leave your drugs at home. You
understand me?"

Stocky nodded.

Gruf said, "Get outa here. And make sure you drive
out even slower than that other asshole did."

At around two-thirty, Danny and I went to work
on the floor in the bar and the front entryway. He
swept, I mopped. About the time we were finished
with that, we broke up a little scuffle over on the back
side of the bar. Bump finished restocking the bar for
the last time, and Gruf headed back to the office to
call his girlfriend Jackson down in Kent and say good
night, and to do the closing paperwork.

Jackson's real name is Lauren King. She'd been in-
spired by Mike Bellini to get herself into college. She
was in her third quarter in the nursing program at

Kent State University. She was paying her way with savings from working summers and holidays at the bar, combined with what she made from a part-time job at a pizza place down there in Kent.

Between her job and her schoolwork, she didn't have much free time. Every couple of weeks, Gruf would make the hour or so long drive down to Kent to spend the night, but, for the most part, he was left almost as high and dry as I was, girlfriend-wise.

I love Jackson like a little sister. I was proud of her for getting herself into college and because she was acing all her courses. She hadn't decided for sure what kind of nursing she wanted to specialize in, but she was thinking about psychiatric nursing because she liked the psychology courses she'd taken so far. She was always telling Gruf about things she'd learned in psychology.

Anyway. At two forty-five, Princess gave last call and the barflies began to wander out into the parking lot. I watched Tiny cram himself into his Carhartt and then drag Mule away from his final longneck. Mule needed a little help getting down the back hall and out the door, so I led the way and opened the doors for Tiny. Any little thing I can do for Tiny.

Cars were crawling slowly out of the dark parking lot. The sound of the frigid tires crunching on the crisp snow set my teeth on edge. There was a Camaro about halfway down the first row that was slow to start. I listened for a minute to the way the engine screamed No no no each time the guy turned his key in the ignition, and thought I might hafta drive him home if he couldn't get the thing started, but it finally caught and I happily watched him roll away.

I walked into the kitchen as Gruf was pulling the last full tray out of the dishwasher. Him and Bump were talking. I only heard the last word of Bump's sentence, which was autopsy.

I said, "Huh? What?"

They both turned to look at me. Gruf said, "How long were you outside?"

"I wasn't. Just stood in the doorway making sure that guy with the Conan O'Brien hair got his Camaro started."

"No shit? Your cheeks are bright red. Is it that cold out?"

"It's cold. What about an autopsy?"

Bump picked up his stack of clean dinner plates and carried them over to the plate shelf. "Ernie Burdett. I was just saying that I don't know when the family's gonna be able to hold the calling hours at the funeral home. He's gotta be autopsied downtown and it hasn't been done yet."

Gruf turned around from the dishwasher. "Oh. Jackson had some news. Hammer, get somebody on the fryers."

Hammer nudged a kid who was standing beside him at the work counter tearing lettuce. The kid whined, "You always make me do it."

Hammer said, "That's because I don't like you," and twinkled his fingers at him.

I turned back to Gruf. "Jackson had news?"

"Yeah. The cousin of some girl she talks to knew Gwen Dillon in high school."

Bump and Danny closed in on us to hear better. Bump said, "Which high school?"

"Bagby. Right before senior year, the Dillons suddenly moved to Black Creek. Nobody could figure out why they moved so suddenly. A rumor went around that Gwen had been involved with a Bagby teacher."

Danny said, "No shit?"

By this time we were standing in a tight little circle. Me, Gruf, Bump, Danny. We looked like a football huddle, only we were upright.

I said, "Speaking of Gwen Dillon, are we gonna

stay out of Alan's way this time like he told us to? Or are we gonna try and find her killer?"

Everybody looked at everybody else. Grins began to appear. In a very short time we were all laughing.

I said, "That's what I thought."

Bump said, "As far as I'm concerned, we can start on Gwen Dillon's murder just as soon as this thing about Ernie Burdett's accident gets cleared up."

Danny said, "Maybe Ernie's autopsy will answer some questions, huh? Like, maybe he had a heart attack or something, and that's what caused his accident."

Bump nodded.

I said, "The guy who's doing it better get a move on, or he's gonna find himself interfering with Cheryl Workman's tropical vacation."

Gruf said, "Cheryl Workman?"

Bump said, "Chrissy's Burdett's mother."

"Ooooh."

Bump said, "Yeah. She can't go on her big vacation in the Bahamas until the coroner releases Ernie's body and they have the funeral. So the coroner better hurry up and get that autopsy done."

I said, "Or somebody'll be autopsying him."

Chapter 9

By the time I woke up Sunday morning, it wasn't any-more. Morning. I farted, stretched, noticed my back was feeling a little tender from moving all those cases of beer, rolled over, looked at my clock radio, and saw it was 12:01.

I staggered out to the kitchen. The coffeemaker hadn't been fired up yet, so I knew I was the first one up. I was just loading the thing when I heard the shower go on down the hall. A minute later Danny's voice cranked up. This morning he was doing a little something by the Mamas and Papas, with his own spe-cial spin. *"Sunday Sunday, can't trust that day. Sunday Sunday, sometimes it just turns out so ga-a-ay."*

It's even worse when he raps. I knew if John hadn't been awake before, he was now.

The phone rang. I answered it. It was a girl asking for John in a sweet little voice. Nervous. "Is John Garvey there, please?" She said it like if he wasn't, she'd practically die of the disappointment.

I yelled, "John. You up? Phone."

He yelled back, "Yeah. Coming." And padded out to the kitchen barefoot. I handed him the phone and heard his voice go quiet and tender and happy when he heard who it was. From his end of the conversation, I could tell she was asking him about our recent bliz-zard. He explained Lake Effect Snow. Then I had a pretty good idea this was a girl from back home in Indiana. John carried the phone back to his bedroom and closed the door.

I got the milk out of the refrigerator and lit a smoke to wait for the coffee. After a while Danny straggled out, fixed himself some coffee, and joined me at the table. I finished my coffee and wandered off to take my shower. When I came back out, John was still on the phone in his room and Danny wanted breakfast. On the way to Brewster's, Danny called Bump and Gruf to tell them we were going. They both said they'd meet us there.

In the parking lot, I pulled into a space next to a big white panel truck. I stared at it in wide-eyed wonder. "Well. Look who's here."

Danny read the red lettering on the side of the truck. "Grodell's Plumbing. Would that be Pookie Grodell?"

I said, "Yes it would."

Danny said, "I never got to meet him."

I was grinning. "Well, you're in for a rare treat."

Pookie and his brothers, Willie and Dirt, used to be regulars at Brewster's. But Pookie had gotten himself in some trouble a year or so earlier, and ever since then, him and his two brothers had been keeping a low profile. This was the first time I'd seen them since. We walked inside and there they were at the front register, paying their bill. Pookie helped himself to a fistful of after-dinner mints, turned away from the register, and found himself looking up at me.

He said, "Hey. You're that one guy."

"Hey, Pookie. How you doing? Willie? Dirt?"

Pookie said, "We've been waiting around all damn morning for you guys. Where's Bump Bellini?"

He was craning his neck, trying to look over first my shoulder, then Danny's. Pookie's a little guy, stands maybe five-six on a good day, and his younger brothers, who were also craning their necks, aren't much taller.

"He's on his way. In the meantime, this is Danny Gillespie."

Danny shook hands with Pookie and his brothers. Then he headed for a booth. When Danny's hungry he doesn't like to be interfered with.

Pookie said, "We'll get another cup of coffee and wait for Bump. Huh, Willie?"

Willie and Dirt were nodding. I wondered what Pookie wanted from Bump. I gave him a look. But he was already following Danny toward the booth. Danny slid in and Pookie slid in right beside him. Danny leaned away from him and gave him a frowning, somewhat alarmed look that traveled over Danny's shoulder and down his arm before it settled on Pookie's upturned, smiling face.

Willie and Dirt slid into the other side of the booth, which left me standing there with my thumb up my ass. I shrugged and parked myself at the adjacent table. In his excitement, and because he's a cokehead, Pookie was bouncing on the bench cushion. Which his bouncing was also causing Danny to bounce. Danny's frown deepened.

Pudgy little Willie opened a menu like he wanted another breakfast, and Dirt's thumbnail was working hard at something deep inside his ear. I wondered what it would be like to be a housewife with a leaky faucet. Look out the window and see *these* three stumbling up the sidewalk.

Since it was Sunday, Mary was off. Our waitress was a sour little teenager who thought she'd seen the last of the Grodells and wasn't happy to've been wrong. She flicked her pencil impatiently on her order pad. Danny ordered, Pookie and Dirt said they just wanted coffee, and I ordered my Number Four. When our waitress looked at Willie, he jerked his thumb at me and said, "What he's havin'."

Pookie grunted, raised his hips off the bench to drag his wallet out of his hip pocket, and thumbed through a bunch of ones, frowning. Then he gave Willie a curt nod. I wondered, So, like, is Pookie the money man, or what?

Bump and Gruf came in and sat at my table. We didn't get our coffee until after our waitress had put in everybody's orders. Then there was the usual sugaring and creaming and stirring and lighting of cigarettes. After what seemed like an unusually long wait, she walked toward us with a trayload of breakfast. Another girl followed with the second tray of plates and a full coffeepot.

Pookie watched them deal out the plates and top off our coffee. When they finished and walked away, he leaned across the aisle toward Bump. "Hey, Bump. We need to talk to you."

Bump was spreading strawberry jam on his Texas toast. "Whassup?"

Pookie said, "It's about Gwen Dillon."

Dirt emptied a fourth sugar packet into his coffee.

Bump said, "What about her?"

Dirt said, "We know who killed her."

On the one hand, a pretty bold statement. On the other hand, it came out of the mouth of a Grodell.

Bump said, "Uh huh?"

Willie said, "Well, we don't exactly know who, like, *who* . . ."

So there you go.

Pookie said, "But we know it was someone from her work."

Bump said, "How do you know that?"

Dirt said, "Because we overheard some of the girls talking out at the Lo-Lites last night."

This is how a conversation with the Grodells goes. They say these one-fact statements and then they stop dead and wait for a question.

Whatever. I said, "What did they say?"

Danny said, "Pookie. If you don't stop bouncing, I'm gonna hurt you."

Pookie stopped bouncing and even folded his hands on the table.

Danny said, "That's better. Now, what did the girls from Lo-Lites say?"

The Grodells looked at each other. Pookie grinned sheepishly. "Well, that's just it. We can't remember, exactly. We were sorta messed up."

I couldn't help it. "No. You were?"

Willie said, "But we remember enough to know that somebody Gwen worked with out there killed her. No doubt."

Pookie said, "No doubt."

Dirt said, "No doubt. Pookie, do we have enough left for me to get a short stack?"

Pookie said, "No."

Bump said, "Do you remember anything—any little detail at all—about what they said?"

Pookie said, "No."

I said, "Who were the girls? Do you remember that?"

Dirt said, "No." He and his brothers smiled at each other like, Mission accomplished. They'd successfully reported to Bump. They didn't seem to realize that they'd come up just a little short, fact-wise.

Bump rolled his eyes at me and we got at our breakfasts. I was just mopping up the last of my egg juice when Dirt said, "Oh, shit. Is that—? It is. Look who just pulled in, you guys."

Willie craned his neck to look out the front windows. Pookie turned around and looked, too. Pookie said, "Oh, no."

I said, "Who?"

Pookie said, "That green Ford pickup? Just parking now? It's Ronny Fish."

Danny and I made eye contact. He mouthed, *"Fish?"*

Dirt said, "Scrunch down in the seat. Maybe he'll only look in the windows."

"So what if he doesn't see us? He'll just do something to the truck again."

I squinted out the front windows. I spotted the green pickup, parked across the aisle from Grodell's white panel truck. A brawny blond guy stood in the middle of the aisle, looking back and forth between Brewster's front windows and the Grodells' white truck, white steam puffing out of his mouth in the cold air.

I said, "What's the problem?"

By this time, the Grodells were sitting at half mast, so their chins came about even with the tabletop. Pookie said, "Ronny Fish has it in for us. If he catches us in town, he'll kill us *dead*. Last time, we saw him coming and hid, so he slashed one of our tires."

Bump said, "Why? What'd you do to him?"

Dirt said, "Nothing. Swear to God. He just decides he's gonna get a hard-on about somebody for no reason. Even ask Lenny Werbel. Ask Fred Oatley."

We all looked at each other. As it happened, we knew both Lenny Werbel *and* Fred Oatley. Neither one of them was what you'd exactly call an upstanding citizen, and neither one of them was what we'd exactly call a friend, but still.

Bump said, "He's just a bully? You swear you didn't do anything to him?"

They all nodded sincerely.

Bump said, "Gimme your truck keys."

Pookie raised a hip and pulled a large ring of keys from his hip pocket.

Danny stared at him. "You were *sitting* on that?"

Dirt said, "Why? What're you gonna do?"

Bump stood up and took the keys from Pookie. Danny pushed Pookie out of his way, slid across the booth bench, and stood. I scrambled to my feet, too, and so did Gruf.

Bump said, "We're going out to get something from our truck. Which key opens the back door?"

Pookie separated a key from the rest and handed the ring back with it sticking up. Me, Gruf, and Danny followed Bump outside to the parking lot.

Ronnie Fish was standing in the slush at the back of the Grodells' truck, looking at the truck and scanning the parking lot. When he saw us coming toward him, he took a step back. Bump walked to the back of the truck. He stuck the key in the lock, then paused and looked around at Ronnie Fish. "What're *you* looking at?"

Ronnie Fish said, "Nothing." He took another step back.

We all turned around and squared off. I looked Ronnie Fish over. He stood just shy of six feet, was my guess. He was built stocky. He had short, sandy hair, little mean eyes, a pug nose, and a belligerent square chin. Real tough guy.

I said, "You know who you look like? You look like Ronnie Fish."

Ronnie Fish said, "So?"

Danny said, "Isn't that the guy who's been bothering the Grodells?"

I nodded.

Danny said, "Are you him?"

Ronnie Fish said, "What if I am?" He took another step back. His hands were hanging at his sides. His left hand was open, but his right hand was closed. I looked closer. You could see the end of a pocket knife sticking out past his thumb.

I said, "Knife."

Ronnie Fish smoothly slid the knife into his jeans pocket and opened his hands to us, smiling.

Bump said, "Somebody slashed a tire on the Grodells' truck a while ago."

Ronnie Fish grinned. "So?"

Bump said, "And now here *you* are, standing by their truck with a knife in your hand."

Ronnie Fish said, "So what?"

Gruf said, "You got a problem with the Grodells?"

Ronnie Fish said, "What if I do?"

Danny said, "They're our friends. If you've got a problem with them, you've got a problem with us. You got a problem with us?"

Ronnie Fish said, "I got no problems with *any*body."

Bump said, "Good."

We stared him down. He shuffled his feet a bit and glanced around the parking lot. Then he turned, walked back to his truck, got in, and slowly drove away. We watched him until he pulled out of the parking lot and headed out Third Avenue away from town.

Back inside Brewster's, the Grodells were laughing themselves sick. They wanted to hear every word that'd been said. They stared at Bump like he was a rock star. You could see they wanted to sit and drink coffee all damn day with us.

As I turned my attention back to what was left of my breakfast, I thought about bullies. I was a skinny little kid up until the summer I was fifteen. But I never had any trouble with bullies because I had five big, bad, cool older brothers. Everybody treated me real nice. At age fifteen, I went to work for Red Perkins as a gofer on my brother P.J.'s crew. It seemed like the minute I did it, I grew ten inches and put on fifty pounds. After that, the bullies stayed away on my own account.

For some reason, I suddenly remembered a night back in . . . it must have been the summer I was fifteen. Because I know I was already working for Red Perkins, or I wouldn't have been trying to go to sleep when most of my brothers were partying with their friends in the backyard. But I wasn't sixteen yet, because I didn't have my first truck yet, or I would've been sleeping somewhere else.

The six of us shared one bedroom. We had three sets of bunk beds in there, with a little space either side of the middle set, so we could get in and out. Over the previous five or six years, this brother or that one had moved out for one reason or another, but that summer they were all back living at home. That night, four of my brothers and their friends were drinking and smoking pot, stumbling around and shrieking in the backyard. Jeez, you could smell that skunky pot.

The only brother who wasn't out there was P.J. He's two years older than me. The rest of them go up from there. Me and P.J. were in bed, the top bunks of two of the sets, me in the middle top and P.J. on one of the walls.

I was lying there thinking. It was a hot, close night, and it would've been awful with four more male Saltzes in there tossing, snoring, smelling of beer and cigarettes and man. I was thinking, Maybe I'll fall asleep first or maybe P.J. will. I thought, Either way would be good. If I fell asleep first, that would be good, but if P.J. did, I could sneak outside and join the party. I knew if I could get away from P.J., the others would be happy to get me high. There was a loud burst of laughter and I thought, I hope some neighbor doesn't call the cops.

I was listening to P.J.'s breathing, trying to hear when he fell asleep. Which he was so quiet and there was so much noise coming from the backyard, I couldn't really tell. I turned my head to look at him. He was lying on his back with his eyes wide open. He glanced at me, then turned his eyes back to the ceiling.

He said, "Listen to 'em out there. What a bunch of morons."

I was shocked. I thought my brothers were awesome, and I thought P.J. felt the same way. By that time, several of them had even been to jail. Nothing hard core. Deke had done a nonpayment, child support, and Berk had gone away for a few months because of a bar fight. Sound familiar?

If the state'd had that *Three DUIs, Say Goodbye* rule then, they'da all been in jail. Between 'em, they'd collected enough DUIs to paper our bedroom walls.

But P.J. had just called them morons. I stared at him. He said, "They think they've got the world by the ass. Fuck. They work their tails off all day, swinging hammers, laying shingles, trimming trees, and then they party away everything they earn. Look at Deke. Twenty-five, divorced, worked like a dog since he was sixteen, and what does he have to show for it? Nothing."

"But—"

"But nothing." He turned on his side to face me. "Think about it, Terry. Us Saltzes, we only know how to do young man's work. We're physical laborers. What happens to Deke in another five years or so, when he's thirty? That's *old*."

Thirty did seem old to us then, when I was fifteen and P.J. was seventeen.

P.J. said, "Huh? What's Deke gonna do when he can't go up a tree anymore? What's Berk gonna do when he's too old to scamper around on a beam anymore? They're gonna be drunk old bums, that's what. Like Dad."

I said, "You shut up about Dad."

And now my other brother Berk was apparently living somewhere right around Spencer. I wondered where, exactly, and what he was doing.

Gruf had stepped out to the sidewalk and bought the morning paper. He was sitting with it spread out in front of him. His voice brought me back from my family. "Pookie, you guys get lost now. We've got things to talk about."

They looked at their new god, Bump. He nodded

and said, "Yeah. Go." They drained their coffee cups and scrambled out of the booth. As they stumbled up to the register and paid their check, Gruf, Bump, and me slid into the booth with Danny. The waitress came to clear the table. Then she came back and topped off our coffee cups.

Gruf folded his newspaper up and set it aside. "There's a story in the paper about Gwen Dillon's murder. It says the body was discovered by 'unidentified laborers.'"

I wrinkled my nose at the slur. Danny grimaced. "Filthy dirty unidentified laborers?"

Gruf understood our reaction and grinned at us. "The filthy dirty part is implied, I guess. Anyway, it says in the paper they're having calling hours for her tonight. From six until eight. We should go."

I said, "Tonight?"

He nodded. "Garrity and Sons Funeral Home."

Danny said, "Garrity and Sons?" He faked a shudder.

I said, "What?"

"I mean, when it's like, Grodell and Sons Plumbing and Heating, that's okay. You picture Mr. Grodell and the boys soldering pipes together, ya know? *Okay, turn on the hot!* But when it's a funeral home, it just doesn't work, does it? I don't know. It just doesn't have the same folksy feel."

Bump laughed and shook his head. "Folksy feel. You crack me up, Danny. But Gruf's right. We need to go to those calling hours tonight. See who's who."

Funeral homes creep me out. I said, "Have fun. I'm not going."

Chapter 10

Danny and me met Gruf and Bump in front of Garrity and Sons Funeral Home just after six. Gruf and Bump were wearing suits and topcoats. They looked amazing, like tall guys dressed to the nines usually do. I'd thrown on a pair of black Dockers that I bought when me and Mike started going to the occasional movie, and then I'd selected a shirt from my extensive collection of threadbare flannels. I didn't feel like wearing my one and only suit, and I had no idea Gruf and Bump were gonna dress like that. I had no intention of taking off my pea jacket once we were inside, anyway, because I had no intention of staying more than a few minutes. Matter fact, I had no idea how they had managed to get me to go in the first place.

Danny didn't even bother with Dockers. He wore jeans and a flannel. Deep down inside, Danny really doesn't give a flying fuck.

There were a lot of people there. I stayed just inside the front door with my pea jacket on while the rest of the unidentified laborers followed the line into the room where the casket was and, I guess, filed past it. Said how lifelike she looked. My opinion was, Go to it, boys, but there wasn't gonna be any gazing upon the face of the dearly departed for me. The whole idea gave me the heebie-jeebies.

And it was a good thing I did stay by the front door, as it turned out. I was standing right there when the trouble started.

The boys had been out of sight for quite a while. I saw some people come in that I recognized from pool league. Mick Wallace, aka Snake Man, was there with some scruffy outlaw biker types. I recognized some people who were on the team we'd played against the night Gwen was murdered. Allison Burgess, looking not a whole lot better than she'd looked tucked under Gruf's jacket just after she'd discovered the body, was huddled near the back of the hall with some other girls who looked like they could hold the interest if they were dancing topless.

After a while there was a buzz of conversation in the doorway of the room where the casket was. I looked over to see an older man and woman walk out. She was clinging to his elbow for support. Their faces looked strained and drained.

They were both trim, neat-looking people. They both wore neat black suits. His gray hair was styled in one of those helmet cuts like a TV newscaster. She wore her gray hair in one of those bubble-looking styles and it looked like a wig, it was so perfect. I watched them, wondering if they were Gwen's parents.

All of a sudden, the woman glanced past me to the front door, did a double take, and her mouth dropped open in shock. She gasped for breath and tugged on the man's arm.

She cried, "What's *he* doing here?"

As the man was still looking, finding, and reacting, she flew away from him toward the door screaming, *"You have the nerve to show your face here?"*

I glanced toward the door myself and saw a pudgy, tired-looking guy in a black three-piece suit and an open black topcoat freeze in his tracks. He stood there paralyzed, not knowing what to do. His eyes skittered around the room looking for help of some kind. When he glanced my way, I recognized him. He was Brown

Suit—the old guy Gwen Dillon had been with the night of the pool match.

He hastily backstepped out the doorway and turned. I guess I had it in my mind to grab his arm. But the woman got between us and stumbled, and instead of a handful of the guy, I found myself with a handful of her.

She screamed, "Let me go. *Let me go*!" And she also screamed, "Murderer! You murdered my *baby*!"

I thought if I let her go, she'd fall on her face, so I held on even when she began to throw her sharp little elbows. One clipped me in the mouth, but I still held on. She was leaning out the doorway, apparently watching him flee. She screamed, "You *better* run!"

I was mostly trying to keep my teeth out of the range of her flying elbows, but I looked up long enough to see a blur of black hurry out to the dark sidewalk in front of the funeral home and disappear into the icy, gloomy night.

By that time, the guy who'd been supporting her was beside me, trying to take her away from me, trying to calm her down. He yelled, "Sherrie. Stop now. *Sherrie*."

Yelling at her wasn't doing any good. In fact, it seemed to stir her up even more. She threw an elbow and clipped him on the cheek. He staggered backwards.

Then someone was pulling him back and someone else was taking her away from me, and I was surrounded by a bunch of reaching, black-suited arms and quiet, soothing male voices. One said, "Come away, Mr. Dillon."

Another said, "Easy, Mrs. Dillon. I've got you."

"Take them into the Serenity Chapel."

"I'll get the whiskey."

The bereaved couple disappeared in a bum's rush of long thin black suits that I assumed must be draped on the able bodies of Garrity and Sons. The crowd of them moved briskly down the wide hall and disappeared into a room opposite the room where the casket was. The doors closed firmly behind them.

By that time, Danny, Bump, John, and Gruf had heard the disturbance and come rushing out. They were all, What happened? What's going on?

I said, "Come on. We gotta catch him."

I raced outside and down the front walk and turned the way I'd seen the black blur go, but there was no one around. Whoever he was, he was long gone.

Bump pounded a few steps past me, stopped, and turned around. "What the fuck was that all about?"

"It was the guy I told you about. That old guy Gwen was with at pool. The woman seems pretty sure he's the murderer."

Bump said, "The woman? What woman?"

I shrugged. "I guess it was Mrs. Dillon."

Danny shrugged. "So we just go ask her who she was yelling at and where we can find him."

I shook my head. "She was hysterical. Anyway, Garrity and Sons took her back to the Serenity Chapel and shut the doors. They're probably pouring whiskey down her throat about now."

Gruf said, "If *she* knew him, someone else in there must know him. Let's go."

I turned and followed them back toward the funeral home porch. "He's in his fifties, balding, sloppy build."

We spread out through the excited crowd and began to ask, but it was hard to get anybody's attention. They were all whispering, speculating, and staring at the closed doors of the Serenity Chapel. We didn't find anybody who could tell us who he was.

Sunday night means everybody heads for our trailer, starting along about six or so, for one of John's home-

cooked meals and a rousing game of Flinch. We all
make sure to keep Sunday nights clear so we can be
there. Usually it's just me, Danny, John, Gruf, and
Bump. Aside from the later-than-usual start, that Sunday night began as no exception. We bundled into our
various vehicles and headed straight from the funeral
home to Chandler's Trailer Park.

John was busy in the kitchen when we straggled in.
Gruf and Bump found out-of-the-way places to change
out of their suits while Danny and me grabbed beverages and got comfortable in our big living room.
Danny tipped back his country-blue recliner and
turned on the TV. Before long Gruf and then Bump
walked out carrying their suits on hangers. They
hooked the hangers onto the oak hall tree and helped
themselves to beverages. Gruf sat next to me on our
three-cushion country-blue sofa and propped his sock
feet up on our oak coffee table. Bump made himself
comfortable stretched out on our plush beige wall-to-
wall carpet.

Bump said, "John. What's for dinner?"

John looked around from the stove. "Beef stew,
mashed potatoes, carrots a la Garvey, baked rolls.
Won't be long now."

Bump said, "Hoo-wah."

Once it was all on the table, we made fast work of
it. After supper, Danny and I cleared the table. Then
Danny and Gruf headed down the hall to Danny's
bedroom to do a little mood adjustment while Bump
and I quickly washed the dishes and put them away.
Since John cooks, he always gets to sit out cleanup.

Danny and Gruf returned from the bedroom and
we all took places around the table. We were just
settling in when Bump's cell phone rang. He didn't
talk much. He mostly listened.

The game we like to play is called Flinch. We used
to play with two regular decks of cards before the

Elliot twins found a couple of actual honest-to-God boxed Flinch sets in a game store someplace. Now we were using those. Five players could get by using one set, but there's more action if you use two.

Gruf shuffled and dealt while Bump talked. Then Bump thumbed his phone off and lit a cigarette. "That was Bud."

Gruf said, "What's up with him?"

"He just dumped Marylou."

I blinked at him. Last time I'd heard from Marylou, she was taking it upon herself to invite me and my crew to remodel Bud's house in the manner to which she hoped to become accustomed. I'd thought I smelled something fishy about her phone call, so I can't really say I was surprised. Clearly, my original suspicion was correct. No more good Marylou. The Bitch was back.

I said, "What'd she do?" Which I figured I was safe in assuming it was something *she* did. Bud Hanratty's totally cool.

Bump shrugged. "He didn't have time to tell me. He wanted to let me know they've found Ernie Burdett's car. It's gonna be towed out to the county maintenance garage tonight, so Bud and I'll be able to be there when they go over it tomorrow. He sounded so bummed, I invited him over here. Try to get his mind off things for a while."

John said, "Poor Bud. I feel for him. Before he gets here, tell me about the calling hours for Gwen Dillon. Anything interesting happen?"

We told him about how Brown Suit had turned up wearing a black suit, and how a woman we assumed was Gwen's mother freaked out when she saw him.

I said, "Brown Suit's name is Ray. Remember, Bump? You talking about your brother reminded me his name's Ray. He's gotta go to the top of our suspect list. If that was Gwen's mother at the funeral home, and if she knows what she's talking about."

Bump pulled his little notebook from the black leather vest he usually wears over his black T-shirts. "Has anybody even made a list of suspects yet?"

I thought about all the stuff we knew about Gwen Dillon so far. "I have a feeling that's not a big enough notebook."

Danny snickered. We thought about suspects as we picked up our cards and got organized.

Bump wrote, "Ray?" in his notebook.

Gruf said, "Start things off, John."

John tossed a one to the middle of the table and discarded a fifteen.

Danny said, "I guess you'd have to consider the whole Lo-Lites crew suspects. Quote unquote the Grodells."

John said, "Huh? What do the Grodells have to do with anything?"

Bump waved him off. "Danny's kidding. The Grodells were blowing smoke over at Brewster's this morning. Believe me. But the Lo-Lites crew all gotta be on the list. We'll have to start eliminating them, one by one."

The discard got around to me. There were three ones down, and a two over one of the ones. The top card on my stash was a fifteen. I was gonna be a long time getting rid of that thing. I have the worst damn luck at cards. I discarded a twelve.

I said, "Lo-Lites. So that includes that biker guy . . ."

Gruf said, "Mick Wallace."

Danny said, "The tomato seed guy Gwen got in a fight with . . ."

Bump was writing quickly. He said, "That was Wes Fletcher."

John said, "Bump. Your turn."

Bump pulled the top card off his hand and discarded it in front of him. He said, "Allison Burgess?"

I said, "For a suspect?"

Bump said, "Why not? A girl coulda done it if she got the right leverage."

Danny said, "You gonna play sometime tonight, there, Boss?"

"Is it back around to me already?" I studied the table, threw a four on a three in the middle and discarded a nine. "And don't call me Boss."

He'd been calling me Boss since he quit his job with Miller roofing and came to work with me and Gruf. It hit me wrong, hearing Danny call me Boss. That's why he did it.

I leaned back and stretched my arms over my head. Danny made to get up. "Who's ready for another one?"

Gruf picked up his empty High Life bottle and twiddled it. Danny took it from him and dropped it into the garbage can on his way to the refrigerator.

John said, "Allison Burgess. How would that have worked? She strangled Gwen when she drove into the parking lot. Then she went inside for a while, and then she went outside and pretended to find the body?"

Gruf said, "Allison's not exactly built like a lumberjack. Would she have been physically capable—"

Bump said, "If she was in the backseat—"

John nodded. "That's what they say. The murderer was in the backseat. Strangled her from behind."

Danny said, "Allison coulda done it. She coulda brought her knees up against the seat back. Used that for leverage."

Bump said, "How *did* she find the body, anyway? Spotted Gwen through the windshield?"

I shook my head. "Gwen's car was buried in snow. Allison said she needed her purse. She went to Gwen's car hoping it would be unlocked, hoping her purse would still be in there—"

Bump said, "Was it there?"

I said, "Yeah. At least, there were two purses sitting on the front seat."

John nodded. "One was Allison's, one was Gwen's. I checked IDs myself."

Bump said, "If Gwen's car was buried in snow, how did Allison know which car was hers?"

I blinked at him. "That's a good question." I looked at John. He looked startled, too.

Danny said, "Maybe Gwen always parked in the same place."

Bump said, "Yeah. Some of those apartment complexes even have assigned parking."

John nodded. "I'll check on that."

Danny threw a two on top of a one and discarded a thirteen.

I said, "Not that any of this matters, but what was that stuff about Gwen going to Bagby High School then moving away right before her senior year?"

Gruf said, "Senior year. Jackson's friend said the Dillons moved to Black Creek all of a sudden."

I said, "Where's Black Creek? I've never heard of it."

Bump said, "East of Spencer."

I said, "There's nothing east of Spencer but farms. Until you get to Pennsylvania."

Bump laughed. "Unless you take Route 77 about thirty miles. Then you end up in Black Creek."

"Oh." I sipped my coffee and tried to think of questions. "We need to find out where Gwen went the night of the pool match."

John said, "Where she went? What do you mean?"

"Allison Burgess put her purse in Gwen's car that night, but when Allison was ready to leave, she couldn't find Gwen. Gwen's car was there, but Gwen was gone. That was why Allison had to leave without her purse. That was why she looked in Gwen's car the next morning. So where did Gwen go?"

Danny said, "And who with?"

I said, "Yeah."

Bump scribbled in his notebook. When he was finished, he sipped coffee, glanced out the window, and squinted. "Is that headlights? I bet that's Bud."

He pushed back from the table and walked over to the door. Bud came in, shed his heavy parka, pried off his shoes, came over to the table, and sat heavily. He was wearing an old red sweatshirt and a pair of worn-out jeans. Bump pulled one of Gruf's High Lifes from the refrigerator and handed it to him. He took the bottle of beer with one hand and rubbed the other palm across his balding head.

I wouldn't have believed it was possible, but he looked even worse than he had the last time I'd seen him. His eyes were sunken and bruised, his face was caved-in and tired-looking, and his mouth was tight. Bump watched him swallow beer.

Bump said, "You get any sleep last night, old man?"

Which I thought was funny, because Bud's only eight years older than Bump. Eight years. It hit me for the first time that Bud and my brother Berk were the same age.

Bud frowned. Then he glanced at me. "I dumped Marylou."

I said, "I know. Bump told us."

He spread his hands flat and muttered, "Sorry. I couldn't hack it anymore."

I laughed at him. "What're you apologizing for? I was *married* to the Bitch, remember?"

Bud nodded. He turned to Bump. "Alan couldn't tell me what time they'll be ready to start on Ernie's car tomorrow. He said he'll call me. Then I'll call you. Okay?"

Bump said, "You told me all that on the phone. Drink your beer and relax, Bud. You're making yourself sick over this thing."

Bud said, "I just—"

Bump said, "You just nothing. Drink up. We'll pick up this hand and deal a fresh one with you in it. You're gonna learn to play Flinch, my friend. Take your mind off your troubles for a little while."

Chapter 11

We hurried through breakfast Monday morning and got to the lawyers' office nice and early. It'd only been three days since we'd been on the job site (Friday was the blizzard, and then it was the weekend), but it felt more like three weeks. Once we got there, we took no prisoners. We clomped straight down to the basement and got at it. After a short lunch we worked right through the afternoon without a coffee break. By quitting time the kitchen was finished except for the lighting, countertops, sinks, appliances, and vinyl flooring.

Danny and I dropped Gruf off at his Jeep in Brewster's parking lot and then we drove straight home. Gruf works at Smitty's Monday nights, but me and Danny always take Monday nights off. I was tired. I was ready for one of John's home-cooked meals and some serious sofa time.

John was already at the trailer. He was standing at the kitchen counter in his sweats, pounding holy hell out of a bunch of boneless chicken breasts with his trusty wooden mallet. The phone rang as we were sitting down to eat.

Bump sounded a little breathless. He said, "Me and Bud are down at the county garage with Alan. We've finished going over Ernie's BMW. Can you guys come down here? We gotta talk."

I really didn't want to. I said, "Why? What's up?"

"Just get down here as soon as you can."

I looked at my steaming chicken cordon bleu and thought, Aw, shit. "Give us half an hour. Where *is* the county garage?"

"Up the driveway from the jail. You know where that is."

"I seem to remember."

"The garage is the big rusty-ass building off to the left of the access road. Hurry up."

John and Danny were both beat, too, but it ended up they didn't wanna miss anything, so we scarfed down supper, piled into John's Geo, and headed south. We followed the long curving access road past the jail to the garage, which looked more like a big warehouse. John parked next to Bud's big red Caddy and we walked through the dark, cavernous, echoing building to a brightly lit bay at the back.

There was a white tarp spread out along the back wall. Parts of Ernie's car were laid out all over it like the twisted pieces of some demented jigsaw puzzle. I recognized the metallic green hood for what it was, and the trunk lid, even though both were crumpled like some clumsy giant hand had tried to make them into bellows. Pieces of engine were laid out, and the four tire rims, all four of them twisted out of shape. A cluster of men stood under a lift looking up at the underside of what was left of the frame.

Bump said, "Here they are." He stepped out of the cluster and came toward us talking. "We went over everything again and again. Come to find out, when we finally saw it, it'd been staring us in the face the whole time."

I said, "What're you talking about? What'd you guys find?"

Bump motioned us over to the lift. Bud, Alan Bushnell, Brian Bell, and a guy in gray overalls that I'd never seen before were all looking up at a tie rod that dangled from what was left of the twisted frame. They stepped back to let us get close. Bump pointed up to the tie rod. Alan handed him a little flashlight.

Bump said, "Here's how it happened. It was an old worn tie rod end and housing, sand blasted and repainted so they looked like new, installed on the passenger side."

We stared up at the flashlight beam playing over the tie rod end. Danny said, "It looks like a new part to me. How can you tell it isn't?"

Bump said, "Look at the shape of the ball. Look how it's distorted from wear. Here's the housing." He walked over to the tarp and picked up a part. "Look at the inside." He played the flashlight over the metal. "They cleaned out the rust and repainted it, too, but you can see the wear. And look."

He carried the housing over to the dangling tie rod end and fitted it onto the ball. "See? You can push it in and out. Thing's totally shot."

Alan said, "Phyllis, got anything on that coffee thermos yet?"

I turned around. Alan had a cell phone pressed to his ear. I elbowed Bump. "What's that about? What coffee thermos?"

"We found Ernie's coffee thermos this morning. It was driven up into the seat springs. There was still some liquid sloshing around. Alan sent it to the county lab for testing."

Alan said, "Call me as soon as you get something. Remember, if you don't find anything, we're sending it out. I'll send it to Virginia if I have to."

I said, "Virginia?"

Bump said, "FBI lab."

I stared at him.

Danny was still examining the tie rod end and the housing. He said, "Would this've held for a short time?"

Bump was nodding. "It held long enough. But the first time it was stressed good, it slipped right out. The tire went where it wanted to go. Instamatic loss of control."

Danny said, "The stress was Dead Man's Curve? That's a left turn if you're eastbound. But he musta made other left turns before he got to that curve."

Bump shrugged. "Bud's thinking maybe there was also something funny in Ernie's coffee."

Bud said, "It's a long shot, but if there was . . ."

Alan said, "Worth checking, anyway."

Bump said, "If he's right, then it prolly wasn't just the curve. As the drug started to work, Ernie would've started to swerve. The swerving as he went into Dean Man's Curve. That woulda been what did it."

I said, "Wait. Drugged? You think Ernie was drugged?"

Bud stepped over. "*Might've* been. *Could've* been. I just want that thermos checked."

I said, "But—okay, the car was definitely tampered with?"

Bump said, "Definitely."

I said, "But then, that means Ernie was—"

Bud finished my sentence. "Murdered. Yes, it does."

My mouth dropped open. I flashed on the scene at the Burdett house the day Bump and I paid our condolences to Chrissy, when everybody there except Sean seemed more interested in their trip to the Bahamas than in the minor detail that Ernie Burdett had just died. I glanced at Bump. I wondered if he'd ever told Bud about the things we'd seen and heard while we were at the Burdett house that day.

Danny was saying, "But how can you tell those parts were replaced deliberately to cause the accident? Maybe they just wore out."

Bump grinned. "That's what I'm trying to tell you.

They were steam cleaned and repainted *after* they were worn out. And there were fresh wrench marks. Here." He pointed to the stud nut. "And here." He held up the housing.

Alan had been listening. Now he said, "Unfortunately, there aren't any prints. Be nice if we had some prints."

As I examined the wrench mark on the housing, John said, "Well, they had to get the used part from somewhere." We all turned to look at him. He shrugged. "We should check the junkyards."

Bud said, "Do they keep records? They'd have a record of selling a used BMW tie rod end and housing?"

John said, "Maybe. Maybe not. But I bet they'd remember. Selling somebody a worn out BMW tie rod? That'd be a pretty unusual sale, wouldn't it?"

Alan shrugged. "Okay. We'll start canvassing the junkyards. Maybe we'll get lucky. Oh. And everybody listen up."

Heads turned toward him. He said, "If a reporter gets onto this and backs me into a corner, I'll admit that Ernie was murdered, and that his car was tampered with. But I'm gonna hold back the details on how it was done. I don't want anyone talking about the details. Hear me now. And I don't want anyone talking about the possibility drugs might've been used. The only ones who know the details are the people in this room and the murderer, and that's the way I want it to stay. Clear?"

Back at Smitty's, the dining room was on the back side of the dinner rush. Bump, Bud, John, and Danny slid into the back booth. I walked on back to the kitchen to tell Gruf to come out when he had a minute. One of the twins was already pouring the guys coffee. I got myself a cup and settled at the next table. A minute later Gruf came out and pulled up a chair.

Gruf stared at us as he settled. "What's going on?"

Bud folded his hands around his coffee cup. "We examined Ernie Burdett's Beemer today. His death wasn't an accident. He was murdered."

Gruf's look of astonishment didn't fade until Bud and Bump had thoroughly explained. When they finished he shook his head. "Holy shit."

Danny said, "What was Ernie doing in downtown Cleveland in the middle of the night, anyway?"

Bud said, "He was at his office earlier that night. He had a closing on some property he was liquidating. It ran late—"

I interrupted. "Where was his office?"

"He owns—owned—a building straight out Route 8, about five miles past Chandler's Trailer Park where you live. Big two-story brick building. Maybe you've noticed the sign. Burdett Properties."

I didn't remember ever noticing a sign, although I'd driven up and down Route 8 many times. I shrugged and nodded.

Danny said, "Where would the Beemer have been parked? In a parking lot outside?"

Bud said, "Why? Oh, you mean where would the murderer have gotten access to it? Well, lemme see. It wouldn't have been parked outside. It would've been inside. Ernie restored that Beemer himself. He loved that car."

Danny said, "There's a parking garage inside the building?"

Bud said, "The land falls away at the back of his building. There's a three-, four-car garage on the back side of the basement. It would've been in there. He even had a hydraulic lift installed in there, so he could work on that Beemer."

Danny said, "Somebody who wanted to tamper with it could've done it right there in his building, using his lift?"

Bud blinked at him. "Well, yeah. I guess so."

Bump said, "Okay, go on. How did he get downtown in the middle of the night?"

"He closed the deal, but the negotiations ran late. He called me, jeez, I guess it musta been after midnight, because Letterman was on. Told me he'd closed the deal and he was going out to Sandusky to see a guy about a boat. He was gonna drive out there that night ahead of the bad weather and get a room, so he could see the guy the next morning."

Gruf said, "Was that unusual? To make a last-minute plan like that?"

Bud smiled tiredly. "Not for Ernie. He always flew by the seat of his pants." His jaw suddenly began to tremble and his mouth got tight. A tear slid down his cheek. I felt so bad for him I had to look away.

Danny lit a cigarette and blew smoke up toward the ceiling. "If he decided to go at the last minute, how would somebody've known to mess with his car that night?"

We all stared at him. Bud said, "Actually, come to think of it, he *didn't* decide that night. He'd called me earlier in the day. That was the Wednesday. He said he was gonna drive out there Thursday morning. He wanted me to come with him. But I'd just watched the noon news, and I told him they were predicting that blizzard. I asked him to put the trip off for a few days, but he didn't want to."

I said, "So he knew by early afternoon that he was going to drive to Sandusky. The only change in his plan was that he went Wednesday night instead of Thursday morning?"

Bud nodded.

Gruf said, "Has there been any word on the autopsy?"

Bud said, "It's done. Finally."

John said, "And?"

Bud said, "Nothing odd so far, but I'm still waiting

for the toxicology report. That's where we'd see drugs, if there were any."

John nodded. We all sat there, smoking and thinking.

Danny said, "So now Alan Bushnell's got two murder investigations on his hands. Gwen Dillon and Ernie Burdett."

I stared at him. That was the first time I'd thought about the two events together. Two murders in the same night. I remembered Alan muttering, "No such thing as coincidence." I glanced at Bump and caught him staring at me. I guessed he was wondering the same thing I was. The next words out of his mouth proved it.

Bump said, "Bud. Do you know of any connection between Gwen Dillon and Ernie?"

Bud frowned. "I can't—unless . . . did I hear somebody say Gwen Dillon lived in Ladonia Hills Apartments?" We all nodded. "Then Ernie was her landlord. He owned Ladonia Hills."

Bump said, "That's not much of a connection. Anything else?"

Bud shook his head. "I can't think of anything. You know, Danny, you raised a good point."

Danny said, "I did?"

Bud nodded. "Alan does have his hands full. I want—I mean, you guys have a couple of murder investigations under your belts. You've done a pretty good job of it, too. Maybe—could you guys look into Ernie's murder for me?"

Bump laughed uncomfortably. "Jeez, Bud. We've just gotten lucky a couple of times. You wouldn't even think of asking if you knew what a bunch of fuckups we are."

The rest of us laughed and nodded. Except John. He looked uncomfortable.

Bud was shaking his head. "No, I don't think so.

Oh, I know Alan'll do his best. He's a good man. But he's gonna be stretched thin. And you guys can do things he can't do. Get people to talk to you that wouldn't talk to him."

Gruf said, "I don't—"

Bud said, "I'm not asking you to, you know, do a full-scale investigation or anything. I know you've got other things going on. I'm just asking you to do what you can. You know?"

John cleared his throat. Everybody looked his way. He said, "Are you gonna tell Alan about this?"

Bud stared at him. It seemed like he suddenly remembered that John was a cop. Realized for the first time what Alan's opinion of his request was likely to be. He said, "Uh. No?"

John rolled his eyes. You could see he wished he wasn't sitting there hearing all this.

Bump shrugged. "Really, you guys, Bud's not asking us to do any more than we would've done anyway. We were already starting to poke around in Gwen Dillon's case. Right?"

I shrugged and nodded. Gruf, Danny, and Bump did the same. John stared off into space.

I said, "I wouldn't even know where to start."

Bud said, "Start by going over to Ernie's office building. Look around over there. Talk to people. Find out who had access to his car. Find out who had keys to the building. I know a lot of people did. Ernie was careless about that. I know his insurance guy used to yell at him about that."

Gruf said, "I guess we could make a quick stop over there after breakfast. Huh, Terry?"

"I guess."

Bud said, "I'll gladly pay you for your time."

We were a perfect quartet. *"Bullshit."* It sounded like we'd practiced for hours.

Bud laughed. "He's got some secretaries, book-keeper, maintenance man. They'll all be there tomorrow. I'll call over there in the morning and ask them to give you a set of keys. The maintenance man can show you around. Lemme think of his name. Uh, it's an unusual name. Uh, Berk. Berk can show you around."

I stared at him. Berk? Well, now I knew where Chrissy Burdett knew my brother from. He worked for her late husband. Danny and I made eye contact. His eyebrows jumped. I caught Bump looking at me, too. He remembered Chrissy asking me if I knew Berk Saltz, and me saying Berk was my brother. Bump and Danny both looked as surprised as I felt.

Danny said, "They said on Court TV that when somebody gets murdered, nine times out of ten, the murderer is the person closest to the victim."

Bump looked around sharply. Bud said, "That's right."

Danny said, "Huh. Well, how was Ernie's marriage?"

That's Danny for ya. He always goes straight to the heart of the matter. I glanced at Bump. He was frowning.

Bud said, "I can't talk about that. Lawyer–client privilege."

Bump said, "Dude. Your client's dead."

Bud flinched. "That was harsh, Bump. And technically, I'm still his lawyer. I'm the executor of his estate. I'm still protecting his interests."

Danny frowned. "You asked us to be your investigators, didn't you?"

Bud nodded.

Danny said, "If a lawyer's working with an investigator, can't he tell the investigator what he needs to know?"

Bud said, "Yeah, but—"

Danny said, "Okay then. How was Ernie's marriage?"

Bud had a wrestling match with himself. Then he

said, "He was planning to file for divorce. But that wasn't gonna get under way until the spring."

Bump was shocked. "Holy shit, Bud. Why?"

Bud shrugged. "I don't know. We hadn't really gotten into the details."

Bump said, "Did Chrissy know?"

Bud shrugged. "Not unless he told her."

Bump said, "*Did* he tell her?"

Bud said, "I don't know."

Bump said, "But why? Why'd he wanna divorce Chrissy?"

Bud shrugged. "He didn't say. I assumed . . ."

Bump said very quietly, "Another woman?" Bud nodded. Bump said, "Was he gonna screw Chrissy over?"

Bud said, "No. We talked about that. He intended to give her a generous package. He'd already started selling off some things, getting a little more liquid so he could set her up."

Danny said, "What about now that he's dead? What are the terms of his will?"

Bud said, "Everything gets split right down the middle between Chrissy and Ernie's son, Sean."

Bump said, "By everything, what are we talking? What was Ernie worth?"

Bud said, "We were just starting to figure that out. It was a lot."

Danny said, "A lot, like, how much?"

"Couple a million plus."

Danny whistled. "So under the will, Chrissy and Sean each get a mil?"

"At least."

Bump said, "Her divorce package wouldn't have been that generous."

Bud said, "Not by a long shot."

Gruf said, "Ernie's car was rigged by somebody who was pretty good with a wrench. So that couldn't have been Chrissy."

Bump said softly, "Yeah, it could. Chrissy knows cars. Her family operated a garage for years, right up until her dad died. The whole family worked right alongside the old man."

I thought about Chrissy's mother. Cheryl Workman. "Chrissy's old lady, too?"

Bump said, "Her, too. In fact . . . shit. That was how Chrissy and Ernie first got together. I remember that now. On slow nights when we worked at the Midway, us guys used to try and stump Chrissy about car problems. You couldn't do it. She always knew the answer. One night, Ernie came in. He sat at the bar listening to us all talking about cars. Then he brought up that he was gonna restore an old Beemer he just bought."

Bud nodded. "Jeez. I remember him telling me about that. He said he'd just met a girl who knew everything there was to know about cars."

It was time for Bump to tell Bud about our visit to the Burdett's house, and he knew it. He looked at me and I could see he was struggling with the problem. His loyalty to his friend Bud versus his loyalty to his friend Chrissy. I said, "*Tell* 'em."

He stubbed out his smoke. Lit another one. He said, "Bud. Remember when we went over to see Chrissy and pay our condolences? Me and Terry?"

Bud nodded. "What about it?"

Bump sighed. "Things weren't the way they shoulda been over there."

Bud said, "You mean you didn't see any tears?"

"We didn't see any tears, except for Sean. Matter of fact, except for Sean, it looked like they were having a fuckin' party."

Bud said, "Aw, jeez."

Chapter 12

Tuesday morning at Brewster's the guys were itching to go. They hurried through breakfast and I could feel their impatience when I lit another cigarette and asked Mary to top off my coffee again. The thing was, yeah, I was eager to go out to Burdett Properties and see Berk again. But I'd had overnight to think about things, and I was a little worried. Maybe worried is too strong a word. Concerned might be closer to it. I was concerned.

I'd been trying to figure out how long it'd been since I'd seen my brother. I seemed to remember partying with him and some other people in a bar down in our old stomping grounds one night. I thought that'd been about four or maybe five years ago, but I wasn't sure. Those years for me had been a blur of hard work and harder partying.

Right after I married the Bitch, I made a serious effort to be a family man. Oh, I didn't expect to make myself over into Ward Cleaver, but that was the goal I wanted to shoot for. I wanted a family. I wanted a family life. I had no idea how to go about it, but I figured if I worked at it, I could figure it out as I went along.

The problem was that the Bitch had other ideas. Once we were married, I went through a brief period of spending hours after work trying to find her, wherever she was, and bring her home. You don't have to use much imagination to picture how that worked out. After a while, I didn't have much interest in going home myself. When a working guy doesn't want to go home to an empty trailer, about his only alternative is to go to a bar. So that was how, four years earlier, or maybe five, I'd ended up partying somewhere with Berk.

For as long as I could remember, and right up to that night, Berk had been a capital-L Ladies' man. My brother could operate. You'd have to see it to believe it. Here's Berk as I remembered him. Six feet tall, perfect athlete's body. Quick. Strong. Always tan and weathered-looking from working outside year round. Curly black hair, rogueish black eyes. Gambler's eyes. He always had a look in those eyes that said he was ready for anything. He used to have to beat the girls off with a stick.

I remembered watching him dance. He had some moves, I can tell you. And slow dancing? I mean, he'd have some girl in his arms that he'd never seen before, and he'd lean back and turn on that smile of his. He could turn on a smile that seemed to have the heat of the sun in it. It seemed to have his whole heart in it, only it didn't. It didn't mean anything at all. It was just the way he smiled.

He'd be dancing with some girl, and he'd smile down at her as if she was the one true love of his life, and you could watch her react to that smile of his, and you knew she didn't have a chance. I'd watch the girl of the hour, or the minute, or whatever, respond to that smile and I'd think, Honey, whatever you've got that he wants, it's as good as his.

Skip ahead to that morning in Brewster's, as I dawdled over my extra cigarette and extra cup of coffee and stalled around about going out to see Berk. I was concerned. Because Berk was Berk, and he'd been working for a guy who was worth a couple of million, and who also had a troubled marriage.

I'd been arguing with myself. I'd been thinking, No, Berk's not mixed up in Ernie's murder. Berk's too cool to get mixed up in anything like that. Berk's too smart. But the thing was, I'd seen Chrissy Burdett. She was a stone fox. And now that Ernie Burdett was dead—murdered—she was a stone fox with more than a million dollars.

Gruf finally said, "Come on, Terry. Get your ass in gear. What's your problem this morning, anyway?"

Bump said, "Yeah. Let's move. I got things to do today."

We left our tips, paid our checks, and headed out to the dark parking lot. It was a little after eight. Dawn wouldn't happen for another hour or more. Danny and Gruf climbed into my truck. Danny crammed himself into my little backseat. Bump followed us out in his own truck.

Gruf turned on the radio as I pulled out of the parking lot. Gruf likes a lot of bass. He adjusted my radio to his taste and looked over at me.

"What's going on with you this morning? Don't you feel good?"

"I'm fine. I guess I'm just—see, this guy we're going to see? This Berk?" The traffic light up ahead turned to green and I shifted into third.

"Yeah?"

"He's my brother."

He blinked at me. "Your brother? No shit. Berk, huh? Is that a nickname?"

"Short for Berkley. As in, California. I think our mother might've been a hippie or something."

Gruf grinned. "And you two don't get along?"

I glanced at him. "No. We get along fine. Matter of fact, I've always pretty much idolized Berk."

"Then what's the problem?"

"It's just that—uh—I mean, I haven't seen him for a long time, or something."

Gruf said, "Oh," and dropped the subject.

Burdett Properties was in a big building. Two floors, redbrick, just like Bud described it. I'd noticed the building plenty of times as I'd driven past it. The reason I didn't know right away which building Bud was talking about was that the sign was small and low to the ground, and you couldn't even see it until after you'd already turned into the driveway.

There was a little portico in front of the main door. There were half a dozen vehicles parked near to the entrance. We parked in the next open spaces and went in. Inside, there was a nicely furnished waiting area with thick off-white carpeting. It was bordered by a waist-high oak rail. Beyond that was a large, open office filled with desks, file cabinets, and a big copier.

There were four women working that I could see. They were all midtwenties to midthirties, and nice-looking. They were all wearing black. They all had Kleenex boxes sitting on their desks close to hand. As we stepped through the door and looked around, one of the brunettes was blowing her nose. She saw us come in and came toward us, dabbing at reddened eyes and trying to force a smile.

"Good morning. May I help you?"

Gruf stepped forward. "Bud Hanratty sent us. He called this morning to give you a heads-up?"

She frowned and looked back toward the other ladies. "Has anyone talked to Mr. Hanratty this morning?"

The other three shook their heads. Our brunette turned back to us. "I'm sorry. What was it about?"

Gruf looked at Bump. Bump said, "Bud wanted us to come out and have a look around. He said he was gonna call . . . Uh, he wanted you to give us a set of keys. He said the maintenance man, Berk Saltz, could show us around."

She frowned. She glanced back toward the other

three ladies. The blonde pushed away from her desk and came toward us. The brunette said, "I don't understand . . ."

The blonde said, "Maybe Berk talked to Mr. Hanratty. Beth, page Berk. I think he's still upstairs." The other brunette reached for her phone and punched in two numbers. The blonde turned back to us and tried to smile. Her nose was red from being rubbed by the Kleenex.

"Sorry if we seem so disorganized. Our office manager has been out sick, and the rest of us are all still so—" She turned away trying to stiffle a sob and hurried across the room and down a hall which led off the back.

The brunette watched her go. Then she turned back to us. "Berk should be down in a minute. If you'd like to have a seat?"

We only had to wait a few minutes. He came out of the same hall the blonde had disappeared into. We stood as he came toward us. He hadn't changed a bit. He was still the same old Berk. He wore a pair of faded straight-leg jeans and a plain white T-shirt, tucked in.

He stopped, leaned back, and exaggerated looking up at us. "Jeez. Where'd all these tall guys come from?" He turned back to the ladies. "Did we hire a basketball team for some reason?"

The ladies giggled.

I said, "Hey, Berk."

He turned and stared at me. "Oh my God. T-Bird?"

I grinned at him. I'd completely forgotten that he used to call me that.

He said, "I didn't even recognize you."

He pulled open the gate in the oak railing, came through it, and wrapped me in a bear hug. Then he stepped back and gave me that smile, but I noticed that his eyes were red, too. Just like his co-workers'.

His eyelids were slightly puffy. Apparently, Ernie's death hadn't been easy for any of them.

He was looking me up and down. "Jeez. I think you're even taller than you were last time I saw you. I'm glad I'm not buying your groceries anymore. Who're these guys? Oh my God. Is that Danny Gillespie?" Danny was laughing. Berk moved to Danny and gave him the same hearty hug. "Jeez, Danny, you little shit, you're as tall as the T-Bird. And look at these other two. T-Bird. Couldn't you find any *tall* friends?"

Danny grinned at Berk like a little kid. Danny had always idolized Berk almost as much as I did. I could see that Bump and Gruf were totally blown away by him, too. As I made introductions, I watched him charm the socks off them.

He turned back to me. "So what are you doing these days, punk? Oh, hey, wait a minute. We don't have to stand around here. Let's go up to my place. I just made coffee. Come on."

We followed him through the office, down that back hall to some stairs, up and around to the left, and down a thickly carpeted hallway to a door that was standing open. Inside was a large, furnished apartment. There was a front entryway with a low cherry table centered under a large gilt-framed mirror. A gray carpeted hallway led off to the left. He turned right and led us through a large living room. There were two black leather sofas at right angles, two black leather armchairs with a cherry table between them in a corner, and the focus of the room was a big-screen TV. CNN morning news blared loudly. On the far side of the living room, divided from it by two large potted trees, was the dining room. There was a gleaming cherry dining room table with black-padded cherry chairs on all four sides. We followed him through the dining room to a large kitchen and he motioned us to tall, padded, cherry stools at the breakfast bar. He

walked around it to the kitchen, where a large coffeemaker was fizzing.

He glanced back at us. "Everybody want coffee?"
We all said we did. While I told him what-all had
happened to me the past four, five years, he poured
us all coffee into tall black coffee cups and carried
them and the black sugar bowl and creamer over to
the breakfast bar. There were only four chairs, and
we were on them. He leaned against the kitchen
counter and sipped his coffee.

I glanced back into the dining room. There was a
massive cherry breakfront facing me across the matching table. There were glass doors all across the front
of it. It didn't look like there was anything on the
shelves inside.

I said, "This is quite a place here, Berk. Whose
is it?"

He grinned at me. "Mine all mine, T-Bird."

"Get the fuck outa here."

"Seriously. Quite the hovel, ain't it?"

I said, "Jeez. You've done all right for yourself."

He nodded, and opened his mouth to speak, but
was interrupted by the ringing wall-phone. He held up
a finger and answered. The conversation was brief. He
hung up and looked around at us. "That was Beth.
Bud Hanratty just called. He said you guys were here
to look around, and that I should give you a set of
keys."

He waited. He obviously wanted an explanation. I
didn't know what to say. I looked at Bump, who
shrugged, then at Gruf. Gruf is rarely at a loss for
words.

Gruf said, "Yeah. Bud asked us to stop over and
take a quick look around. We're not sure why, really.
You know Bud."

Berk frowned. It wasn't a satisfactory explanation.
It wasn't an explanation at all. But he shrugged.

"Okay. Whatever. I think there's a spare set of keys down in the office somewhere."

Bump said, "I'm really surprised you've got an apartment right here in the office building."

Berk nodded. "Ernie wanted a presence here at night. Especially after he put all the new computers in. Plus he's got his cars stored here. Also, he wanted me on call for his tenants, twenty-four–seven. So he said if I'd build me an apartment up here, I could live here rent-free, and he'd pay for the furnishings. And voi- de fuck -la." He spread his arms.

I said, "He paid a fortune for the furnishings. I can't believe this place. That dining room set. It doesn't look like you, Berk."

He grinned. "It *ain't* me. It's nice, though, isn't it? I built the place, but what do I know about decorating? Early American Trailer Park. So Ernie put the missus on the job. Mrs. Burdett decorated it. Did a hell of a job, too, didn't she?"

Gruf nodded. "It's beautiful."

Berk said, "She spent a fortune. I told Ernie, Outfitting that apartment is costing you an arm and a leg, dude. He didn't blink an eye. He goes, 'I want you to be happy and comfortable.' That Ernie. He was—" His voice caught. He fought for control and then let go with a deep sigh. "They broke the mold after they made Ernie Burdett. Well, drink up and I'll give you the tour."

He led us through the building, top to bottom. Ernie's second floor office was at the extreme opposite end of the building from Berk's apartment. There was an outer office where Berk said Ernie's office manager worked. Berk said she'd been off sick since Ernie's death. Ernie's office sat in the front corner so it had large windows in two walls. There was a massive mahogany desk that faced the street, so he could look out to the front or at the woods to the side. There was a workstation on one inner wall where twin iMacs sat, dark and forlorn. The other wall was taken up by bookshelves and file cabinets.

We peeked into each of the other rooms along the second floor hall. There was a big executive bathroom and the rest of the rooms were for storage. Besides the big open office on the first floor, there were bathrooms and several conference rooms. We stopped off long enough for the office girls to find a spare set of keys for us. Then Berk led us down to the basement. To the right of the stairs were the kitchen, lunchroom, and two more bathrooms. To the left of the stairs was a long, open garage. We walked past several cars that were covered by cotton tarps and at the end of the long, open room we came to an open bay with a hydraulic lift in the center.

Berk said, "I think this was Ernie's favorite place on earth. He used to love to come down here and put his Beemer up on the lift. That Beemer—man, that was a beautiful machine. 1972 BMW 3.0 CSC, fully restored." He shook his head sadly. "It's garbage now, I guess."

He walked over to the end garage door and leaned to look out the high windows. "In the summer, we'd work down here with all the garage doors up. It's a beautiful view out there. There's woods, and down the hill there's a little stream. See?"

We peeked out the windows. Dawn was just breaking over the trees beyond the asphalted driveway that gave access to the garages. There was a mandoor just past the garage door where we all stood. I walked over and tried the knob. The lock button in the center of it popped up. I pushed and pulled, but the door didn't budge. Then I saw that the deadbolt lock was engaged.

Berk noticed me fooling with it. "Yeah, I've got it locked. Ernie couldn't remember to lock a door to save his life." He stopped as he realized that the life he'd just spoken of was gone now. He had another brief struggle with his emotions. He sighed. "Dammit. I still can't fucking believe—well, anyway, I used to have to follow along behind him as much as I could, locking things up."

Bump said, "I'm turned around. What's up there?" He pointed at the ceiling.

"That's a storage room. They keep office supplies in there. Shit like that."

Bump said, "And on the second floor?"

"My apartment. My bedroom."

Bump said, "And Ernie's office is—"

Berk pointed. "Far end of the building, and to the front. Opposite corner from where we are."

Bump nodded.

Gruf said, "I guess you must've been pretty happy, working for Ernie."

Berk smiled. "I thank my lucky stars every day."

I said, "You're the maintenance man?"

Berk thought about it. "I guess that's as good a description as anything. I take care of this building, and Ernie owns a lot of rental properties. A couple of pretty good-sized apartment complexes, like Ladonia Hills—"

I said, "Hey. Speaking of Ladonia Hills. How does the parking work out there? Do the tenants have assigned spaces, or does everybody just park where they want to?"

Berk said, "That's a funny question. Why do you ask?"

"You heard about the girl who was found dead out there?"

He nodded. "Gwen Dillon. Awful thing."

"Yeah. Her body was found in her car the morning of that big blizzard. The girl who found the body knew it was the dead girl's car, even though it was buried in snow. We wondered how she knew that."

"Oh. I see. Okay, yeah, the tenants all have assigned spaces across the fronts of the buildings. Guests are supposed to park on the ends or in the middle."

"So Gwen would've parked her car in the same place every night?"

He nodded. "Supposed to, yeah. Okay, where was I? So Ernie owns Ladonia Hills and he also owns Poplar Grove Apartments down in Bagby. A couple of commercial buildings, here and in Bagby. And he's up to twenty-some houses now. Half of those are multiple family."

I said, "Wow."

Berk said, "Yeah. I ride hard on the tenants. Make sure they're not tearing their units up. Sometimes he'll send me when somebody's behind on their rent. If anyone calls in with a clogged drain or a leak in the roof, I take care of it. If there's a bigger job and I need to hire guys, I hire them. No sweat. When a tenant moves out, I line up painters and get it done. It's the perfect job. Something different every day. I never get bored. And Ernie pays me a ton. Uh, paid. *Paid* me a ton."

I said, "Ernie was pretty generous, huh?"

He smiled. "That doesn't even begin to cover it. Plus, he doesn't treat me like a paid employee. He treats me like a partner. He tells me what needs doing and he leaves it to me. I swear, it's not like he's my boss at all. It's like he's my best friend. Was. Was my best friend. I fucking loved the guy."

Bump said, "Do you know most of Ernie's tenants?"

"I know all of them."

Bump said, "Gwen Dillon?"

Berk nodded. "Sure. God. I can't get over that, what happened to her."

Danny said, "Hell of a coincidence. Gwen Dillon and your boss, both murdered on the same night."

Berk stared at him. "Ernie wasn't murdered. What gave you that idea? Ernie died in a car accident."

Bump shook his head. "Bud Hanratty had the Beemer towed out to Spencer. The cops inspected it yesterday. Somebody tampered with it. That was what caused the so-called accident."

Berk didn't want to believe it. He looked at me. I nodded. His mouth dropped open. "No. That—it—that can't be true. Who'd wanna kill—" He broke off abruptly and stared at us.

Danny said, "Good question."

I said, "That's sort of why Bud asked us to come out here. Take a look around, see if we can figure out exactly what happened the night of the murder, before Ernie left the building."

Berk was suddenly agitated. "Listen. I gotta go. I'm meeting some painters in Bagby this morning. I hate like hell to run out on you like this . . ." He edged away across the garage toward the stairs.

The four of us exchanged looks and turned to follow him. He hurried up the stairs, up the hall, across the office, and out the front door. He didn't even go back up to his apartment to get a coat. In the parking lot, he stopped by a blue pickup truck and pulled keys from his pocket. The sign on the side of the truck said BURDETT PROPERTIES. He turned back to me.

He said, "I guess I cut you guys off kinda short back there. Sorry 'bout that. Business, you know? But I'm sure we'll—you know. If you have more questions. Good seeing you again, T-Bird."

We watched in surprised silence as Berk drove away. Bump turned to me. "Was it something we said?"

I shrugged. "Maybe he really does have to meet some painters."

Bump said, "Yeah. Okay."

Danny and Gruf shuffled uneasily. The parking lot

was illuminated by the blue gloom of the rising sun and the air felt even colder than it had when we'd arrived. I've noticed that happens a lot in northeastern Ohio. The temperature seems to drop as the sun begins to rise. Maybe that's what they mean by the cold light of dawn.

Chapter 13

Bump said, "Well, fuck. I got stuff to do. Catch you guys later."

He climbed into his truck and we watched him drive away. I looked at Gruf and Danny. They were frowning. I didn't like the idea of going to work with Berk's sudden mood swing hanging over our heads. I'd had an idea in the shower that morning, and it occurred to me that now might not be a bad time to bring it up.

I said, "As long as we're playing detective this morning anyway, I had an idea."

Gruf smirked at me. "What's that?"

"I was thinking about our mystery man. Brown Suit Ray. The guy Gwen Dillon's mother went off on at the funeral home. Remember?"

Danny said, "Yeah?"

"Well, I was wondering how we could find out who the hell that guy is."

Gruf said, "Easy. Call the Dillons and ask 'em."

I shook my head. "I don't like that idea. That woman was hanging by a thread at the funeral home. But I thought of another way."

Danny said, "You gonna tell us, or should we try and guess?"

I said, "Asshole. It seemed like he's someone the Dillons know. That they've known for a while. What about taking a look around out in Black Creek, where they live? The way you described it, it sounded like it's a small little berg in the middle of nowhere. There can't be that many Rays there."

Danny said, "What all's out there? Gas station? Convenience store? Town hall?"

Gruf grinned. "One of each, as I remember, and that's about it."

I shrugged. "I was thinking we could take a run out there. Ask around for a guy named Ray. Take a shot in the dark."

Gruf shrugged. "Worth a try."

We piled into my Tacoma and headed out through sparsely populated farmland toward Black Creek. Once we passed the Midway Bar, we didn't see a single other vehicle.

It was just coming up on nine-fifteen when we rolled into the Black Creek Sunoco. The sun had struggled above the horizon but the sky was heavily overcast. It was gonna be another dark, gloomy day. We climbed out of the truck. Gruf headed for the front of the gas station, Danny walked across the highway to the little mom-and-pop convenience store, and I went across the parking lot toward the little white town hall. Which the door was locked tight and I couldn't see any lights on inside.

I looked around. The next place was along the road a little bit. It was a tiny little fieldstone house and it was lit up, inside and out, like a carnival. There was a bunch of stuff sticking up out of the snow in the front yard. Stuff like little windmills and little whirligigs and shit. The whirligigs were spinning pretty good in the icy breeze. In among all the little spinners, there was also a little peeling-paint sign which, when I got closer, turned out to say GRANNIE'S TAXIDERMY.

I was standing on the berm of the highway thinking, Euw, when an ancient brown station wagon turned into the drive without signaling. Which, why signal? There wasn't another car in sight and there hadn't been the whole time we'd been there. A little old lady climbed out from behind the wheel. She opened the back door and pulled out a cardboard box. Then she turned around and saw me standing there.

I gave her a friendly wave and walked a few steps up the driveway. Not close enough to alarm her. Not close enough to see what was in the box. Just close enough not to have to yell.

I said, "Morning, ma'am. Do you live here?"

She glanced toward the house like she wanted to verify, and nodded.

"Can I ask you a quick question?"

Her eyes skipped over toward the gas station. I looked and saw that she was watching Danny, who was coming back to the truck from the little convenience store.

I gave her the story we'd worked out as we drove. "We were supposed to see a guy out here in Black Creek who wants to sell some barn siding? We're doing some remodeling for a customer who wants barn siding in his new office. But we lost the guy's phone number. His name's Ray?"

She said, "Ray." She thought about it and shook her head. "Lives here in Black Creek, you say?" I nodded. She shook her head again. "Nope. Can't help ya. Don't know anybody named Ray."

I said, "He's friends with the Dillons. You know the Dillons?"

She frowned. "I know the Dillons, but that doesn't help me any. I still don't know any Rays."

I thanked her and turned to walk back to the gas station. She said, "Young man." I turned back. "The Dillons just had a death in the family. Don't go bothering them with this now. Hear?"

I said, "Yes, ma'am."

She *looked* like somebody's plump little gramma standing there looking all concerned, her white hair curled in a tight little perm. She looked like she ought to be baking oatmeal cookies. Not stuffing squirrels, or the family poodle, or whatever.

I was dying to ask if the sign in her yard was for real, but Danny and Gruf were already sitting in the truck waiting for me, so I just thanked her for her time and headed back. Danny and Gruf hadn't done any better with the little geek in the gas station and the woman in the convenience store than I had with my taxidermist.

At the lawyers' house, we spent the day working on the walls for the basement bathrooms and the hallway that would lead to them. In the early afternoon Danny took a call on his cell phone. It was a brief conversation. He said, "Thanks," and hung up. "That was John."

I looked up from the underside of the bathroom sink I was connecting. "What's he up to?"

"He was letting us know Alan's out at Ernie's office building with some people from the sheriff's department and the county forensics team."

I nodded. That made sense. Now that Ernie's death was officially a murder, that would be one of Alan's logical first moves.

Business was slow at Smitty's that night. The dining room cleared out early and pretty much stayed cleared out the rest of the night. Business at the bar wasn't much better. We had plenty of time to get our cue sticks from the locked cabinet back in the office and get in some practice.

Gruf told Hammer to go ahead and have his crew close the kitchen early. Danny, Bump, and I went ahead and did the closing jobs for the bar. By the time we finished, Gruf and the Elliot twins were sprawled in the back booth. We settled at the next table.

Gruf said, "I was just telling the twins how we struck out in Black Creek looking for your mysterious Ray guy."

Bump said, "Isn't that a bummer? Who the hell *is* that guy?"

Danny said, "Well, he's not from Black Creek. We're just gonna have to call the Dillons and ask them about him."

I winced. I noticed Gruf did, too.

Reginald Elliot said, "Have you checked around in Bagby yet?" The Elliot twins had gotten involved a little bit in our last murder investigation, and they'd loved every second of it. They were following this one with great interest.

Luther said, "Because we know people in Bagby. We could make some calls."

Bump shrugged. "Gwen Dillon lived there when she was in high school like, ten, twelve years ago. Anything you could get about Bagby would prolly be ancient history, wouldn't it? But I guess it wouldn't hurt to ask around. Knock yourselves out."

Gruf said, "Meanwhile, we'll have a golden opportunity at Lo-Lites tomorrow night during our pool match. That'll be a great chance to ask questions."

Princess came over from the bar carrying the register printouts. She handed them to Gruf because he used them for the closing paperwork.

Gruf said, "Princess, are you sure you're gonna be okay here tomorrow night when we go to the Lo-Lites? I'm thinking maybe I should take a pass on pool. Stick around and help you out."

"You do and I'll be really mad." She grinned at him. "I've got Jeff and Deets, and Deets says the new waitress is ready to work on her own. Cindy hostessing, and Hammer and his Smurfs in the kitchen. Not that we don't respect you all to hell, Gruf, but we can manage just fine without you."

Danny hooted at Gruf. "Yeah, so buzz on out to Ladonia where you won't be in the way."

Gruf shook his head and grinned. "If you're sure . . ."

Bump said, "Princess, you live in Bagby. Can you think of anyone in Bagby named Ray?"

I said, "You think he lives in Bagby?"

Bump shrugged. "We struck out in Black Creek. Bagby is the other place where the Dillons lived."

Princess said, "First name or last name?"

I said, "Huh. That's a good question. I assume it's a first name."

She frowned. "I can't think of anyone right off hand. I could ask around."

Gruf said, "As long as we're picking your brain, have you ever heard anything about a scandal involving a student and a Bagby High School teacher?"

Princess said, "Involving? What do you mean, involving?"

Gruf said, "A male teacher involved with a female student."

Bump said, "Where did you get that?"

Gruf said, "From Jackson. Remember? She said she heard the reason the Dillons moved to Black Creek might've been that Gwen was involved with one of her teachers."

Princess said, "Mercy me. Is that why her family moved to Black Creek?"

I said, "So they say."

She shook her head. "I never heard anything like that. But I'll ask around."

Chapter 14

Wednesday we made good progress on the basement bathrooms. We got about half the fixtures installed. We'd stored them upstairs in the hall that led to the old first floor bathroom, so every time you walked down that old dark hall you banged your knees on the edges of things. It was good to have them out of the way.

Since it was pool night, we knocked off early enough so we had time to run home for a shit, shower, and shave. We met over at Smitty's for a little last-minute practicing and a quick supper. Then we headed out to the Lo-Lites.

Here's something interesting about bars. Maybe you've noticed this. Some bars feel public, like you could walk in, never been there before, take a stool, and you'd feel comfortable. Like, This is a public place and you have as much right to be here as the next guy. I've been in plenty of bars like that.

But some other bars feel private. Like they belong to a certain group and no one else is welcome. A lot of times you can pick up the feeling in the parking lot, before you even walk in the door. You know if you *do* walk in the door, you're gonna get looks that feel hostile. Territorial. I guess Smitty's probably was in this second category before we opened the new dining room. I was never in Smitty's at night before we started the remodeling, but I'd guess that's how it was. Same faces every night. Hostile stares for new faces.

It's hard to pin it down, what it is that tells a guy, in this place you're not welcome. It doesn't seem to have anything to do with the size of the place. Take Lo-Lites, for example. It's a big, spread-out place, with a big, busy kitchen cranking out the fries and onion rings and wingdings, and lots of booths back away from the bar and the pool tables, and two runways with poles for where the topless dancers do their thing. A place that big and that busy should feel public. But it doesn't. I felt it right away that night. If I'd been alone, I wouldn't even have parked my truck. I'd have cruised on to someplace else.

Anyway. We rode out there split up between the twins' big-ass Lincolns and trooped in together carrying our cue cases. The twins each had two cue cases, because they each have a special cue stick just for breaking, and one of the twins was also carrying a briefcase-type thing that held their pool league score book, the rule book, and whatever else the efficient pool team captain of the modern world needs.

We followed the twins to two tables at one end of the front pool table and began settling in, taking off our coats, setting out our smokes and lighters, looking around to see where a guy goes to get a drink around here.

Behind me a voice said, "Twin. How's it goin'?"

I finished spreading my pea jacket over the back of my chair and turned around to see Snake Man standing there, tattoos writhing out from under the rolled-up sleeves of his black T-shirt. A big, gold, predatory eagle was silk screened across his chest. Mick Wallace. Leader of the pack. The pack in this case being the Blue River Boys.

Reginald said, "Fine, Mick. And yourself?"

Mick Wallace grimaced. "Same shit, different day. You guys won last week?"

Reginald nodded. "So did you?"

Mick said, "Just barely. Who'd you guys play?"

"Four Corners."

Mick nodded. "They're pussies. You picked up some new guys this session?"

Reginald nodded. "Terry here. Terry Saltz, meet Mick Wallace, owner of Lo-Lites and team captain." Mick and I jerked heads at each other. "And we picked up Gruf Ridolfi. I think you already know him."

"Gruf. Yeah."

"There he is, over by the bar. And next to him over there, the redhead, that's Danny Gillespie."

Mick said, "Okay."

"And also Bump Bellini. I don't see him right now."

Mick grinned. "Bump Bellini? I know him."

"Do you have any new players?"

"Not yet. We've got a vacant slot, losing Gwen Dillon like that, but I just haven't had the heart . . ." I glanced over at him. His mouth tightened. There was emotion in his eyes. I studied his face, wondering what I was looking at. Was it sadness I saw in his face? Anger? *Guilt?* There was something going on inside him, but with a guy like that, it was hard to tell what.

He said, "Well, fuck. Hey, what're you guys drinkin'? Lemme hook you up and we can get started."

Reginald said, "Gin and tonic for me. Terry?"

I said, "Iced tea."

Mick raised his eyebrows at me and nodded.

In a few minutes we were all sitting around the two tables, our backs to the bar, our drinks and smokes in front of us, heads together, talking about who was gonna shoot who and shit like that. The Lo-Lites team was similarly arranged at the opposite end of the pool table, except various members of their team were running back and forth to the bar and chatting with customers, so you could tell most of them were Lo-Lites employees.

Most, but not all. I spotted a vaguely familiar face that seemed out of place.

I nudged Bump. "Isn't that the Burdett kid over there?"

Bump said, "Sean? Where?"

I pointed.

He spotted the guy. "That sure is. What's *he* doing here?"

Luther overheard him and looked up. "Who?"

Bump said, "Sean Burdett."

Luther said, "He's on the Lo-Lites team, precious. Has been for several sessions. Didn't we mention that the other night?"

Bump said, "I guess I forgot."

So did I. I stared at the kid. He was sucking on a bottle of Bud. His eyes moved restlessly around the room.

I said, "I don't remember seeing him at Smitty's last week. Was he there that night?"

The twins thought it over and shook their heads. Luther said, "I don't remember seeing him. I'll ask Mick when he comes back over."

Danny was sitting on the other side of Luther. Evidently his vital juices were flowing, because he said, "Put me up against one of their sevens. I wanna play somebody tough."

A phone rang behind the bar.

I wondered if I was about to get nervous. I said, "I'll shoot first if you want. Either way, I don't care."

A female voice from behind us yelled, "Mick. Phone."

Mick pushed away from his table and walked past us toward the bar.

Reginald came up behind Luther and leaned in to study the team rosters. They both did a lot of pointing, whispering, nodding, and shaking heads no.

Mick came back from the bar looking pissed off and settled in at his table.

Reginald straightened and looked around. He spotted Gruf. "Gruf. Come here a sec, would you?"

The three of them bent over the rosters.

Danny said, "Because I'll *play* a seven. I don't care."

The phone rang again and Mick was summoned again.

I hadn't seen Allison Burgess at all. I guess she was back in the kitchen or something when we first walked in. But after a few minutes, Mick returned to his table and then all of a sudden she was there, leaning over Mick's shoulder, running her finger down the team roster.

That snowy morning she'd found Gwen Dillon's frozen body, she'd been half frozen herself. I remembered her hunched over, shivering, snot-nosed, just this far from screaming for the rest of eternity. And then later I'd caught a glimpse of her at the funeral home during Gwen Dillon's calling hours, not looking much better, huddled in her coat, surrounded by friends. Now that I got a good look at her, I could see that she was a cute little thing.

Mick pushed back from his table and came toward us. He was carrying a quarter. He said, "Flip to see who puts up first?"

Luther nodded. Mick said, "Call it." He flipped the quarter, Luther called heads, and the quarter landed on the table, tails up.

Luther said, "We'll play Terry Saltz."

Mick nodded.

Luther said, "Mick. We were trying to remember. Who did Sean Burdett play last week?"

Mick said, "Sean? Lemme see." He ran a finger down one side of his mustache. "Oh, I remember. He didn't play anybody. He was home sick. Okay, you're playing Saltz? I'll play Allison."

Mick walked back to his table. I stood up and started unpacking my cue stick and putting it together.

Allison was ranked a two. Since I was still unranked, the set was a race to three. Whoever won three games first. Luther told me Allison was inconsistent, but sometimes she was a pretty good shot. Whatever.

I caught her on an off night, I guess, because she never really gave me any problems. I won in three straight games and it was over before I knew it. I didn't have to take any time-outs at all.

Once my set was over, the pressure was off and I could sit back and observe. I entertained myself by watching the next set, which was Danny versus some scruffy-looking guy who had a five rating. Since Danny was a new, unrated player like me, their set was also a race to three.

I sat there half watching Danny's set, half looking around, picking up some of the various sights and sounds around the place. Lo-Lites had a jukebox, but the volume was turned pretty low, so you could hear what was going on. You could even pick up other conversations.

About halfway through Danny's set, Mick Wallace got called to the phone for a third time. This time when he walked back to his table, he didn't sit down. He motioned one of the girls over, pointed her into his chair, and stood leaning over her, talking quietly and running his hands up and down her bare arms. Then he came over to us. He didn't look happy.

He bent over behind Luther and said, "Twin. I gotta go out for a while. Goldie's gonna be acting captain."

Luther looked around at him and nodded. Mick walked out the front door without even stopping to get his leather.

Danny's set was a barn burner right up to the end when his opponent missed a shot on the eight and Danny made it. After everybody had slapped him on the back, he picked up his bottle, looked over at me, and wiggled it in his hand. My iced tea was pretty

much history, too, so we walked over to the bar
together.

Allison was behind the bar. She came over to us
smiling and winked at me. "You did good. Sometimes
I just suck."

I said, "I heard you can be pretty good when your
mind's on the game."

She pursed her lips, thinking. "Sometimes, I guess."
She reached for Danny's bottle and my empty glass.
She wiggled my glass at me with her eyebrows raised.

I said, "Iced tea. Well, Allison. You look a lot better
now than you did the other morning in that parking lot."

She made a face. "Don't remind me. You guys were
very kind to me that morning, though. I should
thank you."

Danny said, "Oh, stop."

She plopped my tea and Danny's fresh bottle down
on the bar. "You guys came to the funeral home, too.
That was nice. Hey." She turned to me. "That was
you in the middle of that riot at the funeral home.
Who was that woman that was screaming? Was that
Gwen's mom?"

I said, "I guess."

"What was that all about? My God."

I shrugged. "Some guy came walking up to the door
and the next thing I knew, Mrs. Dillon was freaking
out. She called him Ray. You guys here must know
him, if he was involved with Gwen. Who is he?"

She was shaking her head. "I didn't see a guy. I just
saw her screaming, starting to fall on her face, you
catching her—"

"She called him Ray. Older guy, maybe late forties,
early fifties, tired-looking, kinda heavyset."

She was shaking her head. "I don't know."

Well, damn. Trying to get this Ray guy identified
was bugging me. I lit a smoke just to have something
to do.

Allison bent down to an under bar cooler, pulled out a Mich Light, twisted off the cap, and drank a healthy slug. "Do you guys only have six players on your roster?"

Danny nodded. He was grinning, watching her chug-a-lug her beer. She was cute. Perky. Danny's on-again, off-again relationship with Deets Duncan, one of the servers at Smitty's, was currently off-again. He settled in, prepared to enjoy a lively conversation with Allison.

Danny said, "The twins are gonna add our other two players when they see what rankings us new guys end up with."

"Yeah. They'll have to be low-ranked players, to balance out all you hot dogs."

Although we'd already heard the full expalanation of why each team had to carry a couple of twos or threes, Danny got a confused look on his face, to keep her talking. "Why's that?"

She said, "See, in each match, the players' rankings can only add up to less than . . ." And she went into a long and confused explanation. Danny didn't make it any easier for her. To pimp her, he kept asking goofy questions that only got her more confused. Meanwhile, I noticed that Sean Burdett was leaning on the bar a few empty stools away from me.

I nodded hi at him. He nodded hi back. Somebody said, "Sean." He turned around. So did I. A fat guy wearing a faded denim vest with a lot of patches and eagle pins and stuff all over it approached. His brown hair was long and scraggly and thinning. He had a scar that extended from the corner of his eye, down his cheek, and into his lip.

The guy said to Sean, "I hadda work late. Goldie's putting me up next. Can I borrow your stick?"

Sean looked at him like he was crazy. *"No."*

The guy was surprised. "Come on, man. I didn't

have time to go home and get my stick. Lemme use yours."

Sean frowned. "No way, Wes. I *never* lend out my stick."

"*Sean.* It's not like I'll beat on it or anything."

Sean was shaking his head. "No, I said. It screws me up when somebody else uses it. It gets the wrong *kharma* on it."

The guy walked away muttering, "Kharma. Fucking little prick."

Sean turned back to the bar, picked up his empty bottle, and waved it. "Allison. I'm getting thirsty over here."

Allison was still trying to get the rules explained to Danny. She broke off and gave Sean a look. "Then tell Ed. I'm not on the clock."

Sean flashed nasty eyes. "You served *them*." He gave us a nasty glare. "God forbid, you should ever lift a finger when you're not—"

Allison said, "Oh, fuck you, Sean. I do more around here in an hour on my night *off* than . . ."

Sean turned his back on her and walked on down the bar toward a guy who was in the process of sliding a couple of frosty mugs toward another knot of patrons. Allison's voice trailed off.

She turned back to us. "I guess I shoulda been nicer. He did just lose his dad." We shrugged. She gave her head a shake. "I'm not usually like this. I've been a bitch this past week."

Danny said, "Understandable, after what you went through, finding Gwen's body and everything. Maybe you should take some time off, you know?"

She frowned. "Time off doesn't pay the bills. Look at him, though. He'll be back down here in a minute to whine. And he wouldn't even lend Wes his stick. Spoiled little rich boy. Oh, that's not fair. Really, I feel sorry for him. I shoulda just got him a beer."

Danny elbowed me. "That Wes guy. He's the one Gwen got in the fight with at pool last week."

I looked back toward the pool table. Wes had found a bar stick and was just starting his practice session. He broke and began to walk around the table, looking for a shot.

Allison said, "You heard that fight last week? Me too. *Man.* Those two got *into* it, didn't they? Tomato seeds on the bread slicer. I thought Wes was gonna go nuts."

She laughed. "That Gwen. She was such a horrible person. What a wench. I know, you're not supposed to speak ill of the dead or whatever, but come on. Gwen thought she was the shit. If sleeping with Mick made you the boss around here, we'd *all* be bosses, if you get my meaning."

Danny looked at me with his eyebrows up.

Allison was reaching below the bar in front of us. I could just see the front edge of a set of sinks. She began to angrily run a few glasses through the suds and into the rinse water.

She said, "I know, here I go again, but excuse me. She was such a whore." She reached to her left, pulled out a towel, spread it on the bar, and turned six glasses upside down on it to dry.

She gave Danny a sly, corner-of-the-eye look and leaned across the bar toward him. "Well, I'm sorry for what happened to her, but she was headed for seven different kinds of trouble. If one didn't catch her, another one would've. Imagine what would've happened to her if Mick would've found out she was dipping the drawers."

Danny stubbed out his smoke. "Do what?"

She wrinkled her cute little eyebrows. "Dipping the drawers. Isn't that what they call it? I think that's what they call it."

I said, "Call what?"

"When an employee's stealing money out of the register. Don't they call it dipping the drawers?"

Danny and I looked at each other. I could tell he was thinking whether he'd ever heard the term before. Me, I was wondering what would happen if someone who worked for Mick Wallace got caught stealing from him. I was thinking it wouldn't be a good thing for the employee.

Danny said, "I don't think I've ever heard that."

She shrugged and grinned sheepishly at us, like she was thinking she'd said something she shouldn't have said.

I said, "Are you sure Mick *didn't* find out?"

She stared at me. "What're you saying?"

I shrugged and grinned at her. "Me? Nothing."

Danny said, "But I was sorta wondering about that fight she had with Wes. He was really mad. Do you think he could've—"

"Wes?" She shuddered. "Oh, I don't wanna think about any of this stuff. I'm going back over with my team. You guys want anything else first?"

I said, "No, we're good."

She came out from behind the bar and headed across the room. Danny and I picked up our glasses and went back to our table.

The next match was just getting under way. Luther versus Wes. I began to lean over Reginald's shoulder, trying to learn how to keep score. Wes was ranked a six, so he had to win six games before Luther won seven. Luther took him to school. The final score was seven–two, and Wes only won the two because Luther was screwing around with his masse shots.

Gruf played after Luther. His opponent was the girl Mick had left in charge of scorekeeping. Her name was Goldie. She was another cute little brunette, just like Allison. She was ranked a three, but she was pretty good. Slow, methodical, and accurate.

It was a race to three. Goldie won the first two games. Gruf racked the balls for the third game and stepped back to watch her break. He smiled as he watched her, and rubbed his chin with one hand, like he was trying to solve an amusing puzzle.

A conversation at the bar caught my ear. I turned to look. Allison was behind the bar again, talking to a couple of guys who had come over and sat where Danny and I had been.

She was saying, "Gwen Dillon was such a slut. She didn't care about anyone or anything. I guess I shouldn't gossip. I've been trying to quit it, I really have. I usually don't act this way."

Bump elbowed me. "That must be what the Grodells overheard that got them all excited, huh? Allison not gossiping."

I grinned at him. "I bet you're right."

A cheer went up around me. Gruf had just run the table. He came walking toward us, grinning. He made a gun out of his hand by pointing a finger and sticking his thumb up. He fired it, brought it up to his mouth, and blew on it. Goldie racked the balls, Gruf broke, sank the ten ball, ran two more, and played a Safety. Goldie shot and missed, and Gruf ran the table. Then he won the next game just as easily.

Goldie dragged back to her team's table in defeat. Her team clustered around her and there was a whispered discussion. Then she looked across the waiting pool table. "Who are you putting up?"

Luther and Reginald had a conference, whether Reginald should play the fifth and final match of the night, or Bump. They decided to play Bump so he could get his second match in and therefore get his ranking.

Luther said, "We'll play Bump Bellini."

Goldie and Wes Fletcher whispered back and forth, and Goldie said, "Okay, we'll play Sean Burdett."

While Sean pulled his stick out of its fancy black

leather case and screwed it together, Bump started his
five minute practice session. Wes Fletcher moved past
us, heading toward the bar. Gruf caught my eye and
pointed after him. Wes balanced on a stool, leaned
over the bar, and began to talk to Allison. Gruf picked
up his empty beer bottle and casually drifted over. My
iced tea glass was down to nothing but a soggy lemon
wedge. I followed him. We straddled stools on either
side of Wes. Danny drifted over and took the stool
next to me.

We sat in silence for a while. I was trying to think
how to strike up a conversation with Wes. Danny
solved that problem by leaning around me and saying,
"I heard that little dick Sean refuse to lend you his
stick. What's up with that guy?"

Wes leaned forward to look at Danny. Danny gave
him his patented Gillespie freckle-faced grin. Wes
smiled back and shook his head. "Aw, Sean's all right.
I shoulda known better than to ask him."

I said, "Still. I mean, you're teammates and
everything . . ."

A cheer went up over at the pool table. We all
turned around. Bump was chalking his stick. Sean was
scowling as he dropped the balls and reached for the
rack.

Wes shook his head. "Aw, cut him some slack. Poor
little fucker just lost his daddy. Anyway, fucked-up
kid like that. It ain't his fault he don't got no people
skills."

But as I watched the set between Bump and Sean
Burdett, it got harder and harder to cut Sean some
slack. At one point, Goldie tried to get him to call a
time-out because he was lining up for a shot that was
gonna be a scratch. Even from my barstool I could
see that. He turned around and loudly told her to fuck
off. He shot and scratched. Then Bump proceeded to
take him to school.

In the next game, Sean missed a bunny shot, got

mad, and threw his stick at the wall, narrowly missing Goldie's head. Instead of apologizing, he yelled at her for talking too loudly while he was shooting. Bump beat him three–zip.

It was a relief when the match was over and Sean walked back over to the bar. Cut him some slack? Fuck, no. The kid was a shithead. I said as much as we rode back to Smitty's.

Gruf said, "You know what he seems like to me? Jackson was telling me about the characteristics of the sociopathic personality. That's what I think he acts like. A sociopath."

Chapter 15

John was sitting at the table tying his cop shoes when I walked out to the kitchen after my shower Thursday morning. He'd made coffee. I poured a cup, stirred in cream and sugar, sat down across from him, and lit a smoke.

"Didja run this morning?"

He nodded.

"How is it outside?"

"Nice. Blue sky, warmish."

"Warmish? Really?" I reached over and opened the window. Sure enough. Warmish. I leaned close to the window so I could see a little patch of the street out front. No ice. Not even much snow, except for the eye-high piles the plows had made. Sweet.

I sipped coffee and had a little drag on my smoke. "So, dude, what's Alan working on lately? How's the investigation coming on his end?"

He shrugged. "I told you guys they were out at Burdett Properties yesterday, right? And a forensics team went over Gwen Dillon's apartment. They didn't find anything at Gwen's they didn't think should be there. Well, traces of pot in a couple of ashtrays. He's had people out checking the junkyards, looking for someone who remembers selling that tie rod and housing. Nothing so far."

I nodded. "Is Alan thinking the two murders are connected?"

"He hasn't actually said so, that I've heard. But yeah. I'm pretty sure that's exactly what he's thinking."

I said, "Boy. They sure didn't like Gwen Dillon out at Lo-Lites. Hey. Have you guys talked to Sean Burdett?"

He looked up from his coffee. "The son? Why?"

I shrugged. "Just wondered. That kid's *all* personality."

He nodded. "That's what I thought, too. Spoiled little rich kid." He glanced up at me with an odd grin on his face. "Speaking of Lo-Lites, how was it last night?"

"We swept 'em.

"But I mean, did you guys have a nice long talk with Mick Wallace?" He still had that odd little grin on his face.

"Barely talked to him at all. He got a couple of phone calls and ended up leaving. Never came back." I looked at him closer. "Why?"

He burst out laughing. "I'll give you one guess who was calling him."

I stared at him. "Who?"

"Alan Bushnell."

"Alan? You're shitting me."

"Nope. He called me last night laughing. He talked Mick into going home so you guys wouldn't get a crack at him."

"That's lame."

He stood up. "I thought it was pretty funny. So did Alan."

I frowned. "Well, any little thing we can do to brighten Alan's day. Speaking of Alan's day, what did they find at Ernie's office building? And Alan musta got the word on that coffee thermos by now."

John stood up and walked to the sink. He drew himself a glass of water.

I said, "John?"

"What."

"The results on Ernie's coffee thermos."

John groaned. "Alan said not to tell anybody the results. Especially not you."

"Okay. You didn't. What did they find?"

He turned around. "He'd kill me dead—"

"You didn't tell me. What did they find?"

He groaned again. "Ketamine."

I blinked. "Ketamine? What's that? Is there a street name for it?"

"I've heard a couple of names. Purple something or other, Special K . . ."

"Special K? That's some nasty stuff. I thought that stuff was injected."

"Sometimes. But this time it was in powder form. Stirred into Ernie's coffee. Half a teaspoon or so would've done the job."

Then we had to sit there with Alan smirking at us all the way through breakfast. Riding out to Ladonia in Gruf's Jeep later, I told Danny and Gruf how Alan had made Mick leave his bar during the pool match. We all shook our heads about it. I mean, because it was so stupid. But I held back the news about the Special K in the coffee thermos. I felt responsible for John's job security. I figured I'd wait a bit on that news. See if it'd come out some other way. Maybe by way of Bud, or something.

For the new kitchen counters, nothing but marble would satisfy the lawyers. One of the lawyers knew a marble guy, so they dealt through him. Marble is tricky. I was only too happy to leave that job to the experts. Three marble cutters showed up at the house Thursday morning just as we were taking off our coats.

We helped them carry the huge slabs down to the basement. Then we hovered over them while they pulled off the wrappers. The marble the lawyers had chosen was really beautiful. It was sort of a slate blue color with streaks of white and muted peach running through it. We stood around the new kitchen for a few minutes and bullshitted with the guys. They'd get their counters cut and installed, and they'd drop in the sinks, because that's tricky when you're dealing with marble counters. When they were all finished, we'd hook up the plumbing and trim everything out.

We worked on the bathrooms all morning. Just before lunch, while Gruf and Danny were wrestling with a toilet, trying to drop it in, I walked back to the kitchen to have a look. The marble guys had all the counter pieces laid. They were having a smoke before they cut the holes for the sinks. I went along the counters admiring the tight seams. Even though the marble was dusty and smeared, you could tell they were gonna look bitchin' when they were cleaned up.

Then I spotted the chip. I said, "Hey, Frank?"

That was the head guy's name. Frank. He turned around. "Yeah."

I pointed to the chip. "What happened here?"

I saw him glance at the guy next to him. He walked over and looked where I was pointing. "Oh, that. Saw chipped the corner a little bit. That happens."

I couldn't believe he was trying to blow me off. "That's not good, Frank."

He laughed. "Oh well. That's the breaks, huh? Anyway, we turned it to the rear. When you guys install the splash guard, that'll cover it up."

I shook my head, pulled out my tape measure, and hooked it on the back edge of the marble next to the chip. "The splash guard's only quarter-inch, Frank. Your chip's more like three quarters. That's not gonna get it."

He showed a little attitude. "Oh, come *on*."

I gave him a look. "*You* come on, Frank. You're gonna have to bring a fresh slab. I can't accept this."

He glared at me. "You're kidding, right?"

"Do I look like I'm kidding?"

He started swearing. I held up a hand. "Frank. These guys are very particular. You must've noticed that when they chose their marble."

He grimaced. "But, Terry . . ."

"Dude. You're gonna have to make it right sooner or later. If I let it slide, the lawyers'll spot it, and I guarantee you they won't let it slide. At least you haven't cut the sink holes yet. You can recycle this piece into another job."

"But—"

"Dude. They're *lawyers*." That chip wouldn't have been acceptable no matter who the job was for, but I figured hinting that he'd get his ass sued was the easiest way to cut the argument short.

I gave him a look. He blinked at me. Then he called his two buddies and they pulled the chipped counter. I felt a little sorry for them, but they'd screwed up and then they'd tried to weasel out of it. That's no way to be.

They'd just loaded the flawed marble back onto their truck and left, and we'd just settled at the old kitchen table with our sandwiches, when there was a knock at the back door. A grinning Reginald Elliot stood on the little back porch holding a copy of the Bagby High School yearbook for Gwen Dillon's junior year.

He said, "We haven't been able to get your questions answered yet, but we did get this. Maybe it'll help."

He said he couldn't stay. I carried the yearbook to the table and the three of us took turns looking through it while we ate. We found Gwen Dillon's thumbnail class photo easily. I squinted at the little picture. She'd been a skinny little thing for a junior in high school. Her hair was all teased up in that horrible mall hair they all used to wear back then. I tore open my bag of Doritos while Danny pulled the year-book over in front of him and continued to turn pages.

Danny said, "Nobody looks right when they're in high school."

Gruf leaned to look over his shoulder. "It's like they have to grow into their faces."

Danny laughed. "Look at this guy. He has to grow into those ears." He continued to flip pages while he chewed his hard salami sandwich. Time passed. I got up to drop my trash in the bag and was stirring up another instant iced tea when Danny said, "Hey. Here's a teacher named Ray."

We all stared at the book where Danny was pointing.

I said, "Holy shit. That's Brown Suit." My eyes dropped to the caption. "Ray Kehoe."

It was definitely my guy. In the photo he was little less pudgy, had a little more hair, and was a little less tired-looking, but it was definitely him. I read the caption: RAY KEHOE, AUTO MECHANICS, VARSITY WRES-TLING COACH. I jabbed a finger at the caption. "He teaches auto shop. He'd have known how to rig Er-nie's Beemer."

Gruf said, "That rumor we heard about why the Dillons moved to Black Creek. About Gwen and some teacher?"

I nodded. "Must've been this guy." I looked from Gruf to Danny. My relief was almost overwhelming, because I'd been a little worried—concerned—about whether or not Berk was in trouble. "Is that it, then? Our murderer is the teacher Gwen had an affair with? A guy who teaches auto shop?"

Danny said, "Sure. You were the witness when she pushed him over the edge that night at Smitty's."

I said, "Okay. But what was his motive for Ernie? We don't even know whether he knew Ernie."

Danny snapped his fingers. "We haven't found out yet why Ernie was gonna divorce Chrissy. Maybe it was because of Gwen Dillon."

Gruf frowned. "Gwen Dillon and Ernie Burdett were having an affair?"

Danny nodded. "And this Ray Kehoe guy found out, and he killed them both. Plain and simple."

Gruf said, "Maybe. Now all we have to do is prove it."

We put a call in for John on Danny's cell phone. When he got the message and called us back, Danny told him we'd identified Brown Suit as Ray Kehoe and asked him to get an address for us. An hour later he called back. Ray Kehoe lived in Bagby in the Poplar Arms Apartments. John hadn't been able to get an apartment or building number.

I repeated John's information to Gruf and Danny. Gruf said, "Poplar Arms? Your brother mentioned Poplar Arms when he was listing the different properties Ernie owned."

I said, "How 'bout that?"

Danny said, "That's not that much of a coincidence. Poplar Arms is about the only apartment complex in Bagby, isn't it? If you wanna live in Bagby and you wanna rent an apartment, that's about your only choice."

I said, "Still."

Smitty's was busy that night, both in the dining room and out at the bar. We told everybody we'd found Ray, and they all found the odd minute to go back in the office and have a look at his picture in the yearbook, but there wasn't a good opportunity to sit around and have a good jaw session about it.

I took my meal break about eight-thirty, but I only had a grilled cheese and fries because I didn't wanna be long about it. I had just carried my dirty plate back to the kitchen when somebody spilled a drink out by the pool tables, so I went right back to work cleaning that up.

Just after ten, there was a little scuffle out by the bar. Gruf and I were the closest ones so we pulled the two guys apart. The one guy was pretty well lit, but he had a buddy there who was in good condition. The buddy said he'd drive the drunk home. I walked them to the front door to make sure the drunk didn't try to swerve around and go back to resume his argument.

They were no sooner out the door than Mick Wallace was in it. I stepped back to let him walk in. Wes Fletcher was right behind him. They were wearing their leathers. I hoped it wasn't a bad sign.

Mick stopped beside me and looked at me, stroking the side of his mustache. Tiny red stones in the eyes of his silver skull ring caught a ray of light and winked at me. He had a black bandana tied around his head like a dewrag. His hair curled out from underneath it like thin, lethal black snakes. He said, "Dude. I forgot your name."

"Terry. Saltz."

"Saltz? Are you related to Berk Saltz?"

Berk again. I said, "He's my brother."

He nodded. "I see the resemblance. Gruf around?"

"Sure. Follow me."

I led them along the bar to where Gruf was still trying to quiet the remaining scuffler. The guy stopped in the middle of his complaint to stare at Mick and Wes. Then he plopped himself on his stool with his mouth shut. Gruf turned around to see why the drunk straightened up so fast. When he saw who was standing behind me, he grinned at them.

"If you guys ever want jobs as bouncers—"

Mick interrupted him. "Gruf. Got a minute?"

"Sure. What's up."

Mick said, "Is there somewhere we can talk? In

private? I don't really want Alan Bushnell or one of
his little narcs to see me in here."

Gruf nodded. "We'll go back to the office."

Nobody invited me along. I let them walk ahead of
me, but I followed. I had no idea why Mick Wallace
wanted to talk to Gruf, but if there was gonna be any
trouble, I was gonna be close enough to jump in.

As they turned into the office doorway, I heard
Mick say, "We're here to talk about Gwen Dillon's
murder. Alan Bushnell doesn't want me and you guys
talking to each other for some reason, but fuck that."

Gruf turned back to the door and almost walked
right into me. "Terry, go get Danny and Bump." He
looked around at Mick and Wes. "What can I get you
guys from the bar?"

Within a few minutes we were all sitting at the long
beat-up table in the office with the door closed, our
drinks and ashtrays all arranged in front of us. It
looked like some kind of weird degenerate board
meeting or something. Wes Fletcher had a faded or-
ange bandana tied around his head in the same style
as Mick's black one. The long scar that ran down the
side of his face and through his upper lip stood out
in the harsh fluorescent light. He chugged his MGD
and let out a loud belch.

Mick said, "So why's Alan Bushnell got such a big
bug up his ass about you guys?"

We exchanged guilty glances. Bump said, "It's a
long story."

Mick said, "He's telling me he doesn't want you
talking to me. Like he thinks you'll be a bad influence
on me, or something." He grinned. "Fuckin', that's a
first. Someone being kept away from me for *my* sake."

I could well imagine.

Mick fixed his eyes on me. He glanced at Danny
and then back at me. "You, Terry. I know these other
guys, but what's your deal? You and him." He glanced

at Danny again. "What do you guys do? Where do you live?"

I shrugged. "We share a trailer out in Chandler's. We have a little carpentry business. We moonlight here for Gruf." I shrugged, like, Satisfied?

Mick said, "Because Alan mentioned your name in particular. He's *really* got a hard-on for you."

I shrugged.

Mick said, "I don't understand how any of you guys are involved in this murder investigation of Alan's. Were you friends with Gwen or something?"

Gruf explained how we had gone running when Allison Burgess found the body that snowy morning. Then Bump explained how we'd interfered in a pair of Alan's previous murder investigations.

Mick listened with growing amusement. By the time Bump finished, he was laughing. "No shit? That's fuckin' hilarious. But why's Alan trying so hard to keep you guys from talking to me?"

Wes had pulled the yearbook over and was looking at it. "Bagby High School? Why's this here?"

Bump said, "It's Gwen's yearbook."

Mick said, "So?"

I said, "Remember the night of the murder, when your pool team was here? The old guy Gwen was with just before she came over by you at the bar? We've been trying ever since the murder to figure out who he was. Now we've got him."

I reached for the yearbook, flipped to the right page, and pointed to the picture. Mick and Wes studied it.

Mick said, "Yeah, I remember seeing him that night. I think I seen him before somewhere, but I don't remember—"

Wes said, "Logan's."

Mick said, "You seen him in Logan's?"

Wes nodded. "A couple times."

Danny said, "Well, that'd make sense. He teaches in Bagby and Logan's is in Bagby."

Bump said, "Wes. Do you remember what night you saw him at Logan's?"

Wes shook his head. He said, "I wonder if he lives in Bagby, too."

I nodded. "Poplar Arms Apartments."

Bump said, "I meant to look and see if he's listed in the phone book." He reached to the desk behind him, pulled the big bottom drawer open, and lifted out the phone book for northern Grand County. He flipped pages, found the right one and ran his finger down the row. "No Kehoes. His number must be unlisted."

Danny said, "If I was a teacher, that's what I'd do. Otherwise, the little shits'd be pranking you all the time."

Mick said, "Why're you so interested in this guy? You think he killed Gwen?"

We all shrugged. Bump reminded him about the scene Mrs. Dillon had made at Garrity and Sons. Mick said, "I wondered what that was all about. I didn't see what started it."

Danny said, "It was him. Kehoe. So he's a suspect, that's for sure."

Mick said, "Well, you're not gonna just *call* him, are you?"

We all gave him pitying looks. Danny said, "Course not."

Bump said, "Be nice if we could catch him in Logan's some night. Strike up a conversation."

Suddenly, Bump, Gruf, Danny, and me were all pulling our little notebooks out of our pockets. Mick's eye skipped from notebook to notebook. He elbowed Wes and laughed again. "They've all got little notebooks. This shit is fuckin' hilarious."

I said, "Dude. We had another question about the

night of the pool match. Maybe you guys can help us with it."

They gave me their attention, but Mick started laughing again. "This is fuckin' awesome. Superfly."

That stopped me for a second. Because I wondered, was Superfly a detective or something? Or was he saying, Super fly? To mean super cool or something. Because I didn't really understand the reference. Anyway.

I said, "Allison Burgess put her purse in Gwen Dillon's car that night. When she was ready to leave, she needed the car unlocked so she could get her purse, but she couldn't find Gwen anywhere. Any idea where she was?"

Wes said, "She was out hiding behind the Dumpster smoking dope with me for a while."

Mick grinned. "Asked and answered. By my *man*." He gave Wes a slap on the back. He certainly was getting a kick out of this.

Bump said, "Any idea what time that was?"

Wes shrugged. "I don't know. Late. Come to think of it, I saw Allison wandering around the parking lot while we were standing there."

I said, "Who's we? You and Gwen?"

Wes nodded.

Danny was grinning at Mick.

I looked at Mick. "You didn't go outside?"

Mick shook his head. "I mighta been gone by that time."

Wes said, "Yeah. He left a while before that." He looked at Mick. "That was after that call you got about that other thing."

Mick nodded.

Bump said, "What other thing?"

Mick gave him a steady look and ran a finger down the side of his mustache. "Other business. Nothing to do with this."

The look meant, Don't ask me about that. Bump did anyway. "Maybe it was something to do with Ernie Burdett?"

Mick's eyes went cold and hard. Up until then, I'd been wondering just how bad and tough this guy was. Because I mean, he'd been acting so pleasant. He'd been acting almost nerdy. Now I caught a glimpse of the other side of Mick Wallace.

Mick said tightly, "Nothing to do with Ernie Burdett. Nothing to do with Gwen Dillon. Okay? Move on."

Bump's eyes got a little cold, too. He spread his hands. "Just asking." Neither of them looked away and just like that, Bump and Mick were in a staredown. They were making me nervous. Finally, Wes started talking and they both relaxed. I noticed Mick was the one who looked away first. Fuckin' Bump. I don't think that dude's afraid of anybody.

Wes said, "Okay. Gwen was going around asking everybody if they were holding. And everybody was telling her no. All tapped out."

Mick nodded. "She asked me, too. That was why she got rid of the old guy that night. That was what she wanted when she came over by me at the bar. She was always asking. The girls complained about it, how she was always doing that. I told them, Just tell her you're bust. That's what I do. Otherwise, she'd annoy the hell out of you."

Wes said, "That's the way Gwen was. When she wanted something, she wasn't gonna let up till she got it. Finally I told her I had some and we went out by the Dumpster."

Mick said, "I can't get over this. I mean, Gwen wasn't the most popular girl who ever lived, but for somebody to kill her? The same night as Ernie Burdett's accident?" He shook his head.

Bump said, "That was no accident."

Mick said, "What?"

Bump told them Ernie's car had been tampered with.

Mick said, "Tampered with? How?"

Gruf said, "Alan hasn't made that public." He gave the rest of us a look to remind us about Alan's warning.

Mick said, "Well, fuck me dead. Did the same person do both murders?"

I said, "Did you know Ernie pretty well?"

He shook his head. "I seen him around a few times, but mainly I just know his son, Sean. You, Wes?"

Wes said, "No. Just know Sean."

Mick nodded. Suddenly nobody had anything to say. I sipped my iced tea and waited for somebody to talk.

Finally, Mick said, "Allison says you guys were asking questions about Wes."

I glanced at Wes.

Bump said, "We're asking questions about everybody."

Mick shrugged. "But why Wes, in particular?"

Bump said, "He was fighting with Gwen the night of the murder. She was reaming him a new one about leaving tomato seeds on the bread slicer."

Wes said, "Ooh, yeah. I remember that now."

Bump said, "She threatened to tell you, Mick. Wes said something about that'd be the last thing she ever did."

Wes looked astonished. "I said *that*?"

Mick nodded at him. "That's you, big man. You say stuff like that." He looked at us. "But that's just Wes. He blows hot and then he cools off. Wes didn't kill Gwen. And just for the record, neither did I."

Bump said, "Allison told you Gwen was stealing from the registers."

Mick blinked. "Wo. You guys are really into this shit, aren't you? So you think I killed her because she was stealing? Fuck. I'd have to kill all of 'em. Including ol' Wes here."

Wes sat up straight. Mick laughed at him. "I know you guys all dip in the registers. Fuck. As long as it's just a buck or two, I don't give a crap. Half the time you end up shorting somebody their change and the total comes out on the plus side anyway."

Gruf looked a little horrified at Mick's easygoing attitude. Gruf wanted *his* registers to come out on the nose every time. He was as upset if a drawer was over as if it was under, for the very reason that it meant some customer got short-changed. He hated thinking some customer walked out feeling cheated.

Mick said, "Anyway." He stretched his long fingers up his sleeve and scratched. I wondered if one of his tattoos itched.

Danny said, "Were you sleeping with Gwen?"

Mick grinned and shrugged. "Sleeping with her? Naw. She's too tall."

Wes laughed. "Mick likes the small girls. Likes to be able to spin 'em."

All of us sorta went like, Heh.

I said, "Then what *was* your relationship with her?"

"Business. Well, friends, too, I guess you could say."

I said, "Did she talk to either of you about stuff that was going in her life?"

Mick grimaced. "Anytime she could corner me."

I said, "Did she ever mention Ernie Burdett?"

"Uh, once. She did once."

That got our attention. Danny said, "Was she sleeping with *him?*"

Mick laughed. "Fuck no. But she was supposed to *act* like she was."

Bump said, *"What?"*

Mick said, "I'm not gonna sit here and act like I know the whole story. Half the time when she started running her mouth, I walked away or tuned her out.

You know? But I guess Gwen and Ernie were friends, or something. I guess sometimes he'd let her skate on her rent for a few days. Stuff like that. Anyway—"

I said, "Skate on her rent?"

Mick said, "Ernie owns—owned—Ladonia Hills Apartments, where Gwen lived."

Bump said, "That's right. Bud told us Ernie owned Ladonia Hills."

Mick said, "A few weeks ago Gwen told me Ernie wanted her to drop a hint here and there that her and him had a thing going. Because he was gonna start divorce proceedings and he didn't want anyone to know the real reason why. See?"

Wes nodded. "I heard that conversation. I was sitting right there. Remember, Mick?"

Mick shook his head. Then he laughed. "This guy. What a memory you've got, Wes."

Bump said, "A fake affair? You gotta be kidding."

Mick shrugged. "Ernie told her certain people would start trying to figure out who his new girlfriend was, and if word got around that it was Gwen, it wouldn't seem like a big deal. Because Gwen saw a lot of guys. Right, Wes?"

Wes nodded.

Mick said, "I thought it was pretty feeble, myself."

Danny said, "It's dumb. Big-deal businessman like that playing that kind of game. Why?"

Mick said, "I'm trying to remember. I think Gwen said it was something to do with Ernie didn't think his wife would pitch a bitch about the divorce unless she thought he was going to turn right around and marry someone else. He thought if he could just keep his real relationship hidden, he'd be able to get through it pretty easy. Right, Wes?"

Wes nodded. "That's exactly what she said. Get through it pretty easy."

Mick said, "I told her my advice was, stay out of it.

Don't get yourself involved in a rich man's games. But she seemed to think it was a hoot. She was impressed by all Ernie Burdett's money. She probably went right ahead and did it anyway."

Danny said, "If she wanted to get next to Ernie Burdett's money, she shoulda gone after Sean."

Mick and Wes looked at each other and burst out laughing. Mick said, "Can you imagine? Sean Burdett and Gwen Dillon?"

Danny said, "Why? What's so funny about that?"

Bump said, "Gwen was a foot taller, for one thing."

Mick said, "The size difference is the least of it. You'd have to know them."

Wes said, "That poor kid. He's one of those little twerps, like, he's there, but he's not there. He opens his mouth, everybody's like, Yeah, okay, Sean. Now shut the fuck up. You know?"

We did know. Everybody knows a kid like that.

I turned to Wes. "One more question about what happened at closing time that night. Mick was gone. You and Gwen were still here—"

Wes said, "I left before Gwen did. I drove Goldie Knight back to the Lo-Lites. Then I went home."

Things got quiet. I was going over my notes in my notebook. Maybe the other guys were, too.

Mick said, "Okay? Is that all the questions?"

We all nodded. Mick punched Wes in the arm. "Let's ride, then." He ran his eyes from face to face around the table. "You guys are all right. Any of you ever need anything, you call me. Huh?"

We all nodded. Mick and Wes got up and shuffled out of the office. Everybody let breath go.

Chapter 16

Alan was waiting just outside Brewster's front door watching the parking lot Friday morning as me, Danny, and John threaded our way through the running streams of melting snow that veined down the asphalt. The only other time I'd seen Alan out front waiting for someone like that had been the time he was waiting with some bad news for me. But when we made eye contact, Alan's eyes rolled past me back to the parking lot, and I was relieved to realize I wasn't the one he was waiting for. We said good morning to him and slipped on by.

At the table, Alan's newspaper was folded and tucked under his coffee saucer. Nelma and Gruf were talking about the Mound Builders for some reason. Bump was working a cigarette like he was the only source of energy for the entire free world. Mary came toward our table carrying a coffeepot.

"Who do you think Alan's waiting for?" John whispered as we settled into our places.

Danny said, "Probably on the lookout for bad parkers. Lookin' good, Mary, you sweet thang."

Mary filled Danny's cup first.

Bump said, "He's waiting for Bud."

Mary filled my coffee cup. "Number Four, Terry?"

"Yes, please."

"Danny?"

He smiled up at her. "A tall stack, and all the bacon you can find."

She giggled.

Bump said, "Mary? Go ahead and pour a cup for Bud Hanratty. He'll be here any minute. And go ahead and order him a Number Four, prolly. Thanks."

Mary said, "Okay, then this'll be Bud's place."

Bump said, "There Bud is now."

We all turned to look out the front window. Bud was just stepping onto the sidewalk. He and Alan talked for less than a minute, mostly nodding at each other, and then they moved toward the door.

I looked at Bump. "What's going on?"

He said, "The toxicology report came back on Ernie. He *was* drugged."

John and I exchanged looks.

Danny said, "Wo. What'd they use?"

Bump said, "Ketamine. Kit Kat. They found traces in his coffee thermos, too."

Danny said, "I thought they called ketamine Special K."

Bump said, "They call it a lot of things."

Danny said, "Pretty clever, putting it in his thermos. He gets it in his system after he's already on the road."

I said, "Whoever it was, they really wanted to make sure, huh? Did his car *and* doped him."

Bump nodded grimly.

I said, "What does Chrissy have to say about all this?"

Bump said, "We're gonna find out right after breakfast."

I said, "Who's we?"

"You, me, and Bud."

I looked at Danny. I really wanted to go with Bump and Bud, but it wasn't right to duck out on Danny and Gruf.

Danny read my mind. "Go ahead, Boss. Me and Gruf know what to do."

Alan and Bud came in, looking grim. Alan buried

himself behind his newspaper. Bud looked at Bump and gave him a tight nod. Bump got up and walked to the pay phone up front. He came back a minute later, gave Bud a somber nod, and settled back into his place.

After breakfast, Bump, Bud, and me piled into Bud's Caddy. On the way out to Chrissy's, Bud told us that Alan didn't want us to mention Ernie being drugged when we talked to her. We could confront her about someone tampering with Ernie's Beemer, as long as we didn't specify that it was the tie rod end and housing.

I didn't understand the logic. "Why?"

Bud shrugged. He has a funny driving posture. He leans against his door with his right arm extended over the top of his steering wheel, apparently steering with his right wrist. He said, "You mean why can't we mention the drugs?"

I nodded.

"He's hoping to find traces of it somewhere. Maybe the murderer still has some leftover ketamine lying around. If they think we don't know Ernie was drugged, maybe they'll be careless about destroying the evidence. Or something."

That made sense. I nodded. I brought up how we'd found out Gwen had an affair with a teacher when she was in high school, and how we'd finally identified him as an auto shop teacher, and how he was the same guy she'd pissed off so bad in Smitty's the night of the murders. Ray Kehoe. Bud listened distractedly. His mind was more on the circumstances of Ernie Burdett's death. He said the name Ray Kehoe didn't ring any bells with him.

Then Bump told Bud about our talk with Mick and Wes the previous night. When we repeated Mick's news about how Ernie Burdett wanted Gwen Dillon to spread a rumor the two of them were having an affair, Bud nearly drove off the road. He regained control and carefully steered the Caddy into Burdett's driveway.

There weren't any cars in the driveway at Chrissy's. As Bump and Bud turned onto the sidewalk that led to the front door, I stepped up to the garage door, shaded my eyes, and peeked inside. The big burgundy Bronco was parked in there, and the metallic blue PT Cruiser. I'd seen the same two vehicles there on our last visit.

I caught up with them on the porch. Chrissy, wearing a fuzzy pink sweater and straight-leg jeans, answered the door as Bump was reaching for the bell. She stepped back to let us in and waited for hugs. The hug Bump gave her was fleeting and cold. Bud and I didn't offer. Chrissy looked up at Bump with her pretty eyebrows drawn together.

She hung our coats in the hall closet and we followed her down the hallway to the kitchen. She'd been busy since Bump had called to tell her we were coming. There was a big coffeepot sitting on a tile on the dining room table, and coffee cups and saucers spread around, and a plate piled with cinnamon rolls. She'd busted ass to get all this stuff laid out for us so quickly. We pulled out chairs and settled. She had a cigarette burning in a little ashtray that looked like half a strawberry.

The vertical blinds on the sliding glass doors were open that morning. Right outside, there was a snow-covered patio with a lot of covered furniture and a covered in-ground pool. Bright red cardinals were hopping around on the covered furniture and the cement birdbath and the cedar bird feeder. You could hear their happy, silly chirping through the glass. Cardinals sing like meth freaks.

Chrissy tucked one leg up under her and watched Bump warily. He cleared his throat.

"Chrissy . . ." Bump's voice was low, full of regret and sorrow.

They stared at each other. Chrissy said, "Bump, what's this about?"

"I . . ." Bump turned to Bud.

Bud was stirring sugar and cream into his coffee. He set his spoon down and looked at her. "Chrissy. Ernie was murdered."

She couldn't have acted the look on her face. She was rocked. *"What?"*

"Someone sabotaged his car."

She was shaking her head. "It was an *accident.* He went into Dead Man's Curve too fast."

Bump said, "No, Chrissy. Someone deliberately tampered with the Beemer. That's what caused the so-called accident."

She stopped with her mouth open. She shook her head. "I don't—what does that *mean*?"

Bud said, "Chrissy. Did you know Ernie was going to divorce you?"

She stared at him. "Oh. Oh, wait a minute. You don't think *I*—"

"Did you know Ernie was going to divorce you?"

She stubbed out the cigarette in the ashtray and lit a new one with shaking hands. She drew smoke, let it out slowly, and set the burning cigarette in the ashtray. "I wondered why you hadn't come over, Bud. You didn't even call. That's so unlike you. I thought, well, he's so overcome with grief himself he can't face me just yet. I know how close you and Ernie were."

Bud said, "I loved him like a brother."

"And you think *I* was responsible? But Bud, why would I have wanted to kill Ernie? How could you think—I would never even *think* of such a thing. Bump? You know me. *Tell* him."

Bump said, "Did you know Ernie was going to divorce you?"

"Well of course I did. How could I *not* know? He was staying out all night a few times a week, giving me the flimsiest excuses. All of a sudden he's selling off property. Of course I knew."

Bud said, "That must've made you pretty angry."

She laughed at him. "Angry? Why would I have been angry? Listen. When I married Ernie I was a bartender at the Midway. I had a nine-year-old car with a screaming fan belt and a one-bedroom apartment in King's Row. *Now* look at me. I've got this beautiful house full of beautiful furniture and I drive a brand-new PT Cruiser."

Bump said, "But—"

She waved her hand at him. "I knew he was gonna be generous. I never had a moment's doubt. Sure, he was a cutthroat businessman. But I knew he'd leave me well provided for. Because he'd feel guilty. That's how Ernie was. He'd do something rotten, but then he'd try to make up for it."

Bump and I exchanged looks.

"Look at this." She stuck out her hand, palm down, fingers spread. We stared at a ring with a big blue stone, surrounded by sparkling white ones. She said, "That's a sapphire and diamonds, Bud. He gave me that last week. *Last week.* Would he have done that if he was planning to screw me in the divorce? I don't think so."

She played with her cigarette, rolling it over in the ashtray, scuffing off the ash. "We were married six years. I'd made a six-year investment in him and I was about to cash out. Not by killing him. Even if I *was* that sort of person, which I'm not, I mean, why would I have felt I had to kill him? He was about to leave me, well, not wealthy, but comfortable. Definitely comfortable."

Bud said, "With him dead, you *are* wealthy."

Bump said, "And you must've been mad. Here

you've given him six years of your life, and now he's gonna dump you for someone else?"

She stared at him and burst out laughing. "Given him six years of my life? What planet are you living on? We were together for six years. We had some laughs. We cared for each other. But I never had any doubts that he'd always have at least one honey on the side. And he knew the same about me. Bump. It's not like I sat home alone."

Bump said, "You mean *you*—"

"Had someone else? Of course I did. *Do.* Grow up, Bump."

Bump said, "Who?"

She said, "None of your fucking business."

Bud reached for a cinnamon roll. I poured coffee and then looked at it. I had forgotten to ask John if Special K was flavorless or not when it was mixed in with coffee. Oh, what the fuck. She wouldn't try to drug all three of us. Would she? I got busy with the cream and sugar.

Bump said, "I *wanna* believe you, Chrissy. I've been so—but come on. You're a lot richer with Ernie dead than you would've been as a divorcée."

She frowned at him and let go with a humorless chuckle. "Ya think? Listen to me, Bump. As a divorcée, I'da been well set up and it all would've been done quietly. Privately. Everybody would've thought, Oh, poor Chrissy. I wonder if she'll be okay. But as a widow, *every*body knows my business. The sharks are circling."

"Sharks?"

"You were here the other day. My mom and my sisters. Yay, Chrissy's taking us all to the Bahamas. Chrissy's rich. All our troubles are over. Barbie's husband can't seem to get his ass off his sofa, except to get another beer from the refrigerator. His unemployment's about to run out and they need a new roof.

Holly wants breast implants. Fuckin' *breast implants*. Oh my God, Bump, my mom thinks I'm gonna set her up for life in the Bahamas. She's already called a Realtor about putting her little house on the market."

Bud said carefully, "Let's talk about your mom."

"What about her? Oh. You don't think . . . Oh, *please*, Bud. My *mother*?"

Bump said, "She knows enough about cars to have rigged it—"

"So do I. So does Sean. Maybe *Sean* did it." She laughed at him and lit a fresh smoke. She blew the first inhale out in a big white puff, then waved at the air in front of her face.

A floorboard creaked above our heads. Chrissy's eyes went to the ceiling.

Bud picked at his cinnamon roll. "Speaking of Sean, where is he this morning?"

"Upstairs asleep. That noise was just the house settling. Sean usually sleeps till past noon."

I said, "Doesn't he have a job?"

She shook her head. "Sean's, oh, trying to find his way, I guess you'd say. When his mom and dad divorced, it hit him hard. He's been in therapy off and on ever since."

Bud said, "That was six fuckin' years ago."

"But, you know, he was the only child. The center of attention. The divorce was a disaster for him, and then his mom moved to Santa Fe. Sure, it was six years ago, but it left him with some pretty serious issues that he was never really able to resolve."

I groaned. Issues, my ass. The kid's got a nice house, his own car, and somebody to pay for him to go to college? Issue *this*, motherfucker. Give me half an hour with somebody that has that kind of issues, we'll get them resolved right now. Oh de well. That's why I'll never be invited to be on *Oprah*.

I said, "Is Sean into drugs?"

Bud shot me a warning look. I hadn't forgotten we weren't supposed to mention that Ernie had been drugged, but I did want to know the answer to my question.

Chrissy said, "Of course not. Oh, well, he experiments. You know. Who *doesn't* go through a stage where they're curious? I did. I'm sure you guys did. But he doesn't have a drug *problem*."

Bump said, "How old is he, anyway?"

"Twenty-four. Still a kid, really."

I thought, A kid? By the time I was twenty-four, I'd been completely on my own, supporting myself, for eight years. Eight fuckin' years.

I said, "How old are you? If you don't mind my asking?"

"Twenty-six."

I thought, she's only two years older than this lump Sean, and she's still cutting him all this slack? What the fuck?

Chrissy continued, "Over time, he's managed to complete two years of college, He dropped out again last year, but he's a good kid. He'll go back and finish, one of these quarters. He just needs a little time."

Bud shrugged, bit into his cinnamon roll, chewed. "Tell us about that night, Chrissy."

"The night of the accident? Uh, murder? Well, let me see. Ernie was out at the office. He called to say he wouldn't be home for supper. He said he had a late meeting coming up. After that he was going to take care of some paperwork and then he was going to drive out to Sandusky instead of going the next day. He liked driving at night. And there was some other reason, but I can't remember—"

Bud said, "There was bad weather coming. That blizzard."

"That's right. He wanted to beat the weather. My mom was here. Sean was supposed to have a pool match that night but after supper he decided to stay home because he didn't feel well. He went to bed early. My mom went up early, too. And I guess I went to bed shortly after she did. I was tired, and there wasn't anything good on TV."

I glanced at Bud and Bump. Both seemed to be lost in thought. I said, "Chrissy, did you know Gwen Dillon?"

She frowned. "I knew who she was. I knew *of* her."

I nodded. "You'd heard the rumor about her and Ernie?"

"Rumor? What rumor?"

"That Ernie and Gwen Dillon were having an affair."

Chrissy said, "What? Ernie and Gwen Dillon?" She burst out laughing. "Where'd you hear that?"

Bump said carefully, "It was a rumor that was going around."

She was still laughing. "What a rumor. Gwen Dillon aggravated the *hell* out of Ernie. She was the biggest freeloading pain in the ass. Listen. She had that two-bedroom apartment out in Ladonia and she was only paying the one-bedroom rate all those years. Half the time she was late with the rent, anyway. She knew she could get away with it. And she seemed to think Ernie was her personal problem-solver. If it wasn't one thing—"

Bump said, "Why was she only paying the one-bedroom rate? And if she aggravated him so much, why didn't he just tell her to kick mud?"

She grimaced. "Ernie was a soft touch with the la-dies. You knew him, Bud. Gwen figured out how to push his buttons. As aggravated at her as he always was, he still thought she was a hoot. But there's no way they were having an affair. She was totally not his type."

My coffee was getting cold. I finished what was

there and poured new. We all sat there fidgeting, fiddling, thinking.

Chrissy said, "More coffee, Bump?"

He nodded. I sipped on mine while she poured.

After a few seconds, I said, "Who else knew Ernie and you were splitting up? Who else knew you were both having affairs? Did you talk about it to your mom and your sisters?"

"Oh my God, no. I didn't talk about it to *anyone*." She laughed. "When you're surrounded by lunatics like I am, you learn to keep your personal business to yourself."

Bump said, "You and Sean don't talk?"

"No. Not about important things. Sean keeps it all inside. Except I think he talks to Berk. Berk is wonderful with Sean. Sean really idolizes him. I think he tells Berk everything."

I said, "About that rumor. If any of your family, or Sean, heard that rumor, would they have said something to you?"

"The Ernie–Gwen Dillon rumor? Are you kidding? The shit would've hit the fan. That would've been *all* they talked about—for *weeks*."

"And nobody said anything about it?"

She shook her head firmly. "No. Absolutely not."

I said, "If Ernie wasn't involved with Gwen Dillon, who *was* he involved with?"

She shrugged. "Don't know, don't care. What difference does it make now, anyway?"

Bud picked at his cinnamon roll. I lit a cigarette. I said, "So you're going to the Bahamas, huh? When are you leaving?"

"The day after the funeral."

Bud said, "They've finished the autopsy. His body's been released."

She nodded sadly. "I know. Garrity's already called. Calling hours are tonight, Saturday, and Sunday, seven to nine. The funeral's Monday at one."

Bud said, "Chrissy, I *wanted* to call you. It's a little late now, I know, but if there's anything I can do . . ."

She nodded sadly. "I know, Bud. Actually, there *is* something. I'd like you to be a pallbearer. You, Bump, Sean, Berk . . ."

Bud was nodding. Bump said, "We will. Just let me know when and where."

She looked up. Her eyes were teary. "Thanks, Bump. I'll call."

Chapter 17

Bud dropped me back at my truck and I headed out to Ladonia. When I got there, the marble guys were hard at work with a fresh slab. They didn't exactly give me sunny smiles when I looked in at them. Gruf and Danny were hard at work in the bathrooms. I quickly told them about our visit to Chrissy Burdett's and then I got to work.

We realized that if we really pushed, we could be pretty much done with both bathrooms by the end of the day. The marble guys finished about an hour before lunch and I inspected their work. It was perfect. Once they took off, Danny went to work in the kitchen installing the faucets and hooking them up, and installing the splash guards.

Bump called us on Danny's cell phone throughout the day. The first time was to tell us we were all going to Ernie Burdett's calling hours at Garrity's that night. I said I'd already been to Garrity's and I didn't wanna go that time and I definitely wasn't going again tonight or any other night. I said I'd tell Danny and Gruf, though. I did, and they said they'd go. The rest of the calls were Bump telling me I was going and me saying I wasn't. By the end of the day, it turned out I was going after all, and I had no idea whatsoever how it happened.

Me and Danny stopped off at the trailer for a quick shit, shower, and shave. When we got to Smitty's, Gruf and Bump were already there. We huddled in the back booth. During supper we sat there with our notebooks in front of us, trying to figure out where the hell we were on this crazy case.

Bump said, "Who's got a suspects list?"

Danny said, "I thought *you* did."

"Oh, here it is. Okay. Who've we eliminated?"

I said, "Chrissy, I guess."

Bump nodded. "Her mom? Cheryl Workman?"

I shrugged. "I'm not so sure on that one. She *does* end up a lot better off with Ernie dead. No motive for doing Gwen Dillon, though."

Gruf said, "How does she end up better off with Ernie dead?"

Bump said, "She wouldn't have gotten anything if there was a divorce. With him dead, she gets a free trip to the Bahamas, and she's angling to get Chrissy to set her up down there permanently."

Gruf said, "Nice."

Danny said, "But why would she've killed Gwen? Unless she heard the rumor about Gwen and Ernie and decided to avenge her daughter."

Avenge. How does he come up with these things? I shrugged. "Chrissy seemed pretty positive no one in the family had heard the rumor. Anyway, Cheryl didn't strike me as the *avenging* type. She struck me as the type, What's good for Cheryl Workman. Period."

Bump said, "Plus, Chrissy says none of them knew a divorce was coming up."

I nodded. "But let's leave Cheryl Workman on the list for now. Who else is gone?"

Gruf said, "Mick Wallace and Wes Fletcher?"

Bump said, "I say scratch 'em." He glanced around the table. Everybody was nodding. "Yeah." He drew lines through their names.

Bump said, "And I'm adding Sean Burdett."

Gruf looked at him. "Sean? Why?"

Bump shrugged. "He got nothing if Ernie and Chrissy divorced. With Ernie dead, he gets half."

Gruf said, "Yeah, but it sounds like that kid had everything he wanted anyway."

Danny said, "Did he know enough about cars to have done the tampering?"

I said, "Chrissy said he did. Remember, Bump? You said her mom knows about cars, and she said, 'So does Sean.'"

"Yeah, you're right. And she said he experiments with drugs, too. Quote unquote."

Gruf said, "But I mean, even if you think he coulda killed his own father. Why Gwen Dillon? That doesn't even make sense. Whatever. Who else?"

Bump read. "Terry's old guy."

I said, "Ray Kehoe. The teacher."

Bump shook his head. "Maybe he had motive to kill Gwen, but why would he want to kill Ernie?"

I said, "There must be more to the story that we don't know about yet."

Bump said, "Dude. Even if he had a motive to kill Ernie, how would he have gotten access? To the car or the coffee thermos?"

I shrugged. "Berk and Bud both said Ernie was careless about locking doors. And Gwen's mom seemed pretty sure it was him. I think we've gotta at least look at him, just on the basis Gwen's mom thinks he did it."

Bump said, "Okay. Cheryl Workman, Sean Burdett, and Ray Kehoe."

Gruf said, "Well, that narrows it down."

Bump said, "Yeah." He glanced at me. "We need to find out where your brother was that night."

That rocked me. "Berk? Why?"

Bump shrugged. "Just to cover all the bases. I mean, he had access to the Beemer. He knew both Gwen and Ernie."

I got my back up. "Bump. Don't *even* tell me you think Berk—"

He gave me a level look.

My heart was pumping way too much blood to my head. I said, "Berk considered Ernie a friend. You heard him say that yourself."

"I'd still like to know where Berk was that night."

I said, "You know what? Fuck you."

Gruf said, "Take it easy, Terry."

Danny said, "What about the mystery woman Ernie really *was* having the affair with? How can we find out who she is?"

I knew he was just jumping in with that to change the subject and calm things down. Still, it was a good question. I lit a smoke. My hand was a little unsteady. Across the table, Bump watched me with a blank expression on his face.

Gruf said, "What about Bud? Think he could find out anything that would help us track her down?"

Bump said, "I'll ask him to check into it."

Danny said, "Why do we even need to find her?"

Bump said, "Because she's the killer?"

Danny grimaced. "Motive? Not. She was about to marry rich. But come to think of it, she might know something."

I said, "She might be scared right now. She might think it shoulda been her instead of Gwen Dillon. The murderer had the wrong other woman." I was still thinking of Cheryl Workman. I really didn't like that woman, and I could totally see her as a double murderer.

People in the kitchen started laughing. Somebody was talking in a high old lady voice, saying, "Nip it in the bud, Andy," over and over. I leaned to see through the doorway. It was Hammer, screwing around. He had a rag mop draped over his head. Every time he said "Nip it in the bud, Andy," the Smurfs erupted in laughter.

Bump gave Gruf a look. Gruf said, "Hammer's doing his impression of Aunt Bea. From the old *Andy Griffith Show*."

Danny snickered. Bump said, "How's he even *know* about the *Andy Griffith Show*?"

Gruf shrugged. "Nickelodeon?"

Danny said, "That kid's crazy."

Reginald appeared to clear away our plates. Gruf looked at the wall clock. "Let's get moving. It's time to head over to Garrity's."

I was stretching my arm into my pea jacket when Bump stopped beside me. I gave him a neutral look. He said, "Look. I'm sorry if I pissed you off by bringing up Berk's name."

I nodded. "All right."

He stepped closer. "But I think you better ask yourself why I struck such a nerve."

I looked at him.

He said, "You've gotta admit to yourself, you've been wondering about him, too."

We walked into Garrity's ten minutes early, but the place was already crowded. Bud was standing near the front door looking ill with grief. We formed a little knot around him. Bump told him we wanted to know the identity of the woman Ernie had been involved with. Bud looked doubtful, but he agreed to see what he could find out.

Bud and Bump headed for the viewing room. Danny, Gruf, and John trailed after them. I stayed where I was, which was just inside the front door, right about where I'd stood during Gwen Dillon's calling hours.

Chrissy Burdett, Cheryl Workman, and some girls who looked like they might be more of Chrissy's sisters were milling around on the far side of the outer lobby and down a ways. They all wore dark skirts, black stockings, and heels. Sean Burdett and some miscellaneous husband-looking guys were there with them. Chrissy caught my eye and nodded at me, like, Thanks for coming. I nodded back.

Sean Burdett spotted me and walked over, which surprised me. In his black suit, he looked like a kid on his way to Sunday school. He shook my hand and introduced himself.

I had no idea what you're supposed to say in a situation like that. I groped for words. All I could come up with was, "Sorry for your loss, Sean."

He nodded, wandered away down the hallway toward the back of the building, and disappeared from view. A few minutes later he returned carrying a Styrofoam cup of coffee. He saw me looking at him and came my way. "There's coffee in the back, if you're interested."

I nodded. "Thanks. Maybe I will." He wandered down the hall again. I noticed he didn't venture into the viewing room. As I glanced in that direction, Berk walked out. He was wearing a black pinstripe suit with a black dress shirt and a gray tie. He looked like a movie star. He looked like he was born wearing a suit. He spotted me, nodded, smiled, and then walked over to join Chrissy and her mother and sisters.

Other people started arriving, in ones and twos at first, then in larger clusters. The outer lobby began to fill up, and I imagined the inner viewing room was probably filling up, too. Nelma Wolfert and her husband, a jolly-looking little guy, came in. Nelma hugged me. I was surprised to see Smitty and his wife come in. I hadn't realized Smitty knew Ernie Burdett. But then I remembered Smitty knew everybody in Spencer. Smitty looked natty in a black suit and tweed overcoat.

People came, people went. Sean stopped by my post a few more times. The first time, he said, "So Berk's your big brother, huh?"

I nodded.

He said, "I feel like he's my big brother, too."

The next time he reminded me about the coffee. The third time he just stood beside me and watched the parade. He didn't seem to know what to do with himself. At last the crowd thinned, and thinned some more, and the unidentified laborers began to form up for the move outa there. I stepped out onto the Astro-turfed front porch and sucked in clean, cold air. Sean appeared beside me.

He said, "Really, Berk's more *my* brother than yours. You haven't seen him for years, but I see him almost every day."

That struck me as an odd thing to say. I blinked at him.

He glanced back in through the open door. He said, "And now, I'm his boss."

I thought, Yeah, that'll work out pretty good. Berk taking orders from a little punk like you.

Chapter 18

Bump called Saturday morning. I rolled over to look at the clock. It was eleven-thirty. After Ernie Burdett's calling hours we'd gone back to Smitty's, where we worked late. It'd been a wild Friday night. I didn't fall into bed until after three-thirty. I coulda slept all day.

I said, "Whassup?"

Bump said, "Me and Bud were talking. I think we've got something."

"Yeah?"

"Remember over at Ernie's office, the girls said the office manager has been calling off sick since Ernie's death?"

"Yeah?"

"She's the one who had an office right outside Ernie's big corner office?"

"Uh-huh."

"Well, Bud says she's hot. We're thinking maybe she's the one Ernie was having his affair with."

I sat up. "Even if she isn't, working that close with him, maybe she knows who it was."

"Yeah. Bud called the office and got her address. She lives down in Bagby. I was thinking maybe we could take a drive down there."

"Okay."

"I'll call Gruf. See if Danny wants to go. Meet over at Smitty's in half an hour?"

"Okay."

Danny was kicked back in his La-Z-Boy watching CNN. I told him Bump's news, and then I hopped in the shower. I'd planned to take care of some chores that day, but oh de well. The chores would wait.

At Smitty's, we piled into Gruf's Jeep and headed south to Bagby. The neat little house sat right on the corner of Prentiss and Route 54. It was a little two-story cottage-looking thing built of fieldstone, which you could barely see the fieldstone peeking out through the ivy. The front yard was outlined by a neat little fieldstone wall that only stood maybe three feet high, with pillars either side of the driveway that were maybe half a foot taller.

Gruf turned into the drive and we sat there looking at the house. Compared to Ernie's big new house in Spencer, it was a tiny little thing, but in my opinion, size was the only thing the house in Spencer had over this place. This place had a feel about it that you just don't get with a new house. This place had character.

It also had a problem. Ivy looks swell all climbing up your walls and shit. But when its roots start working their way into your gutters and up under the eaves of your roof, you're heading for trouble. This place needed the ivy cut back, like, yesterday.

We walked to the front door and Gruf pushed the doorbell.

I said, "What's this chick's name again?"

Bump said, "Beverly Lash."

There was no answer. The windows all sported white miniblinds, and they were all tightly closed. We waited. Gruf rang the bell again.

Bump said, "I know she's in there. I can feel it."

I was trying to think of something witty to say about this when the front door opened. I don't know what I expected exactly, but Beverly Lash surprised me. I expected her to be older, for one thing. But the woman who appeared in the doorway was gorgeous. She was petite, with brown bangs straight across her forehead and the sides curling in around her chin. She had big green eyes and plump little lips and a very worried look on her face.

Gruf introduced us. He explained that Bud Hanratty was executor of Ernie Burdett's estate and that he had asked us to stop by and ask her a few questions. She looked at each of us in turn and I imagined she wondered why it took four of us to do the job, but she stepped back and let us come in.

I was the last one in, so I reached back to pull the storm door closed, but she shooed me on in and stepped past me. Before she pulled the storm door closed, she stuck her head out and looked up and down the street.

I said softly, "You don't need to be afraid with us here, Beverly."

She whirled around, startled. "I'm not afraid. Why would I be afraid?"

I smiled at her. By this time, the other guys were listening. I said, "You seem like you're afraid of something, but you can relax while we're here."

She stared at me like she was gonna say something. Then she shook it off. "Come on back to the kitchen. I'll make coffee."

I glanced around the front room as I walked through. It was furnished simply, with a beige leather sofa and matching recliner. The carpeting was a little darker shade of beige. The curtains were white and I noticed they hung in stiff, crisp folds and the ruffles stood at attention, like they'd just been laundered and starched. There were dried flowers spread in a low flat basket on the coffee table. The room smelled like lavender. There were plump, pale lavender pillows scattered across the sofa.

The guys were already pulling out chairs at the

kitchen table. There was a basket on the table, too, and it was full of what looked like real apples until Bump picked one up and it turned out to be painted wood. Beverly was at the kitchen counter setting up the coffeepot.

Bump said, "Nice place you got here."

Without turning around, she said, "Thank you."

I said, "Were you and Ernie planning to live here after his divorce?"

Boy oh boy, did I ever hit the bull's-eye with that one. Her hands went up to her face, her shoulders slumped, and a second later there was an audible sob. Gruf was up like a shot, standing beside her, rubbing her back. He said, "Go sit down, Beverly. I'll get the coffee going."

She tried to argue with him, but the rest of us joined in and she was seated at the table sobbing into her hand before she knew what hit her. Gruf found a box of Kleenex on the counter and brought it over. Bump pulled one out and slipped it into her hand.

Danny said, "You loved him a lot, huh?"

She nodded and the crying behind her hands seemed to intensify. She kept on crying while Gruf got the coffee going. There were only four chairs at the table, so when he was ready to join us, he pushed a copy of *Vanity Fair* away from the end of the counter and hopped up there.

After a while she settled down. She blew her nose. Then she reached for a fresh Kleenex and dabbed at her eyes. "I'm so sorry," she said softly. "I thought I'd done all my crying."

We all made embarrassed here's-us-not-knowing-what-to-say noises.

Danny said, "Why are you hiding out here? Who are you scared of?" That's Danny for ya. No small talk. Cut right to the chase.

She looked from face to face like she was trying to

decide something. Then she let go with a big sigh. "That's the trouble. I don't know."

Bump said, "I guess the word's gotten to you that Ernie was murdered."

She shuddered and I was afraid the waterworks were gonna start all over again, but she controlled it and shook her head. "No, but I knew it without being told. Ernie and Gwen Dillon both die on the same night? Of *course* he was murdered. I don't know who's responsible, but I know I'm next. I haven't left my house since that night."

I said, "Why would you be next?"

"When they realize their mistake." She shrugged.

Bump said, "So you think Gwen Dillon was murdered because the murderer thought she and Ernie—"

"The rumor he started. Of course. Why else? It was the only possible reason someone could've wanted them both dead."

Danny said, "That we know of."

Beverly sat up straight and alert all of a sudden. "How did you know it was me he was involved with, anyway?" Her eyes skidded nervously to the kitchen window.

I said, "Relax, kid."

Gruf said, "We *didn't* know it till just now. I doubt anyone else—"

"Still—"

I said, "You're safe. Listen, now. We've been looking into this mess in kind of a . . ." I paused, groping for a word.

Bump said, "Half-assed."

"Yeah. Half-assed way. We want to ask you some questions."

She shrugged.

Bump said, "When was the last time you talked to Ernie?"

She rolled her eyes, thinking. "I talked to him off

and on all that last day. After I left work, he had a late meeting, and then later on he was going to drive out to Sandusky."

Gruf said, "Yeah, we know about that."

Danny said, "You know somebody tampered with his Beemer."

She blinked. "No, I didn't know that. Is that what caused the accident?"

Bump said, "Yeah."

Gruf said, "Did Ernie ever talk to you about like, maybe someone who was causing him problems? Or a problem he had that also concerned Gwen Dillon?"

She shook her head. "Gwen Dillon was a tenant of his, out at Ladonia Hills."

We nodded. She said, "But the only reason I know of that someone would have wanted to kill them both was that Ernie wanted people to think he was involved with Gwen, so they wouldn't discover about me. He figured, if they thought he was fooling around with Gwen, they'd think it wasn't a serious relationship. I told him it was a stupid thing to do."

I said, "But who was it he was trying to fool?"

"Chrissy. People who know Chrissy. He wanted to get through the divorce without things turning ugly. He was afraid if she knew he was in a serious relationship with me, that's what would happen. And Sean, of course. He was concerned about Sean."

We nodded.

She smiled. "Ernie and Sean were very close."

Bump said, "Did he want you to help him spread the rumor?"

She frowned. "I told him, Absolutely not. No way was I going to have anything to do with that silly idea."

Danny said, "You were his office manager. You knew his business."

She nodded.

Danny said, "Did he have any enemies?"

She shook her head. "Oh, there were plenty of people who didn't like him. People who were jealous of him. People who ended up on the short end of this deal or that one. But no one was threatening him. I don't know of anyone who was mad enough at him to kill him. And then, what about Gwen? People who might have been mad at Ernie wouldn't have known Gwen Dillon from—"

Bump said, "Adam. Yeah."

Beverly said, "Basically, Ernie lived a quiet, simple life. His greatest pleasure was working on that Beemer. He loved that car. You know he restored it himself. Well, him and Sean."

We all nodded.

"He even had a hydraulic lift installed in his garage at the office."

Danny said, "Yeah. We saw it."

"He had two other cars he was going to restore, too. One was a Mustang and the other was—I forget what it is. But he couldn't move on past that BMW. It seemed like he always had it up on the lift, tinkering with it. Any time I couldn't find him, it turned out he was down in the garage, playing with his Beemer."

Danny said, "You said Sean worked on it, too?"

She nodded. "Oh yeah. It's been their project for years. Like a couple of little kids. Always something to work on."

Gruf said, "Sean." He looked at me. "He had easy access to the car. Could he have—"

Beverly interrupted. "Sean? Oh, no. He loved his father."

Bump was nodding. "Even if he wanted to get rid of his daddy, I mean, what's the motive for Gwen Dillon?"

Danny said, "We don't know for a fact that the same person did both murders."

Beverly said, "It had to be the same person. It's too much of a coincidence, both of them being murdered on the same night."

Bump said, "You said you suspected Chrissy, or someone acting for Chrissy. What did you mean by that? Do you think the murderer is someone in her family?"

Beverly said, "Oh, no. I don't know any of Chrissy's family. I was thinking of one of Ernie's employees. For some time now, I've suspected that he and Chrissy were having an affair. I can't help wondering if he had something to do with Ernie's death."

My stomach clenched as Bump asked, "One of Ernie's employees? Who?"

Beverly said, "His maintenance man. Berk Saltz."

Chapter 19

We excused ourselves pretty soon after that and climbed back into the Jeep. Nobody spoke for a minute. Then Danny said, "Course, she's just guessing."

My chest hurt. I said, "It's a bad guess. Berk said Ernie was his best friend. Berk would never have touched his best friend's wife. No fucking way."

The silence in the Jeep was uncomfortable.

Bump said, "Bagby High School's straight west of here, isn't it?"

Gruf cranked the motor. "Yup."

"And Logan's Bar and Poplar Arms Apartments are both straight east."

Danny was nodding. "That teacher—"

I said, "Ray Kehoe."

Bump said, "Yeah. Ray Kehoe would drive right past here every day on his way to and from the high school."

I figured out what he was getting at. "Beverly's only got a one-car garage. If Beverly's car was already parked inside . . ."

Bump said, "Then the Beemer would've been parked in the driveway."

Gruf said, "Anybody with a hard-on for Ernie would recognize that Beemer. But so what? Where does that get us?"

I said, "I'm starving. We passed a McDonald's in the next block."

Gruf said, "I hear that."

I chewed my McNuggets and gazed absentmindedly out the window. Some kids were out there clowning around in the cold Saturday sunshine in the McDonald's parking lot. The girls looked cute with their fuzzy knit caps and red cheeks and the white vapor clouds streaming from their noses and mouths when they laughed. Some of the guys were wearing navy and gold Bagby letter jackets. Every few minutes a car with one or more kids in it would tool through the parking lot. Sometimes the kids standing in the parking lot would yell and crowd around the driver's window posing and talking. Sometimes the driver of the latest car would park and join the crowd.

Gruf balled the wrapper of his second quarter pounder and tossed it onto the tray. "I'm full."

Danny said, "Of it."

Bump said, "Long as we're down here, we oughtta go see if we can find Ray Kehoe."

Gruf said, "We don't have his apartment number, remember? We don't even know which building. All we know is it's Poplar Arms."

Danny said, "It's in Bagby. We oughtta be able to find him. How many buildings can there be in Poplar Arms?"

I glanced back out the window and waited for the backs of the letter jackets to turn my way in the milling group of kids. Finally I saw what I was looking for. A kid turned to laugh at a girl beside him and showed me his back. The letters said FOOTBALL/ WRESTLING.

I slid out of our booth, walked outside, and approached the laughing boy. "Dude. Got a minute?"

He turned toward me, smiling.

"I'm looking for a Bagby teacher and I've lost his address. I know he's a wrestling coach. Ray Kehoe. I know he lives in Poplar—"

He turned and pointed. "Right down the street. Three blocks, on the right. Mr. Kehoe lives in the second building. First floor, third door on the left."

The girl next to him tucked a mittened hand under his arm and said, "Second door on the left."

The guy shook his head. "I'm pretty sure it's the third."

I said, "Second building, first floor, some door on the left. I'll find him. Thanks."

When Gruf turned into the driveway that led to the Poplar Arms parking lot, Danny, leaning forward in the passenger seat, let out a hoot.

"Look at that. That's him, isn't it? Were we born lucky, or what?"

He was right. Ray Kehoe was standing in front of a car, tinkering with the windshield wipers. Gruf parked in the closest available space and we walked toward the car.

There were two girls standing near Ray, talking to him, giggling. The taller one had short, spiky hair. It was a horrible shade of red that no one has ever been born with in the history of the world. Why do girls do these things to themselves? The other had pale red hair and wore a pair of those horrible over-sized jeans that kids wear to look like badasses. Both had their jackets hanging open, and the dark one stood with one foot tucked back behind the other in a high school girl's version of a fashion model pose.

We believed this guy had an affair with Gwen Dillon when she was a junior in high school, and now here were these two giggly, flirty little girls with him. I jumped to the conclusion this guy had made a life-long habit of being a perv. It made me mad. I penciled Ray Kehoe onto my shit list.

All three of them looked over as we approached.

Danny said, "You kids scamper on outa here now. We need to talk to Ray."

The girls frowned at Danny and looked to Ray for instruction. He frowned, too, and he got his back up. "Just one minute. Who do you think you are, anyway? You don't walk up and start ordering—"

Bump said, "Yeah, Ray, we do."

Danny waved a hand at the girls, like he was brushing them away. "Go on, now. Go play with someone your own age."

The girls stayed where they were. Ray scowled at us.

Ray said, "Oh, hold on, now."

Gruf shrugged. "Okay, Ray, have it your way. We'll talk in front of them. Come to think of it, they might be interested. It's about Gwen Dillon."

That straightened him up. He blinked at Gruf. Then he cleared his throat. "Girls. You go on now and let me talk with these gentlemen."

They didn't want to leave. The taller one took a protective step toward Ray. "Mr. Kehoe, you don't have to talk to them if you don't—"

He patted her arm. "No, it's fine. We do need to discuss a matter. You two go on now. Really."

Reluctantly, with many a lingering and suspicious look back, they eventually reached the end of the parking lot and disappeared around the corner.

Ray went back to the task at hand, but it was obvious he had no idea what he was doing. A new package of windshield wiper blades was sitting on the hood of the green Sunbird, but he didn't know how to take the old ones off. He was yanking the one on the driver's side around impatiently. Any minute now he was gonna yank the whole assembly free from the car.

Bump stepped up beside him. "Ray."

Ray went on yanking the wiper arm.

"Ray." Louder.

Ray looked up. I really mean he looked *up.* Standing that close to him, Bump towered over him.

Bump said, "Move outa my way."

Ray moved. Like, right now. When Bump isn't happy with someone, you can see it in his eyes and you can hear it in his voice. He doesn't hold anything back. Why should he? is how he looks at it.

Bump heartily disapproves of any American male with a driver's license who doesn't at least know how to do minor maintenance on his vehicle. Changing wiper blades is very minor maintenance. So this Ray guy was already on *two* of Bump's shit lists, and we hadn't even gotten into our discussion yet.

Ray let out with a nervous little chuckle. Bump looked over and frowned at him. Ray took another little step back and shut the fuck up.

Danny moved in and tore open the package of new blades. By that time the old blade was off. They exchanged old for new, swish, click, and Bump moved around to the other side of the car. The blade on the passenger side was replaced even faster. Danny handed Ray his old blades and the empty package. Ray stood there holding them in front of him like a dufus.

Bump glared at him.

I said, "Okay. That was fun." I glanced at the guys. "Who's gonna start?"

Danny said, "I will. Ray. Did you kill Gwen Dillon and Ernie Burdett?"

I burst out laughing, but I made sure to keep my eyes on Ray's reaction. He was stunned.

"*What?* Of course not. How can you even ask me that? Who *are* you guys?"

Danny shrugged. "Somebody did. Why not you?"

"Why? Because Gwen was my friend. And I barely even knew Ernie Burdett. He was my landlord. That's about it."

I said, "Gwen's mom seems to think you did it."

"Gwen's *mom*?" He blinked at me.

"At the funeral home she totally went off on you. I was standing right there."

Ray was nervously turning the old wiper blades in his hands, shifting his weight from one foot to the other. "Gwen's parents never understood her *or* our relationship."

Bump said quietly, "I gotta tell ya, Ray, if I was Gwen's father, I wouldn't understand it, either. Course, if I was Gwen's father, *you'd* be the one that was dead right now."

Ray said, "Listen. Listen." He shuffled his weight again and glanced toward the apartment building. "Let's go inside. Where we can sit down and talk about this. I'll make some coffee. Huh? Okay?"

Bump looked at me. I shrugged. More coffee. Jeez. Every damn time you go to somebody's house, they wanna make you coffee. Whatever. Bump said, "Lead the way."

Ray's apartment was small and cramped. Bookcases lined the walls of his living room, and there were books stacked on his desk and coffee table. He led us through his kitchen to his dining room table, where we took chairs and watched him bang around in his little kitchen, getting his coffeepot set up and perking.

I wandered out to his living room and walked around, checking out his books. There were a few books on child psychology, but most of the rest seemed to be about American history. There were sections for each of the wars, and additional sections on topics like Native Americans, American industry, westward expansion and the gold rushes, American geography, the space programs, entertainment, and a big section on sports.

What with his teaching auto shop, and coaching the wrestling team, and diddling the little girls, you wouldn't have thought this guy'd have time to do all that reading.

The coffee cups he brought in weren't exactly a matched set. The one he gave me had a picture of Ronald McDonald on it. When he gave it to me, I looked at his hand. Something about his hand bothered me. I kept watching his hands as he finished bringing stuff out, wondering what was wrong with them. I wondered if they bothered me because I was imagining those same hands pulling the rope tight around Gwen Dillon's neck, but it didn't seem like that was it.

For creamer he set out a pint carton of two percent. Sugar came to the table in its box. He sat down and looked around the table warily.

Gruf finished doctoring his coffee, gave it a stir, and said, "Ray, why don't you tell us about Gwen?"

"What about her? What do you want to know?"

"Start from the beginning. What was she like in high school? How'd you two get together?"

Ray ran his fingers through his thin brown hair. I watched his fingers. What the fuck was it about his hands? Ray said, "Gwen was a screwed-up kid. Too tall. Geeky. No friends. She had no idea how to get along with kids her own age."

Bump said, "The perfect victim. Huh."

Ray stared at him. "Victim? Is that what you think she was? My victim?"

Bump shrugged. "Wasn't she?"

"No. I was trying to help her."

Danny snorted. "Help her get her pants off."

Ray set down his coffee cup. I watched him play with his spoon. He sighed. "Okay. Good. Let's get it all right out in the open. I know the rumors. I've dealt with this crap for most of my career. You think it was about sex."

We all nodded.

He rolled his eyes. "Then why am I still teaching? Huh? If there was anything to those rumors, do you think I'd still be teaching?"

Bump said, "You never had sex with Gwen Dillon?"

"We eventually had a relationship, yes. But that happened much later. I never touched her when she was a student. Or anyone else. Listen. I'm a wrestling coach. To the girls, that means boys. They want to be team statisticians, trainers, anything to be around the boys. Kids have a lot of problems at that age. Girls *and* boys. I try to give them good advice. They trust me."

Bump was frowning. I didn't believe what I was hearing, either. Ray continued.

"Now, in Gwen's case, from the time she was born, she was just one of forty little kids in her mother's day care center. You know Gwen's mom runs a day care center?"

We didn't, but we nodded anyway.

"Her parents are cold, busy people. I don't think they're familiar with concepts like cuddling. Nurturing. Don't look at me like that." This he said to Bump, who was scowling at him. "*I* didn't cuddle her, either. It wouldn't have been appropriate. I did try to nurture her. God knows, she needed nurturing."

Gruf said, "I'm having trouble believing you, Ray."

Ray shrugged. "Here's this little kid, one of the herd at the day care center, watching her mother and the other women care for the other kids. Whenever she tried for some attention, she heard, 'Set a good example, Gwen. Remember, you're Mrs. Dillon's daughter.'

"Her mother's employees didn't like her. The other kids didn't like her. So the way she coped with it was, she sat alone in the office. That's where she spent her preschool years. Sitting in that office by herself. And when her parents saw she was unhappy, did they offer comfort? No. They gave her things. She had more dolls and stuffed animals than she could fit in her closet. By the time she got to high school, she was selfish, neurotic, maladjusted, and she had no concept whatsoever of empathy for another person."

Gruf said, "Was she getting in trouble?"

"Of course she was. Of *course*. I had her in detention hall a couple of times. I could see how unhappy she was. So I tried to help. I listened. It was the first time in her life that someone actually took an interest in her problems."

Danny said, "If you weren't fucking her, how come her parents moved out to Black Creek in such a hurry?"

He sighed. "I don't know. At the time, I thought they must've jumped to a wrong conclusion, because I did spend time with her. Later, it crossed my mind that Gwen might've *told* them it was like that. To hurt them, or to punish them. I can see her doing that. Even then, she was beginning to confuse love with power. She never admitted it, though, if that was the case. So I don't know."

Gruf said, "I don't think you can blame people for jumping to the wrong conclusion, if you spend a lot of time with young girls. I mean, a grown man, alone with a young girl—"

Ray said, "Do you think I'm stupid? I'm never alone with any student. If I talk to a girl at school, even if it's a private conversation, it's out in the cafeteria, where teachers, students, janitorial people are always around. Never alone in my classroom, never in my office, even."

Bump said, "Those two girls out in the parking lot . . ."

"Those two out there only stopped because they were walking by and saw me."

None of us was completely buying his story, but you could tell he was gonna stick to it. There was an uncomfortable silence. Danny sipped his coffee.

Bump and I looked at each other. His eyes said, You got any other questions? My eyes said, Nope.

Ray said, "Anyone want more coffee?"

Everybody shook their heads.

Ray said, "I had hopes for her for a while there. After she got away from her parents. Got out on her own. I urged her to go to college. Her parents would've paid for it. She was smart, you know. But she went to work in that bar. I didn't like to see her settle for that. And those weren't the right people for her to be around." He shook his head.

Danny said, "Was that when things got sexual between you two?"

Ray frowned. "That happened a couple of years ago. Three. Three years ago. I knew it was a mistake almost right away. It was over almost before it started. We did better as friends."

Bump said, "You ended it?"

Ray nodded. "She could be so charming, sometimes. Funny. When it suited her. Other times . . ."

I nodded. "I saw the way she was with you that night at Smitty's. After her pool set."

He looked surprised. "You did?"

I nodded. "She was a total bitch. She drove you right outa there."

He nodded.

I drained the last of my coffee. I was dying for a cigarette, but I hadn't spotted a single ashtray in my cruise through his living room.

I said, "Where did you go that night?"

He said, "Where did *I* go?"

"After she drove you out of the bar. After you doubled back in and saw her hugging Mick Wallace."

He blinked at me. "You saw me come back in?" I nodded. He frowned. "That was Mick Wallace? I thought that was who that was. Huh. He looked just like I pictured him." He saw I was still waiting for an answer. "I got in my car and drove straight home, swearing to myself that was the end of our friendship."

He started collecting the empty coffee cups and loading them back onto the tray they rode in on. I watched his hands again. What was it about his hands? I couldn't see anything wrong with them. They were perfectly normal hands with neatly trimmed nails. I stared at them, trying to figure it out.

Just then, Danny said, "Hey, Ray. What kind of auto shop teacher doesn't even know how to change his own wiper blades?" That was it. His hands weren't busted up enough for an auto shop teacher. His nails were too clean.

Ray blinked. "Auto shop? I don't teach auto shop. I teach American History."

Bump said, "Yeah, you do. It says right in the yearbook. Ray Kehoe, Auto Mechanics, Wrestling Coach."

Ray frowned. "In the yearbook? No it doesn't. Unless . . ." He blinked and then he began to laugh. He laughed pretty hard. He had to set the tray down. When the fit passed, he dabbed at a drop of moisture at the corner of his eye. "*That* yearbook. Where'd you dig *that* dinosaur up?"

We were all looking at each other like, What the fuck? Gruf said, "It was the yearbook for when Gwen Dillon was a junior."

Ray was nodding, trying to stop laughing so he could explain. "That was the winter I bought my new car. See, my old car, when you turned off the ignition, the headlights automatically went off. But the new one, they didn't. So the first day I drove it to school, I don't know, I guess I was preoccupied, thinking about the day ahead. I guess I was in the habit of turning off the ignition and not thinking about the headlights. Anyway, I walked into the building and left my headlights on. When I came out after wrestling practice, the battery was dead as a doornail. Brand-new car."

Bump frowned and nodded. "That's the way it works, Ray."

Ray nodded. "Fortunately, some of my varsity guys were still there. They came over to help. I didn't know how to open the thing—"

Bump said, "Hood. Pop the hood."

Ray said, "Okay, yeah. So they did it for me. Then someone handed me those clip things."

Bump frowned. "Jumper cables."

Ray nodded. "I didn't know what to do with those, either. The kids were very polite about. We're fortunate to have very polite kids here in Bagby. But behind my back, I guess they thought it was hilarious. Anyway, they got the car running for me. Well, the thing was, it didn't just happen the one time. I did the same thing a number of times that winter. Each time, my varsity guys were there to help. Oh, and also, I kept procrastinating about getting a hide-a-key for the new car, so I locked myself out of it several times. They got the door open for me, too." He laughed, shrugged, shook his head at himself.

"So what happened was, some of my wrestlers were also on the yearbook staff. We have a small student body. We encourage the kids to join lots of extracurriculars. Just before the yearbook was ready to go off to the printers, the guys changed my caption from American History to Auto Mechanics. For a joke. See?" He began to laugh again.

Gruf said, "You weren't mad?"

"Mad? Not at all. I thought it was wonderfully creative. And you see? Here it is, fifteen years later—"

Gruf said, "Twelve."

"Twelve? Okay, twelve years later, and it's still funny. One of those treasured memories. I remember every one of those guys." He laughed. Then he stopped and his shoulders slumped. "I'll always remember Gwen, too. I do miss her. You know? Sometimes, I felt like I knew her better than anyone else in the world." He looked up at me. "I hope you guys will catch the person who killed her. But it wasn't me."

We headed back to Spencer after that, split up, and went our separate ways. I got a chance to take care of my chores after all. I pulled a load of jeans from the dryer right before it was time to leave for Ernie Burdett's calling hours at Garrity's.

At the funeral home, we followed what was becoming our regular funeral home routine. The rest of the guys disappeared into the viewing room and I took up my post near the front door. Sean spotted me right away. He hurried over looking puzzled.

He said, "Back again?"

I shrugged. "The guys feel like we should be here for Bud. And Chrissy. And *you,* of course."

That seemed to make sense to him. He nodded. "There's a coffee and pastry table set up in back. If you want anything."

I nodded. "Thanks. Maybe later."

He nodded, too. Then he awkwardly stepped around to stand beside me. And stayed there. Which I thought was odd. Because by that time, Chrissy and her family had set themselves into sort of a receiving line farther down the hall near the doorway to the viewing room. Bud was with them.

Berk was standing there, too. He was wearing the same black pinstripe suit, but this time he wore a white dress shirt and a black tie with it. I was impressed he had two dress shirts and two ties. A blonde who I assumed was one of Chrissy's sisters seemed to be paying a lot of attention to him. He ignored her.

After a while, a guy pulled her away from Berk and
relocated her further down the receiving line. I
guessed he was the blonde's husband.

People coming in the front door saw Chrissy and
her tribe first thing, and therefore they missed me and
Sean, since we were standing on the opposite side of
the long, wide hall. Plus, Sean was more or less hiding
behind me. The two of us mainly stood there and
watched across and down the hall while people paid
their condolences to Chrissy. Time passed. Once in a
while somebody would spot Sean and come over and
shake his hand and say a few words, but most people
didn't even notice him there.

The other guys had come out of the viewing room
by this time. They split up and circulated. From time
to time, one of them would come over and stop beside
me and my new best friend Sean Burdett for a minute
or two, and then move on. Sean asked if I was ready
for coffee yet. I said, Maybe later. I waited for him to
say something else, but he didn't. I glanced at him.
He was watching Chrissy, smiling.

I paid better attention this time than I had the day
before. There were a lot of people there again. Way
more than I'd seen at Gwen Dillon's calling hours.
Bud and Chrissy didn't seem to know a lot of the
people who moved past them through the line. They'd
been strictly friends or business associates of Ernie's.
Berk had to introduce them.

I was happy where I was by the front door. If I
mingled more, I thought I might get stuck talking to
some complete stranger. Standing there in my pea
jacket, I got a blast of welcome cold air every time
someone came or went through the front door. But I
didn't understand why Sean was standing beside me.
Well, I figured, to each his own.

Together, we watched the people move through the
line. Sometimes, someone would recall something

funny from the past, and they'd all laugh sadly. At those times, I'd hear Sean laugh softly beside me, even though we couldn't hear what was being said from where we were.

Visiting hours were winding down. The number of people standing around dwindled. The unidentified laborers wandered down the hall to the coat room and came back buttoning and zipping. I turned to Sean.

"Well, Dude. You take care now."

He said, "Thanks."

Chapter 20

It was a wild and woolly Saturday night at Smitty's. There was a lot of nervous energy in the air. The place was packed, both in the dining room and out in the bar. Everybody was quick to laugh and quick to take offense. Half an hour after Princess gave last call, a ton of people were still sitting at the bar, reluctant to leave.

When we finally had the public cleared out, Gruf cranked the jukebox and we went into closing mode. Alan Bushnell walked in while I was mopping. He went behind the bar and drew himself a Coke. Then he followed us around sipping it while we worked. When all the closing work was done, and most of the crew had clocked out and left, the guys drifted to the back booth in the dining room. I dumped my mop water and joined them.

Alan was talking about Gwen's car. "If that thing'd *ever* been vacuumed, you wouldn't know it. Filthy."

Bump said, "Well, shit. So they didn't find anything?"

"They found yarn fibers. Gray and black. The gray fibers came off a man's winter scarf. The black ones were off a pea jacket. The kind they sell at the Army–Navy Goldfish Store." He looked at me. "Your brother owns a black pea jacket, doesn't he?"

I shrugged. "Berk? I wouldn't know. But I've got one."

Bump said, "Who doesn't? I've got one, too. I have no idea where the fuck it is. . . ."

Alan was watching me. He said, "How long has your brother worked for Ernie Burdett?"

I really did not like Alan asking me questions about Berk. I really did not like the way he was watching me. "I don't know, Alan. Why don't you ask him?"

Alan gave me a slow smile. "Oh, I already have. Rest assured."

Gruf said, "Have you looked for the scarf?"

Alan gave him a look. "No. We're not interested in finding the scarf at all," he said sarcastically. "Of *course* we're looking for it."

Danny said, "Even if you find it, what would that do for you? All that would mean is the scarf had been in Gwen's car. So what?"

Alan shrugged. "We just keep collecting information. Sooner or later, it all adds up to something. Now, the pea jacket is different. Fibers from the pea jacket were under Gwen Dillon's fingernails. She tore her nails scratching at the sleeves while she was being strangled. Some of the broken nails bled. If we can find the jacket, we should be able to find Gwen's DNA on it."

I said, "What about the Special K? Found any of that yet?"

Alan gave me a blank look. "Special K? Oh. You mean the ketamine." He smiled. Then he said, "You guys have remembered to keep that information under wraps, haven't you?"

We all nodded.

"Keep quiet about that. I don't want the murderer to know that *we* know Ernie was drugged."

Danny said, "Still?"

"Still."

I lit a smoke. Alan had avoided answering the question of whether they'd found traces of the ketamine. I wondered if that was significant. I thought of something else, too. "You guys were gonna contact the junkyards. See if anyone remembered selling that worn Beemer tie rod."

Alan nodded. "Nothing came of it. We even did the junkyards north of Fairfield. If anybody did sell one, they don't remember it now."

Bump said, "Oh well. It was worth a try."

Alan gave me that look again. "Your brother Berk. He knows a lot about cars, doesn't he?"

I'd had about enough. I said, "Alan. My brother considered Ernie Burdett his best friend. He loved his job and he thought Ernie was a great boss. I don't know what kind of a game you're playing here, but get off it."

Alan doesn't like it when you talk to him that way. He opened his mouth to say something ugly, but Danny jumped in and headed him off. "Alan, did anyone tell you about the rumor Ernie wanted to start?"

Alan snapped his mouth closed and turned to look at Danny. "What rumor?"

Gruf said, "Ernie was planning to get a divorce in the spring, and he had the next Mrs. Burdett all lined up, but he didn't want Chrissy to know who she was. So he asked Gwen Dillon to start a rumor that *she* was seeing him."

Alan said, "Oh, that. Yeah, Mick Wallace told me about that. But it doesn't amount to anything. Mick was the only one Gwen ever mentioned it to, and he didn't tell anyone. It's a dead end."

John had mentioned to Alan that we'd finally identified Brown Suit. Alan asked us about that. We told him about tracking down Ray Kehoe and talking to him.

Alan said, "Okay. I never had much interest in him, anyway. If he'd been gonna do something to Gwen, he'd have done it in the heat of anger, then and there.

And where's his motive for Ernie Burdett?" He turned to Bump. "Talked to Bud Hanratty lately there, Bump?"

He said it like there was something wrong with Bump talking to Bud. Bump said, "Bud and I talk frequently. Why?"

Alan said, "Frequently like, every day?"

"Frequently like, every couple of hours. Why?"

"I guess Bud has his own theories about the case, huh?"

Bump frowned. "If he does, he keeps them to himself."

Alan said, "Me, I keep going back to the basic theory in a case like this. In the vast majority of these crimes, the perp turns out to be somebody who was very close to the victim."

Danny said, "That's just what *I* said."

Bump said, "We don't even know who Gwen was close to. But in Ernie's case, that puts us back to somebody in his family. Chrissy, or—"

Gruf said, "Chrissy, and or her mother, and or Sean."

Alan gave me a look. He didn't have to say it. I knew what he was thinking. He was thinking, And or Berk.

Danny said, "If it was one or more of Ernie's family, you've got a little time problem, huh?"

Alan frowned at him. "What do you mean by that?"

"They're all going to the Bahamas the day after the funeral."

Alan frowned. "I hadn't heard that."

Danny said, "And the funeral's Monday. Last visiting hours are tomorrow night and the funeral's Monday."

Bump said, "So that means Tuesday they'll all be climbing onto that big silver bird."

I said, "You can't let 'em go, Alan."

Alan said, "Stopping 'em could be a little tricky, if they're determined to do it."

Bump called Sunday morning. He'd just talked to Bud Hanratty. Bud had something he wanted us to check. Bump wanted me and Danny to meet him at Brewster's for breakfast. He'd already talked to Gruf.

At Brewster's, Bump was reluctant to talk. He didn't manage to get started until after the plates had been cleared away and we were all lighting smokes.

Bump exhaled smoke and forced out the news. "Bud thinks we have to go talk to Berk again, Terry. So do I. This morning. Right now. There's no way around it."

I should have seen it coming, but I didn't. I was tongue-tied. I couldn't argue the point. Berk hadn't told us anything the first time we'd talked to him. Not really. And the second we told him that Ernie had been murdered, Berk suddenly remembered he had to meet some painters somewhere. Bud and Bump were right. We did have to talk to Berk again. I didn't want any part of it, but I was stuck.

Since it was Sunday, the Burdett Properties office building was dark and empty. Bump still had the set of keys Berk had given us. We went in through the front door, locked it behind us, and filed up the stairs. The second floor hall was dark and quiet. Bump knocked on Berk's door. We couldn't hear anything stirring inside. Bump knocked again, louder. After a minute, the door swung open. Berk stood there in a white T-shirt and white briefs, blinking at us. His black hair stood up on the side that'd been mashed against his pillow.

Berk blinked at us. "What the fuck?"

Bump said, "Dude. We've got some questions for you."

Bump's voice was aggressive. Berk glared, took a

step back, and balanced his weight for action. "Fuck
your questions. I spent a good part of the night fixing
an overflowing toilet out in Ladonia. Next time, call
first."

Berk tried to close his door. Bump tried to push
past him. Berk tried to hold his ground. They were
headed for a major tussel. Gruf and I quickly got in
front of Bump. Danny pushed through and backed
Berk up. "Calm down, Berk. Just give us a couple of
minutes, huh? It's important."

After a hairy minute or so, we ended up in Berk's
kitchen. Berk sat at his table and lit a cigarette. I
loaded his coffeepot and got it going. Danny tried to
make small talk to settle everybody down. It seemed
like it took forever to get everybody hooked up with
coffee, but eventually we were all stirring in our cream
and sugar.

I was as uncomfortable as I'd ever been in my life.
I hated that we were there confronting the brother I'd
idolized my whole life, and I dreaded hearing him give
answers I didn't want him to give. I decided to start
things off easy and hope for the best.

I said, "Berk, I saw you at Smitty's the night of the
murders. What were you doing there?"

He blinked at me. "At Smitty's? Oh. Were you
there?"

"I work there. I told you that."

"Oh, that's right. You did. Uh. What was I doing
there? I went there looking for Sean. Wes Fletcher
told me he'd called and said he wasn't coming. He
was home sick."

I said, "Why were you looking for Sean?"

Berk flicked his ash into his ashtray. "Huh. I don't
remember. Must not've been important."

I glanced at Bump. He glared at me.

Gruf said, "Berk, did you know Ernie was planning
to divorce Chrissy?"

Berk paused before he answered. I didn't like how careful he seemed to be with his answers. He said, "Of course I knew. Ernie told me everything."

Bump said, "That was gonna make it nice for you and Chrissy, huh, Berk? You woulda been able to stop sneaking around."

Berk looked at Bump and his face went blank. Then he turned to me. "T-Bird, your friend here has six inches and fifty pounds on me, but if he says one more word about Mrs. Burdett, I'm gonna do my best to give him a pretty strenuous couple of minutes."

Gruf and Danny both let out with nervous laughter and jumped in, trying to defuse the situation. Bump just sat there. Berk kept that same deadly, blank look on his face as he turned back to Bump. "Ernie Burdett was my friend. I told you that. I admired him. I respected him. Even though he's gone, I'll still lay my life on the line for everything that belonged to Ernie. That includes Chrissy. And Sean."

I said, "You and Sean Burdett are pretty close, huh, Berk?"

He sighed and shrugged. "He's Ernie's kid."

I said, "Chrissy told us Sean confides in you."

Berk smiled for the first time. "When Sean needs to talk about something, he likes to talk to me."

I said, "What's Sean been talking to you about lately?"

He gave me a long, neutral look that made me want to go crawl in a hole somewhere. Then he said, "That's nobody's business but Sean's and mine."

Everybody went silent. The silence turned uncomfortable. Gruf seemed to decide we weren't going to get anywhere by sitting there. He pushed back from the table. "We'll get out of your hair now, Berk. Sorry we woke you up."

Berk said, "I had to get up anyway. The cops have

released Gwen Dillon's apartment. We'll be painting it today and tomorrow."

I said, "On a Sunday?"

He shrugged. "Can't re-rent it till it's painted."

Chapter 21

In the Jeep, Bump apologized for getting in Berk's face. My head was pounding. I told him to forget it. He wanted us to all go to Smitty's. Get some lunch. Talk things over. Clear the air. We stopped off at Brewster's parking lot on the way and picked up the extra vehicles. After we ordered lunch I walked over to the bar and bought a little pack of Nuprin.

Over lunch the guys rehashed everything we knew. I sipped on my iced tea, waited for the Nuprin to kick in, and listened. They were talking in circles. I began to think about that fucking Gwen–Ernie rumor. Out of everything we'd learned so far, it seemed like that was the most important connection between Gwen and Ernie. It seemed like that rumor was the only thing we knew about that could've somehow triggered their murders. I wasn't satisfied that no one but Mick and Wes had heard it. There had to be something else there that we hadn't turned up yet.

When there was an opportunity, I brought it up. "That rumor. I keep thinking we've missed something important there. That maybe someone besides Mick and Wes heard it and believed it was true."

Bump shrugged. "Maybe someone else besides Wes was around when Gwen and Mick were talking. Someone Mick and Wes didn't notice."

Gruf said, "There's only one way to find out. Talk to Mick again. I'll call Lo-Lites and see if he's there."

He wasn't, but they expected him in half an hour or so. We decided to drive out to Ladonia. Mick and Wes ambled in together about fifteen minutes after we arrived. Mick led us back to a cramped office and closed the door. Wes nodded at a row of folding chairs. We each opened one and sat. Wes leaned against the closed door. As Mick settled himself behind his desk, he said, "I talked to Alan Bushnell yesterday."

We all nodded. Bump said, "How'd that go?"

Mick grinned. "About how it always goes when I talk to Alan." Wes snickered. "Mainly he wanted to pick my brain about Sean Burdett."

That surprised me. I said, "About Sean? What about him?"

Mick lit a smoke and Wes took a long pull on his Corona. Mick exhaled and watched the ribbon of white smoke get drawn up into the fluorescent light. "What kind of a kid is he? Who does he hang out with? Does he have a girlfriend? That kind of thing."

He sucked in one side of his cheek then let it go with a wet little *pfft.* "I felt like he was wasting my time. I don't really see how he could think a little candy ass like Sean Burdett did a double homicide. Something woulda had to really set him off."

Danny said, "*Does* Sean have a girlfriend?"

Mick snorted.

Danny said, "I guess we can take that as a no?"

Bump said, "We've got some more questions. When Gwen told you Ernie wanted her to start that rumor?"

Wes said, "Yeah?"

Bump said, "You said you two were the only ones who heard her."

Mick said, "Right. Well, she told me, but Wes was there, too." He turned to Wes. "Right? You were sitting there or something?"

Wes said, "Right. I came over to ask you for a night off because I—"

Mick waved a hand. "Whatever." He turned back to Bump. "What about it?"

Bump said, "We're wondering if that rumor got around a little more than just you two. Was anyone else there while Gwen was talking? Anyone maybe sitting at a table nearby, or walking past?"

Mick shook his head. Wes rubbed his chin. Wes said, "Wait a minute. Allison was there."

I thought, Allison? Holy shit. I barely knew the chick, but I knew she was a total gossip. Anything that went in her ears would come right out her mouth.

Mick frowned at him. "No, she wasn't."

Wes nodded. "Yeah, she was. She walked up with a hundred dollar bill for me to look at." He looked at Gruf. "Mick makes the girls bring fifties and hundreds for us to look at, so we don't get stuck with any bogus bills. Gwen was telling you about the rumor and Allison walked up. I reached to take the hundred from her and she wouldn't let go. She was staring at Gwen. I had to jerk it away from her."

Mick laughed. "How do you remember this shit? What'd I tell you guys? My boy Wes has the memory of an elephant."

I said, "What did she hear? I mean, did she hear enough to know it was a lie, or did she walk away thinking it was true?"

Wes shrugged. "Ask her. She's here now. I'll go get her."

He reached for the doorknob but I stopped him. "Hang on. We need to be a little careful how we ask her." I could see nobody understood what I meant. "If the murders happened because she repeated that rumor like it was true, that means she talked to the murderer. See what I mean? The way she runs her mouth, we don't wanna *give* her more information than we get."

Mick said, "Oh. She could go straight to the murderer and repeat anything we said?"

"There ya go."

Bump said, "So you think the murderer is someone she talked to?"

"Could be."

Bump said, "Who does she talk to?"

Wes laughed. "Allison talks all the time. Whoever happens to be around, that's who she talks to."

Gruf said, "Mick, you mentioned you know Berk Saltz. Does he come in here?"

I thought, Berk again, and hoped the Nuprin would see me through.

Mick said, "Not often. He comes in once in a while with Sean Burdett. I think he only comes around trying to give Sean some bonafides, you know?"

Bump said, "I don't follow."

Mick said, "Sean's kind of a—he's got looks and he's got money but he comes up a little short in the balls department."

Wes nodded. "Balls and personality."

Mick said, "Yeah. Personality, too. It seems like Berk looks out for the kid, you know? He'll come in with Sean, and it seems like he's trying to kind of set him up. He'll get the girls around . . ." He grinned at me. "And your brother knows how to get the girls, Terry. Then he'll kind of push Sean forward a little bit. That kind of thing."

I said, "Is Allison friends with Sean?"

Wes said, "She's friendly with him, I guess. Fuck. The kid's got money. Allison likes money. I don't think there's any more to it than that, though. Allison had a boyfriend until just recently."

Danny grinned. "Yeah, that's right. We watched her dump him the morning of the murders."

Bump said, "And she's friends with Berk, too?"

I watched Wes think about it. "She knows him. I've seen her talking to him. Friends? No, I don't know if you could say they're friends."

I said, "All right. Let's get her in here and ask some

questions. But don't give her any more information than she already thinks she has."

Wes went out to find Allison, returned with her in a short time, and guided her to a chair, closing the door behind him. She fidgeted nervously.

I said, "Hey, Allison. How's it going?"

Her eyes were darting from face to face. She seemed more nervous than she ought to have been. "What do you guys want? Because I've got stuff to do."

Mick said, "Relax. We just wanna ask you a few questions."

I said, "Allison, a week or so ago, you had a hundred dollar bill you wanted Wes to look at. Remember that?"

She remembered, all right. She knew exactly what we wanted to ask her about. You could tell by the way she fidgeted in her chair. But she said, "No. I mean, I get hundred dollar bills all the time."

Gruf said, "You remember this particular time, though. Wes was sitting with Mick and Gwen Dillon. Gwen and Mick were talking."

She avoided eye contact. "Were they? Whatever."

I said, "You overheard something, didn't you?"

"No. Who knows? I don't think I did."

I said, "Yes you did. We know you did. Tell us what you overheard."

She was becoming upset. Her cheeks turned red and she was suddenly blinking back tears. "No, I didn't. I don't know what you're talking about."

Mick leaned across his desk in an intimidating way. "You're not talking to Alan Bushnell now, baby. You're talking to *me*." He hardened his voice. "Answer the question."

She burst into tears and tried to stand but Wes put a hand on her shoulder. "Answer the question, Allison."

"Gwen said she was having an affair with Sean's father. That filthy bitch. Okay? Happy now? *God*." Her nose was running. She didn't have a Kleenex, so she wiped it on the back of her hand. I looked around for paper towels or something, but I didn't see anything like that and I didn't wanna interrupt the questioning so I just let her.

I said, "Hearing her say that made you mad."

Gruf said, "You were shocked, huh."

Allison was sobbing. "Of course. She was a horrible person. It wasn't my fault, what happened to her. It was her own fault, what happened."

I said, "The *murders* weren't your fault? Why would anyone think the murders were *your* fault?"

Bump said, "Because you told someone what you heard Gwen say, didn't you? Who did you tell?"

"Nobody."

Mick said roughly, "Allison."

She blinked at him, sobbing. "Nobody. I *swear*."

Mick said, "You're lying. Tell me the truth."

She screamed, "I told *Sean*. Happy now? He had a right to know. It was his *father*."

Now she did fly off her chair. She pushed Wes out of the way, pulled the door open, and ran from the room. Wes reached for her but we stopped him. Gruf said, "Let her go. She told us what we wanted to know."

Mick looked confused. "Does this mean *Sean's* the murderer?"

I felt just as confused as he looked. "I don't guess he would've been too thrilled to think that his dad and Gwen Dillon were involved, but I don't see how he would've been upset enough to *kill* them both. Am I missing something here?"

Bump was shaking his head. "I don't get it."

Gruf said, "Maybe Sean repeated it to somebody else."

Bump said, "Maybe Sean told Berk."

*   *   *

Gruf drove us back to Brewster's. Me and Danny climbed into my truck and I drove us home. I swallowed another dose of Nuprin and fell onto my bed. The next thing I knew, Danny was telling me it was time to get up if I was going to the final calling hours at Garrity's.

The early going at the funeral home was just like the previous nights. I stayed close to the front door and Sean Burdett hid in my shadow. Only now, Sean seemed a little hostile toward me. I puzzled over this for a while and decided it was some kind of juvenile jealousy because of my relationship to Berk. I noticed he watched Berk almost constantly.

I watched Berk, too. Tonight under his pinstripe suit coat he wore a gray dress shirt and a black tie. He shook the hands of the people who filed through the receiving line and turned on that hundred-watt smile of his as he thanked them for coming. I guess I'd been standing there for maybe forty-five minutes when I felt Sean touch my arm.

He said, "I'm going for coffee. Want some?"

I was just about to turn to answer him when I saw Berk leave his place in line and walk toward Chrissy Burdett. He stopped beside her and bent to say something in her ear. She turned toward him and he smiled at her. She smiled back. The whole thing happened in a fraction of a second. I'm sure I was the only one in the whole place that saw it. But in that instant I knew beyond any doubt that they were majorly involved with each other. They might as well have shouted it at the top of their lungs.

Sean said, "Huh? Terry?"

I said, "What? Oh. No coffee, thanks. I'm gonna go out and get some air."

I felt sick. I went outside, stood in the deepest, darkest shadow I could find on that long front porch, and tried to make myself face my worst nightmare. Was there any way that Berk could have murdered two people?

I tried to put aside that Berk was my brother and figure things out. I thought, Okay, Berk and Chrissy are involved. No doubt about that now. Allison tells Sean that Gwen and his father are having an affair. Sean is probably upset, maybe really upset. Does he repeat the story to someone? Sure he does. We've already learned that there's one person Sean admires and trusts. Only one person he confides in. Berk.

So Sean goes to Berk and tells him that Ernie and Gwen Dillon are having an affair. Then what? Berk doesn't believe him, because Ernie hasn't told Berk any such thing? Berk does believe him? Then what? Berk gives some thought to what will happen if Ernie divorces Chrissy to marry Gwen Dillon. Does Berk decide he'd rather make Chrissy a rich widow than watch her become a divorcée on a budget?

The Berk I'd grown up knowing was careless about money, but then again, he never had much. I thought about the furniture in his apartment at Burdett Properties. That big screen TV, all that cherry wood, those leather sofas. How vulnerable was Berk, now that he'd spent some time on the edge of some real money? I didn't think he would've been tempted to kill for it. Not the brother I'd grown up idolizing. But I had to face the simple fact that I didn't really know.

Berk could easily have kept track of Ernie Burdett's movements that night. And Berk had access to the Beemer. And Berk had gone to Smitty's that night. I'd seen him there myself. He said he'd gone there looking for Sean for some reason. Why? Maybe he didn't go there to see Sean at all. Maybe he was making sure Gwen Dillon was there, so he could follow her home and strangle her. But what was his motive

for killing Gwen Dillon? Money could've been his motive for Ernie Burdett, since, as Chrissy's lover, he
could reasonably expect to benefit from her inheritance. But why Gwen?

And if Berk wasn't the murderer, then who was? It
seemed to me that our suspects list was down to Berk
and Sean. I realized I couldn't make nearly as good a
case for Sean being the murderer. He might've been
upset to learn that his dad and Gwen Dillon were
having an affair, but so what? Another divorce would
mean another upheaval in his life, but would that
prospect have made him angry enough to kill the dad
he loved and a girl who was only a casual acquain-
tance? No. Sean wasn't nearly as good a suspect as
my brother.

I stood in the dark on that cold porch, alone, and
tortured myself until my friends came out.

John had wrapped three pork loin roasts in foil and
stuck them in the oven that Sunday night before we
left for Garrity's. He chose pork loins as a favor to
me. I'ma loves the roast pork. By the time we returned, they were ready. The trailer was filled with
the tummy-tickling fragrance. Gruf helped himself to
a High Life, Bump grabbed a can of Coke, and me
and Danny set the table while John tossed a salad.

The phone rang as we sat down to eat.

Danny reached for it. He answered and then said,
"Boss. Phone." He held it out to me.

"Don't call me Boss." I took it from him. "Yeah?"

A voice said, "Yeah, Terry. I wanna give you a
heads-up about something."

I didn't recognize the voice. "Who is this?"

He said, "Mick." Like, You asshole, who else would
it be?

"Mick Wallace?"

"Listen. I didn't think to mention this before, but

me and Wes have been talking. We think you oughtta know this. Last night after closing, some of us were sitting around, and Sean Burdett was there. He came in after the visiting hours at the funeral home. He brought up about that he's going to the Bahamas after his dad's funeral."

"Yeah?"

"So then Wes brought up about that me and him went over to Smitty's that one night to talk to you guys about Ernie Burdett and Gwen Dillon. Wes mentioned that you guys were looking into the murders. Wes and me were laughing about it. Not about the murders, but about you guys interfering with Alan Bushnell. You know. How cool it is that you guys are doing that. How much it bugs Alan."

"Uh-huh."

"So then Sean, he starts asking questions. What are you guys doing, exactly, who are you talking to, shit like that."

"Yeah?"

"He kept asking all these questions. He wanted to know, were you guys asking any questions about *him*."

"Uh-huh."

"Yeah. So I didn't think anything about it at the time, but me and Wes were talking about it after you guys left this afternoon. Because Sean was acting pretty funny last night. You know?"

"Funny?"

"Upset, I guess you'd say. He kept asking questions about you, in particular. Because Wes mentioned that you're the one that really twists Alan's shorts. Sean wanted to know, What's your deal. Where you live. What you drive."

"What I *drive*?"

"What you drive."

I said, "That's odd."

He said, "Yeah. That was the question that really

bugged Wes. He was all, why would Sean ask what the dude drives? That hit both of us funny. And we were thinking, if Allison gets on the phone and tells him about us questioning her today, that could make Sean's bad attitude worse. So we thought about it and decided I should call you. Let you know."

"Yeah. Thanks. I appreciate it."

"Yeah. You ever need anything, have a problem with anybody, you call me. Yeah?"

"Yeah. Thanks."

I handed the receiver to Danny and he hung it up.
• Bump said, "What was that all about?"

I told them. When I finished, Danny said, "Well, well, well."

We all watched him, waiting for him to share his thoughts, but he just sat there pulling the tender pork apart with his fork, plowing it around in his gravy, and shoveling it into his mouth. We gradually realized he didn't have any further thoughts to add at the moment.

Gruf said, "Does anyone think Sean's our murderer?"

I said, "What? He's the murderer, and now he thinks I'm on his tail, and he's getting ready to tamper with my truck?" Which I was treating it like a big joke.

But Gruf said, "Dude. I think we have to take him seriously. If he's the murderer, and he thinks you're onto him, he could be getting ready to give you some payback before he leaves the country."

I said, "Why? Because I asked a few questions about him? Because Berk's my brother, and not his? I don't think those things give him a motive for trying to fuckin' murder me, but if they are, well, let him bring it, then. What the fuck." Because I still thought the whole idea was too out there to be taken seriously.

John frowned. "I don't see Sean trying to kill *any-*

body. He had no motive whatsoever for killing Gwen Dillon. And anyway, the kid had everything he wanted. Why would he have wanted to kill his dad?"

Bump said, "According to Bud Hanratty, Ernie's will gave him more than a million reasons to kill his dad."

Chapter 22

We got six inches of new snow overnight. The weather forecast was that temperatures would be up near forty by noon Monday, and that would easily take care of the new snowfall, so there really wasn't a pressing need to go out into the icy darkness and shovel the driveway early Monday morning, but I did it anyway. I shoveled Mrs. Carmody's driveway, too. I was just crossing back over to my own side of the dark street when I heard a shout.

"Hey!"

Once I heard the voice, I realized that was the second Hey I'd heard. I stopped, turned around, and looked up and down the street. John came jogging around the corner up at the top of the quiet street. He ran through the yellow glow of the corner streetlight and pounded through the darkness toward me, rhythmically puffing big white clouds of exhaust out around his head. But nothing else was moving anywhere that I could see that early in the morning. I shook my head.

"Up here, moron. In the window."

My eyes went across the street to Mrs. Carmody's trailer, and there she was, her pinched, warty head sticking out her front window, her hand waving impatiently.

Now what? I waved back at her and said, "Morning, Mrs. Carmody."

She said, "There was a car parked in front of my driveway last night after all your lights were off."

"There was?"

"Little shit sat there a while and then he got out and snuck over to your driveway."

"Huh?"

"Whadda ya mean, huh? You deef? He even turned off his overhead light so it wouldn't light up when he opened his car door. I let him get as far as your truck, and then I ran him off."

"My *truck*?"

"Was sneakin' up toward the driver side door, runnin' his hand along the top of the bed. I yelled, *'Hey, you. I already called the cops, you little shit. You git now.'* " She cackled. "You shoulda seen him jump. He ran back to his car and lit outa here!" Her cackling laughter ended in a coughing fit.

I waited till the fit passed. "You didn't see what he looked like, by any chance."

"Five-eight, five-nine. Brown hair, medium length. Younger than you. I'd say late teens, early twenties. You know him?"

I nodded. It sounded like Sean Burdett to me. Exactly like Sean Burdett. By this time, John had reached our driveway. He puffed, jogging in place. He was wearing several layers of gray sweats and had a white bath towel draped around his shoulders. Steam was rising from his buzzcut and hovering above it in the cold, still air. It looked like he had a leaf fire in his hair.

I said, "I think so. You didn't notice what kind of car it was, didya?"

"Burgundy Bronco. I couldn't get the license plate number."

I nodded. I remembered seeing that burgundy Bronco sitting in the garage over at Burdett's house. "Yeah, I know who it was. And he wasn't here to do me any favors, that's for sure."

Wow. I guess it's true what they say, huh? What comes around and all that bullpucky? Mrs. Carmody was turning out to be better than a watchdog. How many watchdogs can give you a fuckin' description of your prowler?

I said, "Are you sure he didn't have time to do anything to my truck? You ran him off as soon as he got close to it?"

"Course I did."

I said, "Well, thanks. I owe you one."

But she was already slamming her window and pulling her curtains. I thought I heard her mutter, "Beatnik."

What? *Beatnik?*

John said, "What was that all about?"

"Did she just call me a *beatnik?*"

"I didn't hear. What's going on?"

"Come on. I'll tell you over coffee."

At Brewster's, when everyone had left except me, Gruf, Danny, and Bump, I repeated what Mrs. Carmody had told me.

Bump said, "He *did* move on you. Or try to. That's fuckin' weird."

Gruf said, "I've been thinking about this, and I think we need to talk to Berk again. Make him give us some answers. And we gotta do it this morning, before the funeral."

Danny nodded. "That's exactly what I was thinking. He's probably still at Ladonia Hills today, repainting Gwen Dillon's apartment. Let's go talk to him."

I didn't like the idea. I didn't want to hear any answers Berk might have for us, and also, we were already losing half a day's work for the funeral. I didn't want to cut into what was left to go harass Berk. But I was outvoted.

We made a little convoy of vehicles out to the lawyers' house, then we parked and jumped into Gruf's Jeep for the ride around the corner into the Ladonia Hills parking lot. It was easy to figure out which building Berk and his painters were working in. Berk's blue Burdett Properties pickup truck was parked right in front of it. After that, all we had to do was follow the smell of paint.

Berk was working with two other guys. They had a radio set up in a corner of the vacant living room. *Pickin' Up the Pieces* by Average White Band was playing. All three of them looked around when we walked through the open door. Berk climbed down off the low scaffolding, ushered us out into the hall, and closed the apartment door. He jerked his thumb at the closed door and said, "They don't need to hear us talk."

I said, "Berk, we need—"

He held up his hand. "Hang on, T-Bird. I've been doing some thinking, and there are some things I want to tell you guys."

Bump said, "Finally."

Berk nodded. "This has been tough. Different loyalties, and all that bullshit. But I've had second thoughts about this. The number one priority is, I want Ernie's killer to pay. No matter who it is."

Gruf said, "That's what we all want."

Berk sighed. "Let's go outside. I need a smoke."

Out on the sidewalk, Berk pulled his cigarettes from a deep pocket in his white painter's coveralls, lit up, and let go with a big smoky exhale. "First of all, I've been having an affair with Chrissy Burdett."

I saw red. I already knew he was, but to hear him say it, so easily, so casually. I said, "You fuckin' bastard. 'Oh, I thought the world of Ernie. Oh, he was my best friend.' And you were fucking his *wife*?"

He shook his head at me. "I *did* think the world of Ernie. He *was* my best friend. I wasn't being disloyal to Ernie. I never would've touched Chrissy if Ernie still loved her. But he was about to divorce her. He had a hot thing going with Beverly Lash."

I noted that Berk knew the identity of Ernie's lover, when even Bud Hanratty didn't know that.

I braced myself to get right to the heart of the matter. I said, "Berk. A week or so before the murders, did Sean Burdett tell you a rumor he heard from Allison—"

Berk was shaking his head. "I don't know anything about any rumors, and don't interrupt me. There's a few more things I have to tell you. *God.* I hope I'm doing the right thing here. But the bottom line is, my loyalty is still to Ernie. I'm gonna get this off my chest, and you can tell Bud Hanratty or fuckin' Alan Bushnell, or whoever's got you guys out here asking me these questions, or don't tell them, I don't care. I'll have a clean conscience."

He dropped his smoke on the sidewalk and smashed it with his hightop.

"A few days before the murders, Sean was really hot under the collar about something. I asked him what was wrong. He said he was mad at Gwen Dillon about something, but no matter how hard I tried to get him to open up, he wouldn't say any more about it. That was really unusual for him. He usually talks nonstop when something's bothering him. The day of the murders he came out to the building again, and he was still pissed off at Gwen, and he seemed to be mad at Ernie for some reason, too."

Bump said, "Did he say—"

Berk didn't let him interrupt his train of thought. "We were down in the garage. I was cleaning my tools and sorting out my tool bucket because I had to go down to Bagby to do some— Well, anyway, Ernie came down for something and Sean hid behind one of the cars until Ernie went away. He didn't want to talk to his dad or even see him."

I said, "Was that unusual?"

"That was fuckin' weird, is what that was. Sean and

Ernie were very close. I couldn't understand what'd happened, and Sean wouldn't talk about it. He left pretty soon after that. Later on, I couldn't get it out of my mind, how angry he was. I remembered that Wednesday was Sean's pool night, and that Gwen Dillon was on his team."

We all nodded.

"I started to worry, with Sean as mad as he'd been. He goes flat stupid when he's mad about something, and now he'd be seeing Gwen at pool. I was afraid he'd get himself in some kind of trouble. I remembered Lo-Lites was shooting at Smitty's that night, so I took a drive over there, thinking maybe I could stop him from doing something he'd regret. But I saw Wes Fletcher over there, and he said Sean had called off sick, so I thought, that takes care of that."

He lit another smoke. "Here's where it gets tough. *God.* I saw Sean in the office building later that night."

Bump frowned. "The night of the murders? You couldn't have seen him at the office building. He was home sick in bed."

Berk shook his head. "No he wasn't. He was in the office building. I was laying in bed, in that la-la land right before you fall asleep? And I heard the mandoor close down in the garage. That door makes a sound when it closes. The metal of the lock plate scrapes across the metal of the door frame and makes a high-pitched squeal that I can clearly hear all the way up in my bedroom, because my bedroom is right above it. I got up and looked out my window, and there was Sean going around the corner. He had parked his SUV around the corner there, close to the blind wall of the building. I was surprised. He never parks there. But I saw the reflection of his red brake lights in the snow and I heard him start the engine."

Bump said, "Holy shit."

Berk said, "Yeah. The first time you guys came out to talk to me, when you guys told me Ernie was murdered, and that it had been done by somebody tampering with his Beemer, that was the first thing I thought of. Sean was here that night."

I said, "That was why you cut off so fast."

Bump said, "You told us you had to go meet some painters."

Berk nodded. "And Ernie'd left the Beemer up on the lift."

Danny said, "Up on the lift?"

Berk nodded. "He was down there tinkering with it right up until the guy came for that meeting. A little while after Sean left, I heard Ernie lower the lift, open the garage door, start up the Beemer, back it out, and close the door. The thing is, ever since you guys told me Ernie was murdered, I've been worried sick that Sean did it. But I haven't said anything, and I don't even know if I'm doing the right thing telling you about this now, because it doesn't make any sense to me. Why would Sean have done such a thing? Lemme ask you guys this: are you absolutely sure the same person did both murders?"

We looked at each other. I said, "Not absolutely sure, no, but it looks that way."

Berk said, "Because it just doesn't make any sense to me that Sean could've done it. He worshiped the ground his dad walked on, and he was madly in love with Gwen Dillon."

I think all of us said it at once: *"What?"*

Berk said, "About Gwen, you mean? You didn't know Sean was in love with Gwen? Well, no, I guess you wouldn't. He wouldn't have told anybody but me. But, yeah. He was crazy about her. Sick in love. Poor kid. So, that's what I'm saying. Even if he was mad at her about something, how could he ever have killed her?"

We all stood there, struck dumb, scuffing our shoes in the slush. Gruf said quietly, "Have you talked to Sean about all this? Asked him about it?"

Berk said, "Fuck, no. And I ain't gonna, either. You guys might get off on all this shit. I don't."

We didn't let on until we were back in Gruf's Jeep, but we were stunned by what Berk had told us. When we got back around the corner and parked in the driveway at the lawyers' house, Bump came inside with us. We made coffee and huddled around the table in the old kitchen.

I said, "Sean must've gone nuts when Allison told him what she'd heard from Gwen. Spoiled, selfish kid like that."

Gruf said, "*Sociopathic* kid like that."

I said, "Whatever. He must've gone ballistic. His own father. He must've been outraged. There's his motive for both of them."

Bump shook his head. "I hate to say this, but it's time for a reality check. No one else but Berk puts Sean in the office building that night. No one else but Berk has said Sean was in love with Gwen. No one else but Berk has said Sean was mad at Gwen and Ernie in the days leading up to the murders. We only have Berk's word for all this, and he could be lying. He could be trying to frame Sean for murders he did himself. Think about this: Berk could've killed Ernie, figuring he'd marry Chrissy for her inheritance. If he can also frame Sean for it, he and Chrissy'll get Sean's share, too."

Chapter 23

Ernie Burdett's funeral was held at St. John's in Spencer. It's a big church, and it needed to be for Ernie's funeral, because the place was packed. We got there ten minutes early and it was already SRO. Bud and Bump hustled around trying to get the older people seats and keep things organized. They were pallbearers along with Sean Burdett, my brother Berk, two of Ernie's brothers, and two of Chrissy's brothers-in-law.

The priest did some talking and then a few people stood up to say a few words. Bud choked me up when he spoke. Bud has a way of doing that. Then it was over and everybody was filing out and going to their cars. At the intersection of routes 89 and 114, we passed John, who was in the middle of the intersection doing traffic duty while the procession crawled through.

I wouldn't even wanna guess how long the procession was out to Grand County Memorial Gardens. I know we had to hike forever to get from our car to the graveside. There were a few more words there which the cold wind blew away unheard, at least by me. Then Chrissy and Sean each gave the coffin a last good-bye and it was over.

We got in line to say something to Chrissy, but the wind was so fierce that Bud, Bump, and Berk hustled her away to the waiting limo before we ever got anywhere near. We struggled back to Gruf's Jeep.

Which there was no relief from the biting cold there,

either, because Gruf's heater doesn't work and really, the thing doesn't even have any windows to speak of. By the time we got back to Smitty's we were dudesicles.

Alan Bushnell came in right behind us. He stepped inside looking cold, tired, and haggard. He waved at us to walk on in with him. In the dining room, he walked straight back to the waitress station for a pot of coffee and a cup. Reginald Elliot gave him an annoyed look as he struggled out of his heavy cop leather. The Elliots don't like it when somebody gets their own coffee. Even when it's Alan.

Alan waited until the rest of us were settled. He sat there with his glasses off, rubbing his tired eyes.

Hammer appeared in the doorway to the kitchen. "Gruf. Can I see you a minute?"

Gruf turned around. "Whassup?"

"I wanna show you some menu plans. I wanna start doing a special every—"

Alan said, "Gruf's busy right now. He'll be with you directly." Hammer frowned and disappeared from view.

Alan put his glasses back on. "Where's Bump?"

Gruf said, "Still with the funeral party. He'll probably be a while."

Alan said, "Dammit. Well, I can't wait for him. We found a pea jacket with blood on the sleeves. It was stashed in a storeroom at Burdett Properties. When the tests come back, they should tell us a lot. Also, we found the junkyard where the tie rod end and housing were purchased. A part-timer there did the transaction. He was off the day we stopped out there and nobody mentioned it to him until this morning. Anyway, he knows Sean Burdett and he's certain Sean's the one who bought the parts."

The relief I felt was almost overwhelming. I said, "Holy shit."

Alan said, "Yeah. And I guess I can tell you now.

But keep it to yourselves. We found traces of the ketamine."

Danny said, "Where?"

"In the bottom of the sugar bowl in the lunchroom at Burdett Properties. The way I figure it, the murderer knew Ernie would take a thermos of coffee. Maybe his thermos was already sitting on the counter. I checked with Chrissy. Ernie liked a lot of sugar in his coffee. The murderer probably emptied the bowl down to about how much he thought Ernie'd use and stirred in the ketamine powder. Ernie used what was there. The next person to want sugar refilled the bowl, pouring the new sugar in right on top of the ketamine residue and sugar that was left in the bottom."

Gruf said, "That makes sense."

Alan said, "Yeah. But me and Wally Flynn have been banging our heads against a brick wall all damn day. He says we still don't have enough to get an arrest warrant from Urquhart. Especially since he's still sore about the Sutton case."

I'll translate. Wally Flynn is Grand County Prosecutor. Judge Urquhart doesn't like it when Alan brings him arrest warrants for three different people, one after another, all for the same murder, which is what happened in the Sutton case. And unfortunately, Judge Urquhart has a really good memory.

Gruf said, "An arrest warrant for Sean Burdett?"

Alan said, "Of course for Sean. Who else would it be for? I'm tearing my hair out here, so I gotta ask you. Have you guys turned up anything, anything at all, that could help me?"

We looked at each other. Gruf gave me a subtle shake of the head, turned to Alan, and said, "No. Sorry."

Alan said, "*Fuck*. All right. You get anything, any little thing, you get hold of me right away. Pass the word along to Bump when he gets here. And keep all this to yourselves." He hauled himself out of his chair and we watched him disappear down the back hall.

I said, "Well, it's as good as over for Sean now."

"But, dude. Why'd you shake me off? We shoulda told him everything we have."

He frowned. "What do we have?"

I shrugged. "That Sean was sneaking around my truck, and that—"

"What does that prove? Nothing, by itself. And everything else is a big jumble. We need to at least wait till Bump gets back. Talk things out. See if we can come up with a way to fill in some of these blanks. And if we can't . . ." He shrugged. "Well, then I guess we give it all to Alan and let him try and untangle it."

I lit a cigarette and inhaled deeply. Relief at hearing it was Sean who bought the worn Beemer parts continued to spread through my system like some kind of warm, golden liquid. We sat quietly for a few minutes, drinking coffee and thinking things over. Then Danny said, "Berk was telling the truth when he said he and Ernie were close. Berk knew Ernie's lover was Beverly Lash. Even Bud didn't know it was her."

Gruf said, "Yeah. And the one time Ernie *didn't* confide in Berk, it ended up costing him his life."

Danny said, "How do you figure that?"

"If Ernie had told Berk he wanted to start that Gwen rumor, Berk woulda warned him off. He'd have said, 'Don't use Gwen. Your son's in love with her.' "

Danny said, "I don't think Berk ever *did* hear that rumor. If he did, he woulda understood right away why Sean was suddenly so mad at his dad and at Gwen. He woulda known right away that Sean had heard the rumor."

I said, "Yeah. And if he'd known about the rumor, as soon as he heard about Gwen's murder, he'd have known Sean did it."

Danny said, "If he didn't know it then, he'd have

known for sure when we told him Ernie's death wasn't an accident."

Gruf played with his spoon, clinking it around in his cup. "I hate to say this, but Bump's not here to play devil's advocate. I don't think all the questions are answered. Not by a long shot."

Danny said, "Explain?"

Gruf said, "That pea jacket with the blood on it could be Berk's. And just because Sean bought that worn part for the Beemer, that doesn't mean he's the one who installed it. Berk could've done it."

I groaned. "Oh, come on. You don't still think . . ."

Danny said, "What about Sean sneaking around Terry's truck last night?"

I said, "Yeah. What about that?"

Gruf shrugged. "Suspicious, yeah. But it doesn't prove anything. Maybe we shoulda told Alan about our talk with your brother."

I said, "Too late now. *Shit.* Tomorrow Sean and Chrissy and her tribe of amazons will be gone."

We sat quietly thinking about that little detail. Then Gruf said, "I better go see what Hammer wants." He walked into the kitchen. Danny waved his coffee cup at Reginald and we got refills. We sat there lost in thought. It was down to Sean and Berk. One or the other of them had done the murders. But how could we prove which one was guilty? I chewed on the problem.

We had some levers. The innocent one knew Ernie's car had been rigged, but he didn't know how. Alan had forbidden us talking about the tie rod end and housing. The innocent one didn't know Ernie had been drugged, and neither one of them knew that the *cops* knew Ernie had been drugged. And I realized that if the murderer was Sean, we had a big ol' ace in the hole. He still didn't know that the rumor which had set him off in the first place was false. He still believed that his father and the girl he loved had been getting it on.

A vague idea began to take shape in my mind. If we could just get Sean and Berk together, maybe get them drinking, maybe start tripping on them until the guilty one lost his cool and made a mistake . . . I went back to the office and called Mick Wallace. Me and Mick talked for a while. Then I went out to the bar, got myself a fresh iced tea, and sat down to wait for Bump.

Chapter 24

At Lo-Lites that night, Danny, John, and I got there first. We sat at a table in the middle of the big room and ordered drinks. There weren't many customers there yet. It was Monday night and it was only a little past seven. A few biker types hovered over their beers at the far end of the bar, and there were a couple of hard-looking girls sitting at a nearby table, but that was it. Somebody kept dropping quarters in the jukebox, playing "Takin' It to the Streets" by the Doobie Brothers, over and over again. Worry had me twisted up like a pretzel. All those lyrics about I'm your brother made it worse.

After we'd been there a few minutes, Berk arrived. He looked puzzled as he sat down next to me. I introduced John as Danny's and my roommate, but I didn't mention that he was a cop. I noticed that Berk ordered a Coke instead of a shot and a beer like he'd favored in the old days, and I wondered if he was on the wagon. I also saw him react when I asked for a fresh iced tea. His eyes moved from my eyes to my glass and back, and we smiled at each other.

After a while Gruf and Bump came in and pulled up chairs at our table, and, finally, Mick, Wes, and Sean arrived. Sean smiled when he saw Berk. He started toward our table, but Mick steered him to a table at the back of the big room and into the corner chair.

Wes walked over behind the bar and returned carrying three bottles of MGD. Sean reached to pull his wallet from the hip pocket of his jeans, but Mick waved him off. I heard Mick say, "You're drinking on the house tonight, kid." Sean grinned at him like a little kid.

Wes settled onto a chair opposite Mick. The way they were sitting, they had Sean trapped in the corner.

We passed the time at our table by telling Berk about the job at the lawyers' house. It looked like Mick and Wes weren't having any trouble keeping the small talk going with Sean. Sean looked happy. I guessed it was probably because he wasn't used to having somebody pay for his beer. He probably wasn't used to having Mick's undivided attention like that, either.

I glanced at them from time to time to see how things were going. It wasn't long before I saw Mick wave at someone behind the bar. Goldie brought out three fresh MGDs and carried away the empties. Berk kept looking back toward that corner table with a puzzled look on his face.

Time passed. While Wes waved for the third round of beers, Mick gave me a nod.

I said, "Hey, you know what? Let's go sit with those guys, huh? Make it a little going away party for Sean."

Wes was already dragging two other tables over, one to each side of the corner table, as we all drifted back. Bump maneuvered Berk so that he ended up on the chair next to Sean. By the time we were all seated, Sean was in the corner on one side of the table, and Berk was in the corner on the other. They were both completely blocked in.

You could see that Sean was beginning to feel a little trapped, hemmed into the corner like he was. His eyes darted around between our unsmiling faces.

Berk seemed more interested in Sean's discomfort

than in the fact that he was also blocked in. He nudged Sean's arm. "You okay, kid?"

Sean said, "What's the matter with these guys? Everybody looks so mad. What's going on?"

Berk said, "They're not mad. You guys aren't mad, are you? No, they're not mad. Relax."

I hadn't told Berk anything on the phone, except that I wanted him to come to the Lo-Lites that night and that it was really important. I could tell by the way he looked around that he knew something was up. He was trying to figure it out. All eyes were beginning to focus on Sean and Berk. Wes and I lit cigarettes. Nobody said anything.

Goldie came over carrying the three MGDs. I asked for a fresh iced tea and it turned out the rest of my guys were ready for more, too. She brought out another tray of drinks and passed them around.

Berk gave me a stare and then turned to look at Sean, and I knew he was beginning to guess what was going on. He frowned, reached over to give Sean's shoulder a squeeze, and said tightly, "You poor kid."

I relaxed a little, thinking if Berk was our murderer, he'd be more worried about himself than about Sean.

I said, "Well, I guess you two are glad to have the funeral over with, huh?"

Sean nodded energetically and a brief smile flitted across his face.

Berk frowned at me. "That's an odd way of looking at it, T-Bird."

Bump blew off his straw wrapper and dropped his straw into his fresh Coke. "Ernie's funeral reminds me of a story about a guy I knew."

Danny said, "Yeah? What story's that?"

"The guy's name was Rod. He had to go out and buy a suit and tie for a funeral. He ended up with an unbelievably ugly tie. When his friends saw it, they laughed their asses off. He goes, 'What's so funny?' They were all, 'It's about your tie, Rod.'"

When we'd talked things over earlier at Smitty's, we hadn't really gotten into details about how we were going to do this. We figured we'd get Sean and Berk together at Lo-Lites and start tripping on them until we had them good and stirred up. If there's one thing guys like us know how to do, it's how to pimp somebody. We figured we'd lay it on thick and see if we could get the guilty one to expose himself some way, but we didn't get into specifics. So Bump's opening took me by surprise. I laughed and nodded my approval at him.

Berk thought Bump really was talking about neckties. He nodded. "I know. You wonder why they even *make* some of these—"

But the rest of us knew it had nothing to do with neckties. Sean knew it, too. Everybody but Sean and Berk burst out laughing. Berk broke off his sentence, looking puzzled. I was so happy to see that puzzled look on his face that I didn't know what to do with myself.

Sean looked scared. That made me happy, too.

Several of the guys were repeating the line and laughing. "It's about your tie, Rod."

I interrupted. "Sean was creeping around my truck last night. What were you gonna do to my truck, dude?"

Sean jerked like he'd touched a live wire. Then he tried to cover it up with an angry outburst. "That's a lie. I wasn't anywhere near your truck." He turned to Berk. "He's lying."

Berk said, "Why would he lie about that?"

Bump said, "Sean. You poor kid."

I was laughing. "You're busted, Sean. My neighbor saw you. That lady that yelled at you? She gave me a description of you and everything. What were you gonna do?"

Gruf said, "Maybe you were gonna do a little something to the tie, Rod?"

We all laughed again.

Berk was beginning to understand what was going on. He said, "Wait a minute. Tie rod? Are you guys saying that's how Ernie's car was—"

Sean panicked and tried to stand up. Mick pushed him back down, told him to finish his beer, and waved for another round. Sean chugged.

Berk stared at Sean like he'd never seen him before.

Danny said, "Sean, you poor kid."

Sean said, "Stop saying that."

Bump said, "Yeah. How can he be a poor kid when he's going to the Bahamas tomorrow?"

Gruf said, "He's going away, but not to the Bahamas."

Sean said, "Yes, I am. The Bahamas.

The stools along the bar were beginning to fill up. I scanned along the row. "Where's Allison tonight?"

Mick said, "I gave her the night off."

Danny said, "She's a cute little thing, but she sure is mouthy. Right, Sean?"

Sean said, "Huh?"

Gruf said, "Allison talks too much. You know that, don't you, Sean? You know what a little gossip Allison is. Don't you?"

Sean shook his head, confused. He looked at Berk like he thought Berk could explain what was going on. Berk stared at me. Then he turned back to Sean. "Is there something you need to tell us, Sean?"

Sean gave him a blank look.

Bump said, "We already know, anyway."

I said, "I've got a story. I know this kid named Sean. He's all about good nutrition. Like, every morning he breaks out his Special K."

Sean's head jerked.

Berk said, "Special K? What's that about?"

I shrugged. "Ask Sean."

Berk looked at Sean. Berk said, "You told me you bought some Special K, Sean. Two, three weeks ago.

I told you to flush it. I told you it was fuckin' dangerous. Did you flush it?"

Sean said, "You're lying. He's lying. He's the one who bought some Special K."

Berk shook his head sadly.

Gruf spoke up. "I know a story. This guy I know told me. It's about a junkyard."

Sean jerked like he'd been tagged on the chin.

Bump said, "I know a guy that works in a junkyard."

Gruf acted surprised. "A junkyard? You do?"

Bump said, "Sure I do."

I said, "So do I. What's your story, Gruf?"

Gruf said, "It's about a kid who buys a worn-out part for a Beemer."

We all watched Sean as we talked. He was flat-out scared.

Berk frowned at Sean. "Why would a kid buy a worn-out part for a Beemer?"

Gruf said, "That's what this guy wanted to know."

Bump said, "Sean. Do you believe in ghosts?"

Sean stared at him.

Bump said, "Ghosts. The undead. People who die with unfinished business they can't leave behind."

Sean said, "Huh?"

I said, "I know a story. It's about a kid named Sean."

Berk said kindly, "Sean. There's something you need to tell us, and you need to do it right now."

Sean was agitated. He tried to stand. There was a brief scuffle as Mick put him back into his chair.

Sean said, "You guys are all nuts. I don't know what you're talking about."

I said, "You're right. You don't. Not all of it, anyway. Lemme tell you my story. It's about this kid named Sean. He hears a rumor his daddy is fucking the girl he loves."

Berk said, *"What?"*

Gruf said, "Wait. I think I heard this story. Some girl tells him a rumor and he believes it."

Berk said, "What? Are you guys talking about Ernie and Gwen Dillon?"

Sean said, "Berk, no. Shut up."

Bump said, "I heard this, too. Instead of asking around to find out whether the rumor's true or not, the kid just goes ahead and freaks out."

Berk said, "What do you mean, freaks out? What are you talking about?"

Bump shrugged. "Freaks out. Murders them both. *Pfft.* Early Eight. Both in the same night, just like that."

Berk looked horrified. The rest of us shook our heads and laughed. Sean said, "It wasn't a rumor. It was true." He turned to Berk. "It was true."

Berk said, "Oh my God. I can't believe it."

I said, "Wait a minute. I didn't even get to the best part yet."

Sean said, "Don't. Shut up."

Berk said, "You poor kid. Are you gonna tell us, or not?"

Sean said, "I don't know what you're talking about."

I said, "Sure you do. Now here's the end of the story. The kid believes the rumor, but he's a fuckin' idiot. The rumor's not true."

Sean said, "Yes it was."

I said, "No. It wasn't. The rumor was a lie. The dad wasn't fucking the girl. But the kid killed them both anyway. He drugged his daddy and tampered with his daddy's car, and while his daddy was dying in a car wreck, he strangled the girl."

Bump said, "Who would be crazy enough to do something like that. Huh, Sean?"

Sean was completely panicked now. "I didn't do it. I was home sick. Even ask Chrissy. Ask Cheryl."

Anger crept into Berk's voice now. He said, "No, you weren't. You were in the building that night. You were in the garage. I saw you."

"That's a lie." Sean's voice went higher and louder by several notches. "Berk's lying. *He* did it. He snuck in the kitchen and *he* stirred the Special K into the sugar."

John said quietly, "What did you say, Sean?"

Sean was too wired to stop himself. "He went in the kitchen and saw the coffee thermos sitting there, and he *knew* all he had to do was dump the Special K in the sugar bowl . . ."

John pulled the tape recorder from his jacket and set it on the table, still running. Then he pulled out his radio and said, "Alan. Come on out. We've got him."

I was surprised. I didn't know John had arranged for Alan to be waiting there.

Sean was yelling, "What? You don't have me. Berk did it."

John Mirandized Sean as Alan and Brian Bell walked toward us from where they'd been waiting in Mick's office.

John said, "It was you, Sean. Nobody mentioned anything about the coffee or the thermos or the sugar bowl. The only way you could have known about it was if you're the murderer."

Alan placed Sean under arrest and confirmed John had read him his rights.

Sean couldn't control his anger. He went right on talking and the machine went right on taping. "She should've known how I felt. I bought her that perfume for Christmas. It was so obvious. Any idiot would've seen that perfume and known. But no. She had to go screwing around with my dad. And *he* should've known. Gwen was mine. Not his. He should've known. He was my father, wasn't he?"

Bump said, "Hellooo. She *wasn't* screwing around with your dad. It was all a lie."

Danny said, "That was a pretty good idea hiding your pea jacket in the storeroom."

Sean was beyond thinking rationally. He took Danny's remark as a compliment and smiled. "I know. It was, wasn't it? It had blood on it, so I couldn't take it home. I took Berk's home, instead. That way, if somebody found mine in the storeroom, they'd think it was his."

He giggled. He continued to giggle as Alan pulled him out of his corner seat, turned him around, cuffed him, and steered him toward the back door and the cruiser waiting outside. Brian Bell and John followed them out.

The rest of us sat there and watched them go. Then Mick turned to Bump. "Wow," he breathed. "That was something."

The DNA tests confirmed that the pea jacket found in the storeroom was Sean's. Gwen's blood and tissue were found on both sleeves. A little packet of waxed paper was found in the bottom of a can of tennis balls in Sean's bedroom closet. The powder residue proved to be ketamine, and tests showed it came from the same batch they'd found in the bottom of the sugar bowl and in Ernie's coffee thermos. All that, added to the tape John had recorded in Lo-Lites, made the case against Sean airtight.

Because Sean had murdered his father, Chrissy got his share of the inheritance in addition to her own. It amounted to nearly three million dollars. Her mother and sisters went through with their planned trip to the Bahamas, and Chrissy picked up the tab, but Chrissy stayed behind to give moral support to Sean. She was the loyal little stepmother right to the bitter end.

Another reason she skipped the Bahamas trip was that she wanted to be with Berk. She wanted Berk to take over running Burdett Properties, since he knew the business inside out, and she also wanted Berk to marry her. He jumped at the chance to run the business, but he had a little trouble making up his mind about marrying Chrissy. I thought that sooner or later he probably would. I wondered how money and power would change my brother. I hoped it wouldn't change him too much.

Once Sean had been cuffed and guided out of the bar that night, we sat around talking quietly. Berk was bummed. He seemed almost crushed by sadness.

I was surprised how many different emotions were all tumbling around inside me. I was very relieved that Berk was in the clear, but I didn't feel good about nailing Sean the way we did. I didn't see how I could possibly feel sorry for a spoiled, selfish little rich kid who had done a double murder, but there it was. Everybody else seemed pretty subdued, too. Maybe Berk's sadness was working on all of us.

At one point, Bump looked across the table at Berk and said, "I got a little hard-ass with you a couple of times. I hope there's no hard feelings?"

Berk took a second to think it over. Then he said, "You're a friend of the T-Bird's. That makes you a friend of mine." He stuck out a hand and they shook.

We told Berk about all the different things we'd done, investigating the case. Mick and Wes joined in where they could. Berk listened, but we didn't take much joy in explaining things to him, and he didn't take any joy at all in hearing it.

After a while he collected his cigarettes and lighter and pushed away from the table. "Fuck. Well, I better go break the news to Chrissy. She really cares about that kid. It'll be better if she hears it from me."

We sat in silence and watched him walk out. It was a few minutes before the talk started again, and even when it did, it was halfhearted. I wondered why we were all so bummed. It hadn't been like this the other times we'd interfered in one of Alan's cases. I wondered what the difference was. The only thing I could think was that the other two times, the murderers had been more hateful. They'd known exactly what they were doing. It didn't seem like Sean did, really. Even when Alan was taking him out to the cruiser, it didn't seem like he understood what was happening. Maybe that made him seem sort of pitiful. Whatever.

About the time we started to realize we were repeating ourselves, we split up and went our separate ways. Back at the trailer, Danny, John, and me watched a little bit of Letterman, and then we turned in. I tossed and turned for a long time before I finally fell asleep.

Sometime that night, I dreamed my baby was sitting on my bed beside me. Her hand was in mine and she was whispering that she loved me. I woke up to see that I wasn't holding her hand. I was gripping a twist of blanket and sheet. The whispering was the hiss of sleet which was being driven against my window by the high, cold wind.

Mike wasn't sitting beside me. She was somewhere in Africa. And I was in Spencer, Ohio. All alone.

I was sitting in Brewster's one Friday morning in the middle of November, happily mauling my number four breakfast like a healthy growing boy. I was enjoying my friends' goofy small talk and watching the weather out Brewster's big front windows. Lightning ripped through black, boiling storm clouds, and sheets of cold, wicked rain slapped at the vehicles in the big parking lot.

Ah, late autumn in northeastern Ohio. Nothing else like it.

My name's Terry Saltz. I'm a carpenter. Breakfast at Brewster's every weekday morning is sort of a ritual for me and a few friends. Eat. Shoot the shit. Get our natural juices flowing by ragging on each other before we head out in different directions to earn our daily pack of Marlboros. As I sipped my coffee and glanced around that particular morning, I was lazily speculating whether or not to go ahead with a fairly radical plan.

I was thinking about maybe getting a haircut.

My hair's long. I've worn it long since I was thirteen. At first, it got long because my old man wasn't around to spot me the cost of a haircut, and I wasn't willing to hand my hard-earned paper-route money over to a barber. In those days, I was using that paper-route money for food half the time.

My hair grew down over my collar. Teachers started

getting on me about it, and I discovered that I liked being a bad boy. When it got longer, the girl I'd been watching for a while suddenly got interested in me. Sometimes after school we'd go stand behind the middle school building and she'd reached up and run her hands through my long black hair and say how silky it was, how good it smelled.

After that, I was enthusiastic about three things: my girlfriend, my long hair, and what kind of shampoo and conditioner smelled best. No shit. I spent the better part of a year sniffing bottles all up and down the shampoo aisle in the drug store.

When I was fifteen, my older brother P. J. got me and my best friend Danny Gillespie jobs as gofers for Red Perkins Construction. P. J. and most of the other carpenters who worked for Red wore their long scraggly hair in ponytails, so me and Danny split a pair of leather shoelaces and tied ours back like theirs. That's how we've had it ever since.

Only recently I'd been thinking about getting it cut. All that long black hair is a lot of trouble. That November morning, while I chewed my Texas toast and watched the rain, I was thinking how much easier it would be if I just got it all chopped off.

The absolute last thing on my mind was my wife Marylou, also known as the Bitch. Which, by that time, she was supposed to be my ex-wife. Except that the divorce she'd so cold-bloodedly initiated six months earlier while I was sitting brokenhearted and forlorn in jail, somehow got canceled once I was out and on my feet again, in a new town, with new friends, new money, and a new outlook on life.

The talk around the table that morning turned to names. Gruf Ridolfi mentioned that if your initials spell a word, it makes you lucky all your life. Danny Gillespie piped up right away with the information that his initials spell "dig."

I looked at him. "I? What's your middle name?"

He got a look on his face like he'd stepped in something. Which he had.

Bump Bellini grinned at him. "I can't even think of a name that starts with I."

Danny got busy stirring sugar into his third cup of coffee. He said, "Don't even start with me. Everybody has a weird middle name."

John Garvey said, "Mine's Thomas."

Bump said, "Mine's Edward."

Gruf grinned. "Andrew."

I said, "William."

Gruf said, "William? So your initials are T.W.S.? Ouch. Sorry, Terry."

I said, "T.W.S. spells something. It spells Twees."

Bump said, "Nice try."

I said, "Hey, you know? Twees wouldn't be a bad nickname."

Bump groaned. "Here we go."

I said, "No. Really. You guys didn't like Muzzy for my nickname. So let's go with Twees."

I saw them all make eye contact. Four pairs of eyes making connections all around the table. Well, fuck 'em if they can't take a joke.

I said, "Yeah, I'm going with Twees from now on. That's what I wanna be called."

There was a heavy silence. Then Bump turned back to Danny with an evil gleam in his eye. "So where were we? Oh, yeah. What's the I stand for?"

We all watched Danny and waited. He squirmed.

John poked him. "Well?" He was grinning.

Finally, he blurted out, "Okay, it's Ignatius. Happy now?"

I'd have to say we *were* pretty happy. Everybody howled.

And just at that point, Danny glanced toward the front door.

He said, "Uh-oh."

I followed his eyes and there was the Bitch, bearing down on me like a mall surveyor. All up and down the table, my friends saw her coming and got the squirms. It looked like Danny, Gruf, Bump, and John had all suddenly gotten infested by some kind of specialized flea that only enjoyed the rich red blood of mid- to late-twentysomething males.

She walked down the side of the table and stopped behind me. An expensive cloud of Jessica McClintock perfume wrapped itself around my head. I put my fork down and turned to look at her. She smiled down on me, but you could see that behind her eyes, lots was stirring.

She said, "Hi, Terry. Can I talk to you a minute?"

I said, "Shoot."

Her eyes flicked briefly around the table. "In *private*?"

In my brain, I said, Oh shit. I looked mournfully at what was left of my breakfast, picked up my coffee cup and my cigarettes, and looked around. The only open table in the place was a booth right behind the pushed-together tables where me and my friends always sit. That was way too close for comfort, but what was I gonna do?

We slid in across from each other, and she nodded when Mary, the waitress who takes care of all of us every morning as if we're her own family, asked her if she wanted coffee. Mary glanced at me and gently patted my shoulder. I noticed the slight rise in her sweet little eyebrows as she turned away.

She brought the Bitch a cup and topped me off. She said, "Don't you want your plate over here, hon?"

I shook my head. I wasn't hungry anymore.

There were a million thoughts flying around in my brain, but the main two were: How did the Bitch know where to find me, and What did she want? I wanted to say something to her about, Where did she get off bothering me during my leisure hours, then I realized it wouldn't make any sense.

So then I thought, Okay, what I was really feeling was that she must have been spying on me to know where and when I ate breakfast. Because ever since I got out of jail and moved to Spencer, I'd been pretty careful not to let her know how to get in touch with me. I should demand to know where she got off doing that. But I didn't.

I thought about saying that I didn't want her coming around me anywhere, anytime, anymore. I didn't want to always be looking over my shoulder, thinking she might turn up here or there. But I didn't really want to say anything hurtful. That was more in *her* line, if you catch my drift.

I ended up not saying anything. I just sat there looking at her, waiting for her to start, while my friends sat at the next table with their ears sticking out. You could almost see their little pink lobes quivering, waiting to pick up every word.

Oh, jeez, look at that. Bump and Gruf were laughing. Danny, too. Now John was leaning over to Danny. Yeah, Danny had said something to make Bump and Gruf laugh and now he repeated it to John, and they were all laughing behind their hands.

One thing, I knew it wasn't anything mean directed toward me. These friends of mine, they're the loyalest bunch of humanus erectus you could ever find anywhere. I doubted it was anything mean directed toward Marylou, either.

What it was, it was just one of Danny's wry little comments on the situation in general. Danny can come up with some pretty good ones sometimes. But it wouldn't have been mean. Danny doesn't have a mean molecule in his body.

I looked at Marylou, sitting there with her big blond

seventies mall hair and her two-fisted makeup covering up all her natural good looks. I lit a cigarette and waited. She took a sip of her coffee. Then she looked up at me through her heavy black mascara, combed out into what looked like millions and millions of long, long lashes.

She smiled like she was flirting with me and said, "You could at least act like you're glad to see me."

I didn't want to say anything hurtful to her, but I wasn't gonna sit there and lie, either.

I said, "Why? I'm not."

She poured it on, turning her head a little and batting those eyelashes. "Not even a little bit?" There was actually self-confidence in her voice.

"Not even a little bit," I said coldly. "What do you want?"

Mary was over at the guys' table with the coffeepot. She stopped by Bump, bent down to whisper something, and stayed bent down to hear the answer. It looked like he was whispering into a microphone hidden in the red carnation she had pinned on her green waitress dress. I swallowed a chuckle and turned my eyes back to the Bitch, who was busy pushing her cuticles back from her pearly white nail polish.

I said, "Marylou, say what you want and leave, so I can finish my breakfast in peace."

She gave me a hurt face and puckered her lips. "You don't have to be so grumpy."

I drummed my fingers and waited.

She drew breath and said, "Okay. I want you to help me move."

I thought about hauling her out of the booth, pointing her toward the door, giving her a gentle shove, and saying, There. You're moving. Happy now?

Instead I said, "Move. To where?"

But I already knew to where. A few months earlier,

she'd been in Carlo's, the little pizza place where I worked nights as a driver, and she'd told Debby the waitress that she was going to sell our trailer down in the southern part of the county and move into a townhouse here in Spencer. I'd been horrified at the news.

She said, "Green Meadow Townhouses."

There it was. It was really gonna happen. Not only that, she wanted me to help her do it. I got pissed.

I said, "I'm not gonna help you move up here. I don't want you up here. Find yourself another sucker."

I reached to pick up my cigarettes and go back to my place at the table, but she put her hand on mine.

She said, "You have to help me."

"No. I don't. Get some of your friends to help you."

"You're my friend."

"No. I'm not."

"But I love you."

"That's your problem."

You're probably thinking, Why does this guy have to be such a hard-ass? Would it kill him to help the poor girl move?

If you're thinking that, Chief, it's because you don't understand women. Or at least, you don't understand *this* woman. Neither did I, back when she and I were together. Which it wasn't even that long ago. Just about a year. But I'd learned a lot about women since then, and I knew for a fact that she wasn't here about moving. She could get plenty of help with moving.

Why she was here, she wanted her and me to get back together. The moving was her excuse. She figured, get me to help her move, wear some Daisy Duke cutoffs, something along those lines. Then the whole time during the move, she'd keep brushing against me, keep posing and giggling, keep saying how much she missed me. Keep saying things about how nice the townhouse was and didn't I think I'd like to live there with her? Look, we could get a recliner and put it right there for me. Wouldn't that be nice?

I could see it all happening right before my eyes. And it would've worked once. But not now.

She tried to work up a tear. Her lower lip even got a slight tremble going.

She said, "You loved me once. It's not my fault if your feelings changed."

Making a conscious effort to keep my voice soft and calm, I said, "Oh, you've wrong there. It's entirely your fault that my feelings changed."

She looked away. "Anyway. We're still married. You have to help me."

This made me laugh. "We're not married anymore. Our marriage was over the day I got your divorce papers in jail."

"But—"

I interrupted, making my voice even quieter. "But there's still a piece of paper in a file cabinet somewhere that says we are married?" I shook my head. "It doesn't mean squat to me. We're not married anymore. Plain and simple."

She looked down into her coffee cup.

I said, "And as far as that piece of paper goes, I don't care anything about it. It can sit in that file drawer until hell freezes over, for all I care. If it bothers you, you go pay a lawyer to make it disappear."

She said, almost whispering, "I don't understand your attitude, Terry. You make it sound like you almost hate me."

I said, "I don't hate you. I don't feel anything for you at all, except I want you to stay out of my life. Starting now."

Now I did pick up my coffee cup and my cigarettes and move back to my place at the table with my friends. They were looking at me curiously.

I stole a glance at Mary. I studied her kind face like it was my own conscience, but couldn't tell whether she looked sympathetic or disapproving.

Well, whatever. I'd explain it to her later if she didn't understand. Because I was pretty sure I felt great. I'd stood up to the strongest of the old forces that had led me down a self-destructive path that ended in a jail cell, and I'd said no. Loud and clear.

Mary came over with the coffeepot. "More coffee, Terry?" she asked softly.

"Thanks, yeah. Top it off."

I heard a little rustling sound behind me. In peripheral vision I saw a figure moving toward the front door. I turned to watch her go. Her short little black skirt bounced side to side like windshield wipers as she walked away.

All of a sudden, everybody was moving and coughing and talking at once. I looked around, waiting to hear what they thought.

A strand of long, golden hair had escaped from Bump Bellini's ponytail. He tucked it back behind his ear and grinned at me. "Whew! I guess you told her!"

Daniel Ignatius Gillespie gave me a high five. He was laughing. "No offense, dude, but I really didn't think you had the balls."

They were all grinning and laughing. I started laughing, too. We all sat there, laughing like a bunch of idiots.

Everything would've been different if I'd helped the Bitch move that rainy November morning. Some stuff probably would've still happened, just in a different way. Some other stuff probably wouldn't have happened at all. If I were the kind of guy who sits around thinking about what might've been, I guess I could log some serious hours wondering about this. But I'm not, so I won't.

SIGNET

THE WORKING MAN'S MYSTERY SERIES
L.T. FAWKES

COLD SLICE
0-451-20835-8

Terry Saltz gets drunk and wakes up in jail the next
morning to learn he has lost his job, his wife, his truck,
and his mobile home. When he gets a job
delivering pizza, things begin to look up—until
one of the other drivers turns up dead.

LIGHTS OUT
0-451-21133-2

Someone is shot and killed in Terry Saltz's trailer park,
and his soon-to-be-ex-wife Marylou is caught holding
the gun. Terry has no love for Marylou, but he
knows she's no killer. Now Terry has to get her off
the hook and find the real killer.

**Available wherever books are sold or at
www.penguin.com**

ONYX

USA Today **bestselling author**
JEFF ABBOTT

CUT AND RUN

Whit Mosely, a Texas judge, investigates
his own past in a harrowing search for the
mother who abandoned his family years
ago. What he finds is a nightmare of
double-crosses, viscious schemers, murder,
and a conniving woman who may be
plotting the cruelest betrayal of all...

"A master of white-knuckle suspense."
—Harlan Coben

0-451-41114-5

Also available:

A Kiss Gone Bad	0-451-41010-6
Black Jack Point	0-451-41050-5

**Available wherever books are sold or at
www.penguin.com**

o505